# STAR TREK
## THE NEXT GENERATION

Written by
**David Brin**

Painted by
**Scott Hampton**

Lettered by
**Tracey Munsey &
Comicraft's Albert Deschesne**

Designed by
**Alex Sinclair**

Edited by
**Jeff Mariotte**

STAR TREK: THE NEXT GENERATION — FORGIVENESS. 2001. Published by WildStorm Productions,
an imprint of DC Comics under exclusive license from Paramount Pictures Corporation.
Editorial Offices: 888 Prospect St Suite 240, La Jolla, CA 92037. Copyright © 2001 Paramount Pictures. All Rights Reserved.
STAR TREK and all related marks are trademarks of Paramount Pictures. DC Comics authorized user.
Any similarities to persons living or dead are purely coincidental.
PRINTED IN CANADA. ISBN# 1-56389-850-0
DC Comics. A division of Warner Bros.—An AOL Time Warner Company

## DEDICATIONS

For Sarah, Nathan, Miriam, and their generation--
whose adventures will span all the way to a better
world they help create...

### DAVID BRIN

To my paint pals--Dave, Chris, Ray, George,
Mark, John, and Durwin.

### SCOTT HAMPTON

## ACKNOWLEDGMENTS

First and foremost — A huge bear hug and pat on
the butt to Durwin Talon, who captained the
H.M.S. PhotoShop with the inspired assistance of
Glen Osterberger and Rob Talon. You guys
saved my bacon.

Thanks to George Pratt and John Van Fleet for
ongoing computer tutorials; take it from me, folks,
sometimes it's better to meekly go where
some men have gone before.

And a huge hug and sincere butt-pat to Letitia.

If I forgot folks (and I'm sure I have), my apologies.
This project is not quite finished and I have miles
to go before I sleep.

### SCOTT HAMPTON

JENETTE KAHN President & Editor-in-Chief  PAUL LEVITZ Executive Vice President & Publisher
JIM LEE Editorial Director — WildStorm  JOHN NEE VP & General Manager — WildStorm
SCOTT DUNBIER Group Editor  JEFF MARIOTTE Editor  RICHARD BRUNING VP — Creative Director
PATRICK CALDON VP — Finance & Operations  DOROTHY CROUCH VP — Licensed Publishing
TERRI CUNNINGHAM VP — Managing Editor  JOEL EHRLICH Senior VP — Advertising & Promotions
ALISON GILL Exec. Director — Manufacturing  LILLIAN LASERSON VP & General Counsel
CHERYL RUBIN VP — LICENSING & MERCHANDISING  BOB WAYNE VP — Sales and Marketing

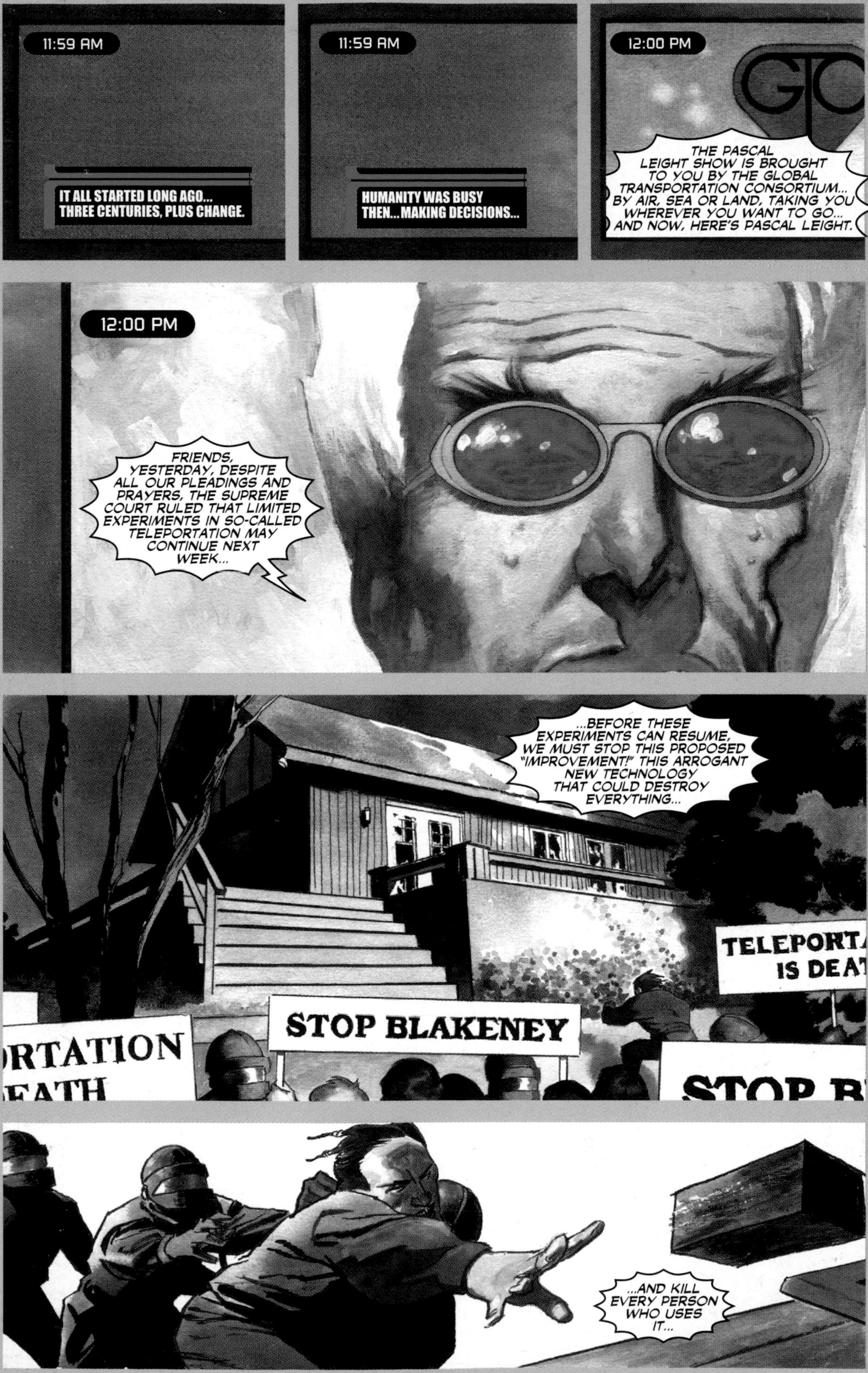
11:59 AM
IT ALL STARTED LONG AGO... THREE CENTURIES, PLUS CHANGE.
11:59 AM
HUMANITY WAS BUSY THEN... MAKING DECISIONS...
12:00 PM
GTC
THE PASCAL LEIGHT SHOW IS BROUGHT TO YOU BY THE GLOBAL TRANSPORTATION CONSORTIUM... BY AIR, SEA OR LAND, TAKING YOU WHEREVER YOU WANT TO GO... AND NOW, HERE'S PASCAL LEIGHT.
12:00 PM
FRIENDS, YESTERDAY, DESPITE ALL OUR PLEADINGS AND PRAYERS, THE SUPREME COURT RULED THAT LIMITED EXPERIMENTS IN SO-CALLED TELEPORTATION MAY CONTINUE NEXT WEEK...
...BEFORE THESE EXPERIMENTS CAN RESUME, WE MUST STOP THIS PROPOSED "IMPROVEMENT!" THIS ARROGANT NEW TECHNOLOGY THAT COULD DESTROY EVERYTHING...
TELEPORTA IS DEAT
STOP BLAKENEY
ORTATION EATH
STOP B
...AND KILL EVERY PERSON WHO USES IT...

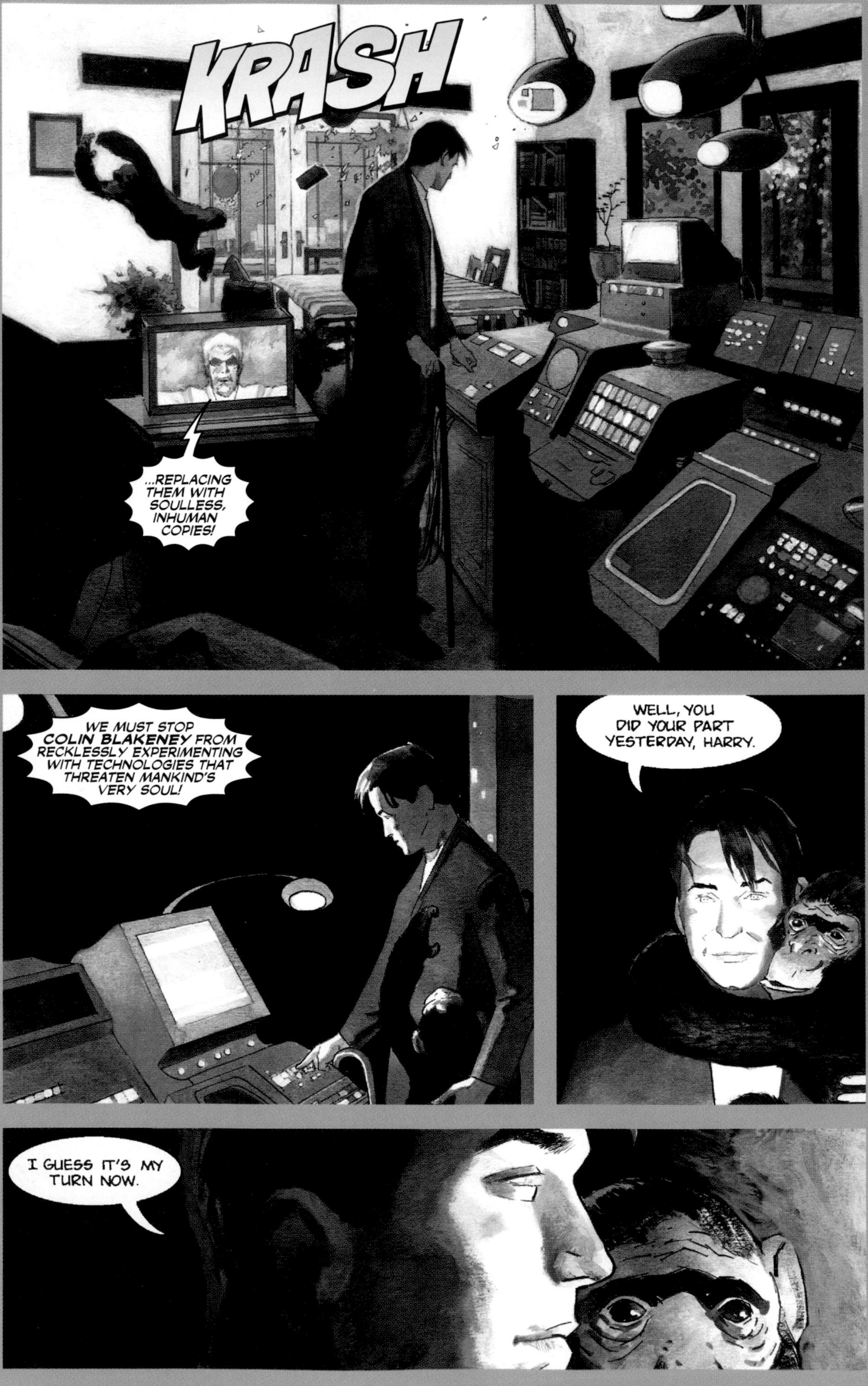
KRASH
...REPLACING THEM WITH SOULLESS, INHUMAN COPIES!
WE MUST STOP COLIN BLAKENEY FROM RECKLESSLY EXPERIMENTING WITH TECHNOLOGIES THAT THREATEN MANKIND'S VERY SOUL!
WELL, YOU DID YOUR PART YESTERDAY, HARRY.
I GUESS IT'S MY TURN NOW.

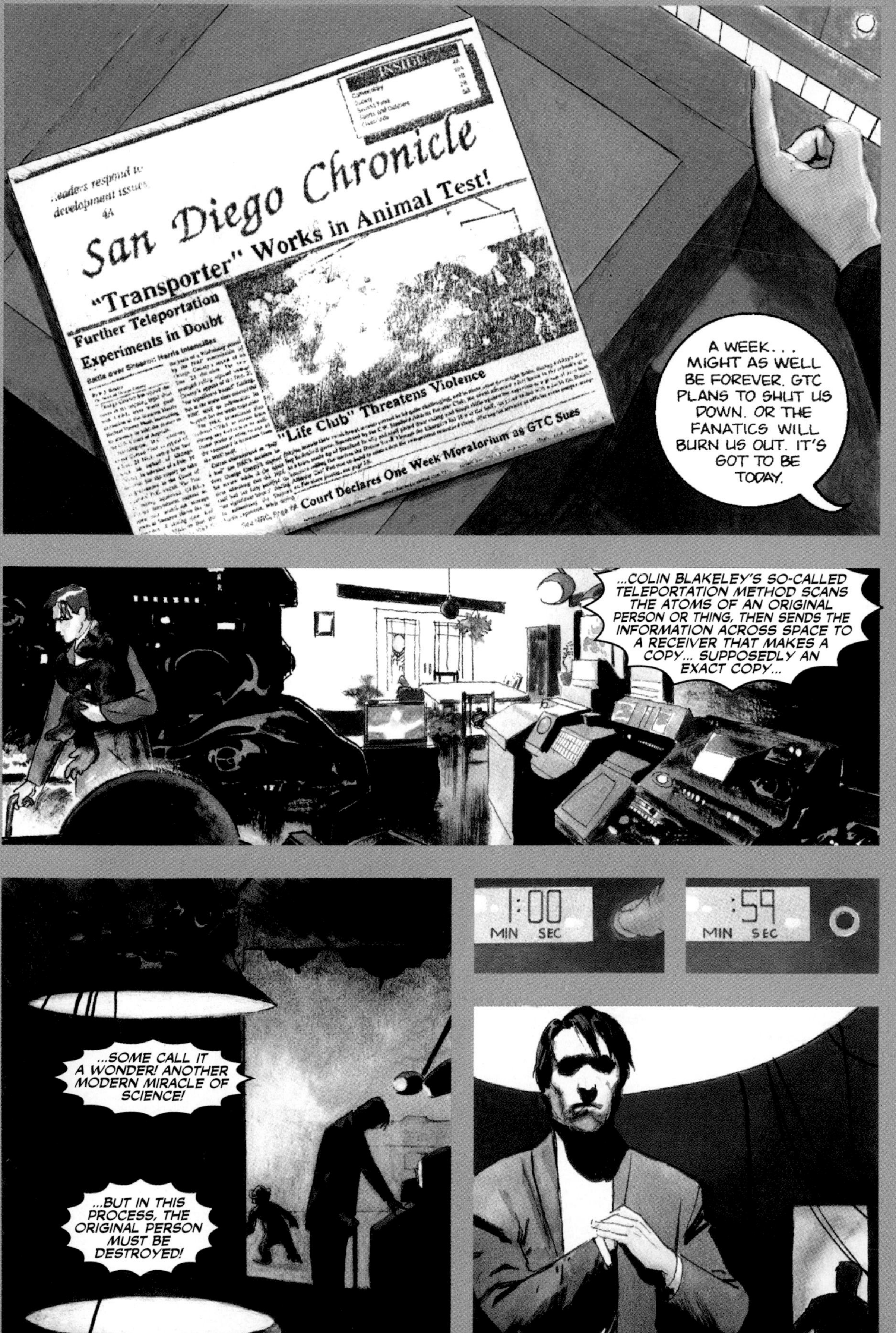
San Diego Chronicle
"Transporter" Works in Animal Test!
Further Teleportation Experiments in Doubt
"Life Club" Threatens Violence
Court Declares One Week Moratorium as GTC Sues
A WEEK... MIGHT AS WELL BE FOREVER. GTC PLANS TO SHUT US DOWN. OR THE FANATICS WILL BURN US OUT. IT'S GOT TO BE TODAY.
...COLIN BLAKELEY'S SO-CALLED TELEPORTATION METHOD SCANS THE ATOMS OF AN ORIGINAL PERSON OR THING, THEN SENDS THE INFORMATION ACROSS SPACE TO A RECEIVER THAT MAKES A COPY... SUPPOSEDLY AN EXACT COPY...
...SOME CALL IT A WONDER! ANOTHER MODERN MIRACLE OF SCIENCE!
...BUT IN THIS PROCESS, THE ORIGINAL PERSON MUST BE DESTROYED!
1:00
MIN SEC
:59
MIN SEC

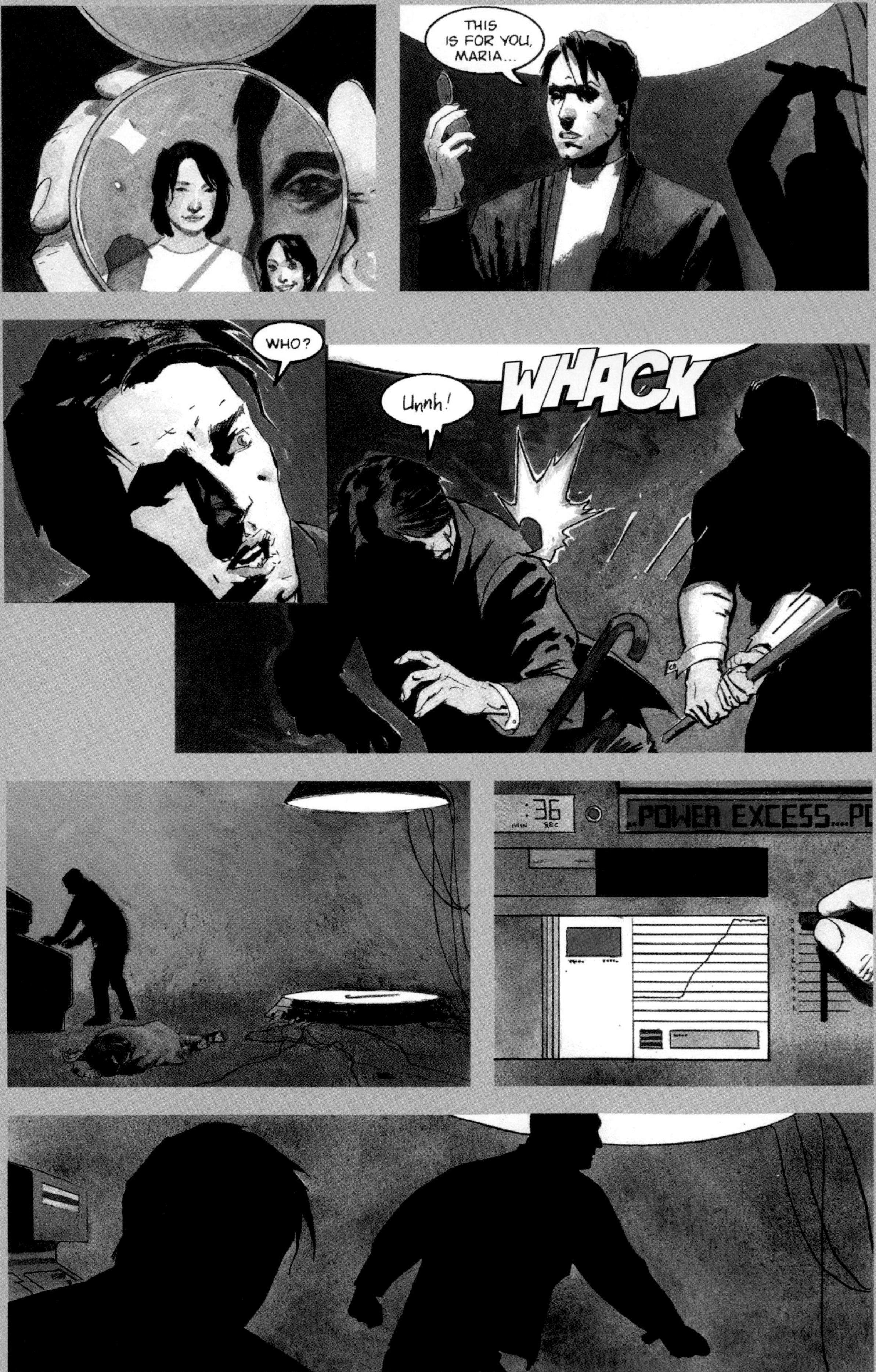
THIS IS FOR YOU, MARIA...
WHO?
Unnh!
WHACK
:36
MIN SEC
..POWER EXCESS....PO

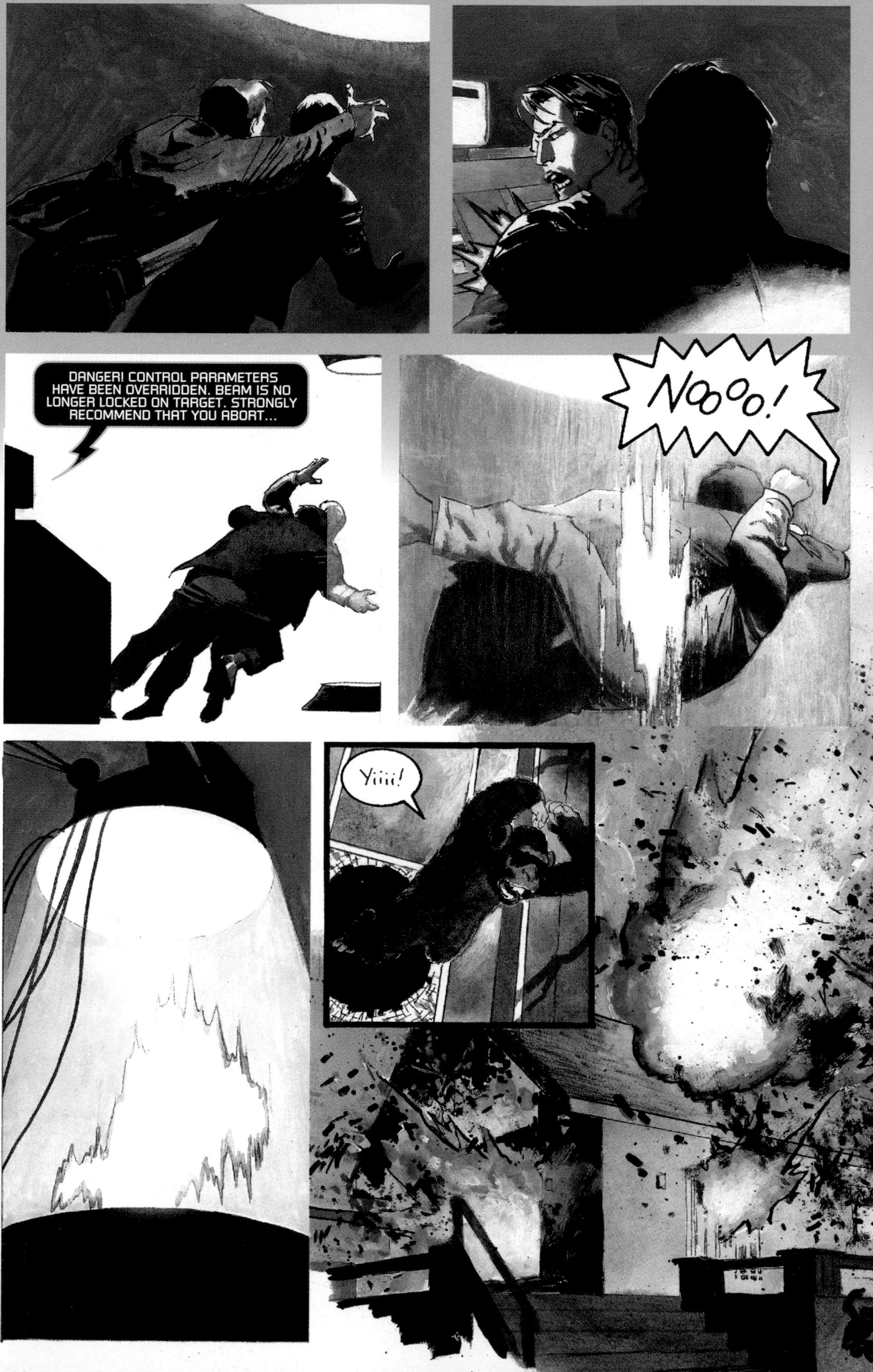
DANGER! CONTROL PARAMETERS HAVE BEEN OVERRIDDEN. BEAM IS NO LONGER LOCKED ON TARGET. STRONGLY RECOMMEND THAT YOU ABORT...
Noooo!
Yiiii!

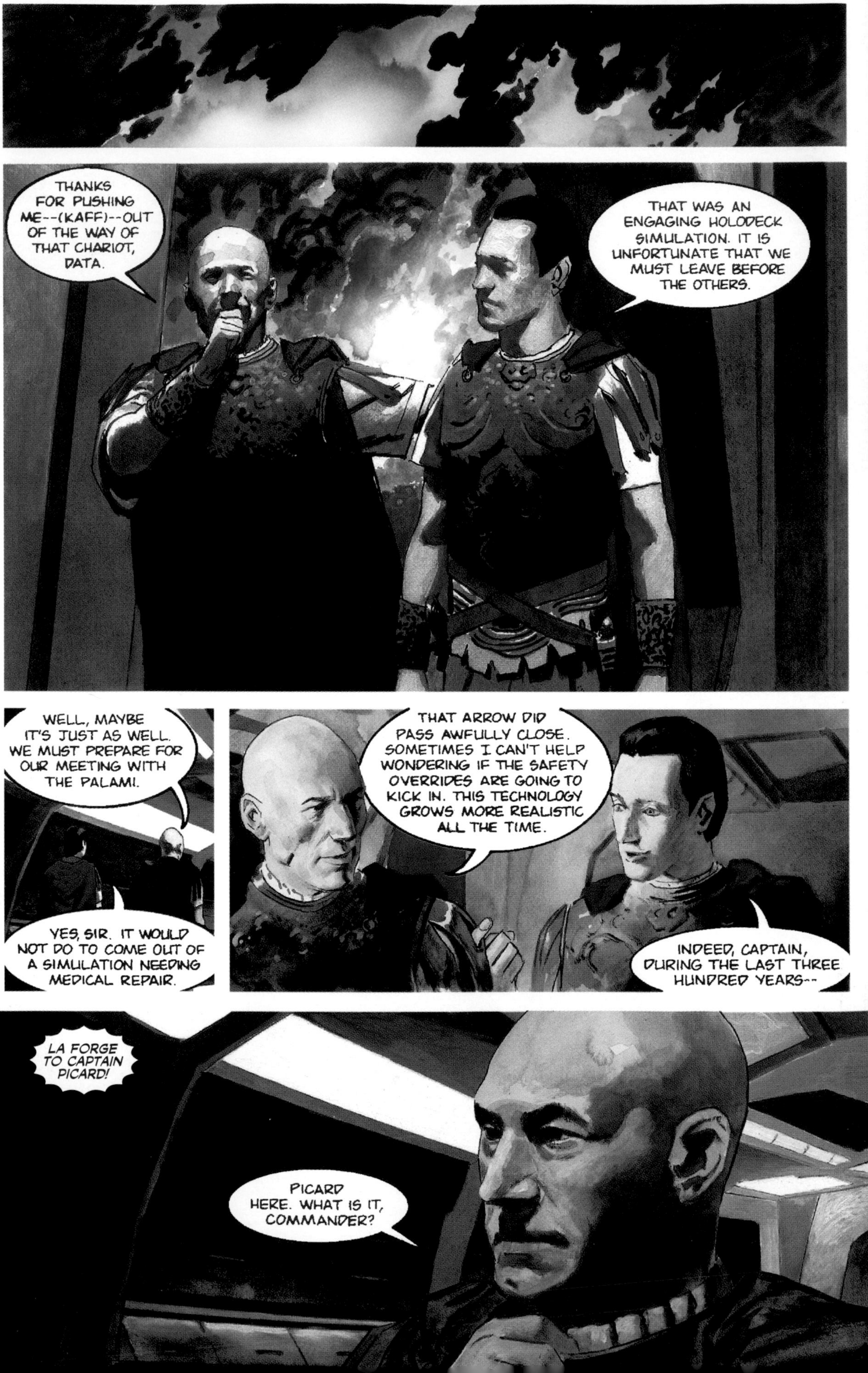

THANKS FOR PUSHING ME--(KAFF)--OUT OF THE WAY OF THAT CHARIOT, DATA.
THAT WAS AN ENGAGING HOLODECK SIMULATION. IT IS UNFORTUNATE THAT WE MUST LEAVE BEFORE THE OTHERS.
WELL, MAYBE IT'S JUST AS WELL. WE MUST PREPARE FOR OUR MEETING WITH THE PALAMI.
YES, SIR. IT WOULD NOT DO TO COME OUT OF A SIMULATION NEEDING MEDICAL REPAIR.
THAT ARROW DID PASS AWFULLY CLOSE. SOMETIMES I CAN'T HELP WONDERING IF THE SAFETY OVERRIDES ARE GOING TO KICK IN. THIS TECHNOLOGY GROWS MORE REALISTIC ALL THE TIME.
INDEED, CAPTAIN, DURING THE LAST THREE HUNDRED YEARS--
LA FORGE TO CAPTAIN PICARD!
PICARD HERE. WHAT IS IT, COMMANDER?

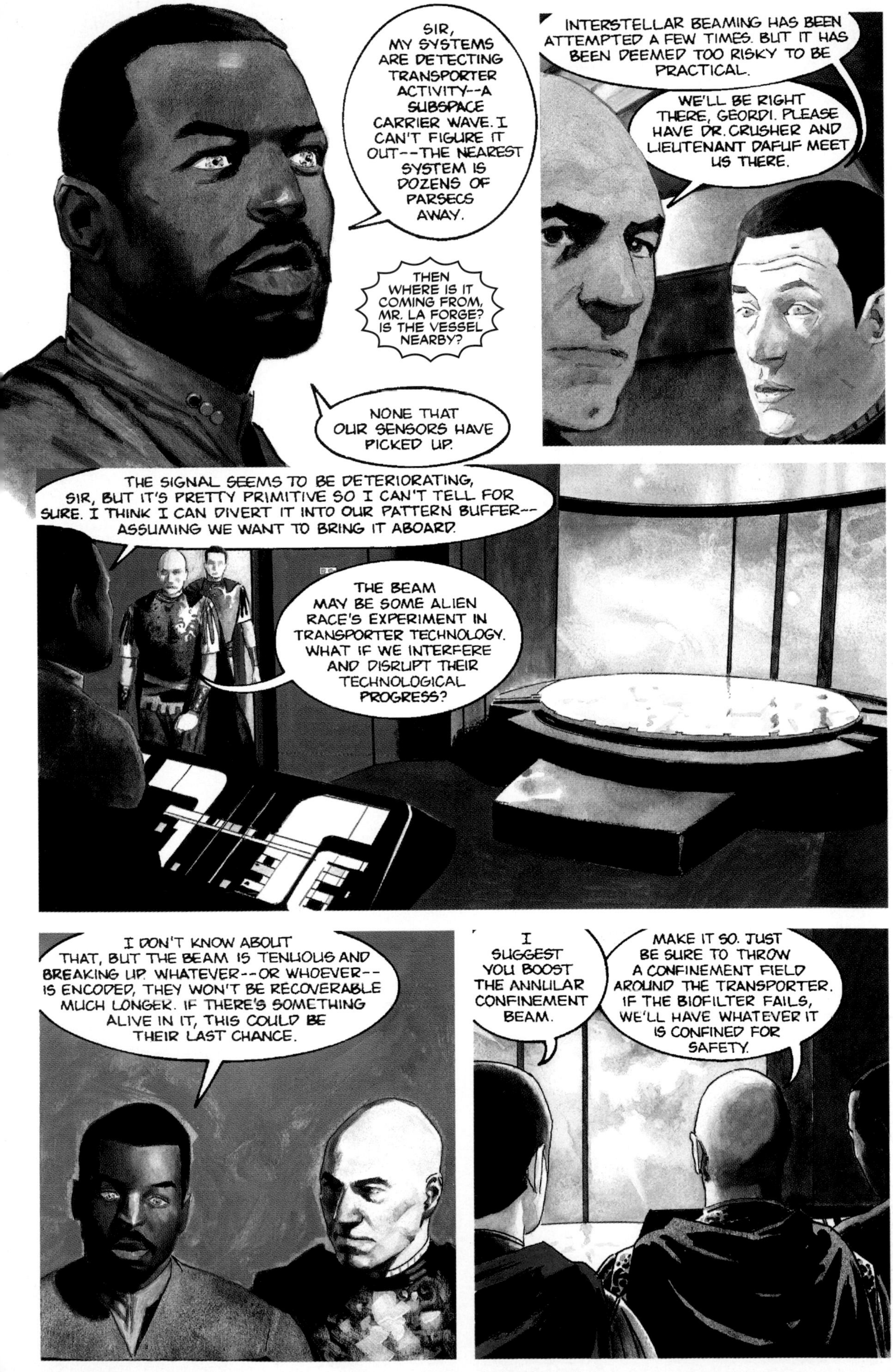
SIR, MY SYSTEMS ARE DETECTING TRANSPORTER ACTIVITY--A SUBSPACE CARRIER WAVE. I CAN'T FIGURE IT OUT--THE NEAREST SYSTEM IS DOZENS OF PARSECS AWAY.
THEN WHERE IS IT COMING FROM, MR. LA FORGE? IS THE VESSEL NEARBY?
NONE THAT OUR SENSORS HAVE PICKED UP.
INTERSTELLAR BEAMING HAS BEEN ATTEMPTED A FEW TIMES. BUT IT HAS BEEN DEEMED TOO RISKY TO BE PRACTICAL.
WE'LL BE RIGHT THERE, GEORDI. PLEASE HAVE DR. CRUSHER AND LIEUTENANT DAFUF MEET US THERE.
THE SIGNAL SEEMS TO BE DETERIORATING, SIR, BUT IT'S PRETTY PRIMITIVE SO I CAN'T TELL FOR SURE. I THINK I CAN DIVERT IT INTO OUR PATTERN BUFFER--ASSUMING WE WANT TO BRING IT ABOARD.
THE BEAM MAY BE SOME ALIEN RACE'S EXPERIMENT IN TRANSPORTER TECHNOLOGY. WHAT IF WE INTERFERE AND DISRUPT THEIR TECHNOLOGICAL PROGRESS?
I DON'T KNOW ABOUT THAT, BUT THE BEAM IS TENUOUS AND BREAKING UP. WHATEVER--OR WHOEVER--IS ENCODED, THEY WON'T BE RECOVERABLE MUCH LONGER. IF THERE'S SOMETHING ALIVE IN IT, THIS COULD BE THEIR LAST CHANCE.
I SUGGEST YOU BOOST THE ANNULAR CONFINEMENT BEAM.
MAKE IT SO. JUST BE SURE TO THROW A CONFINEMENT FIELD AROUND THE TRANSPORTER. IF THE BIOFILTER FAILS, WE'LL HAVE WHATEVER IT IS CONFINED FOR SAFETY.

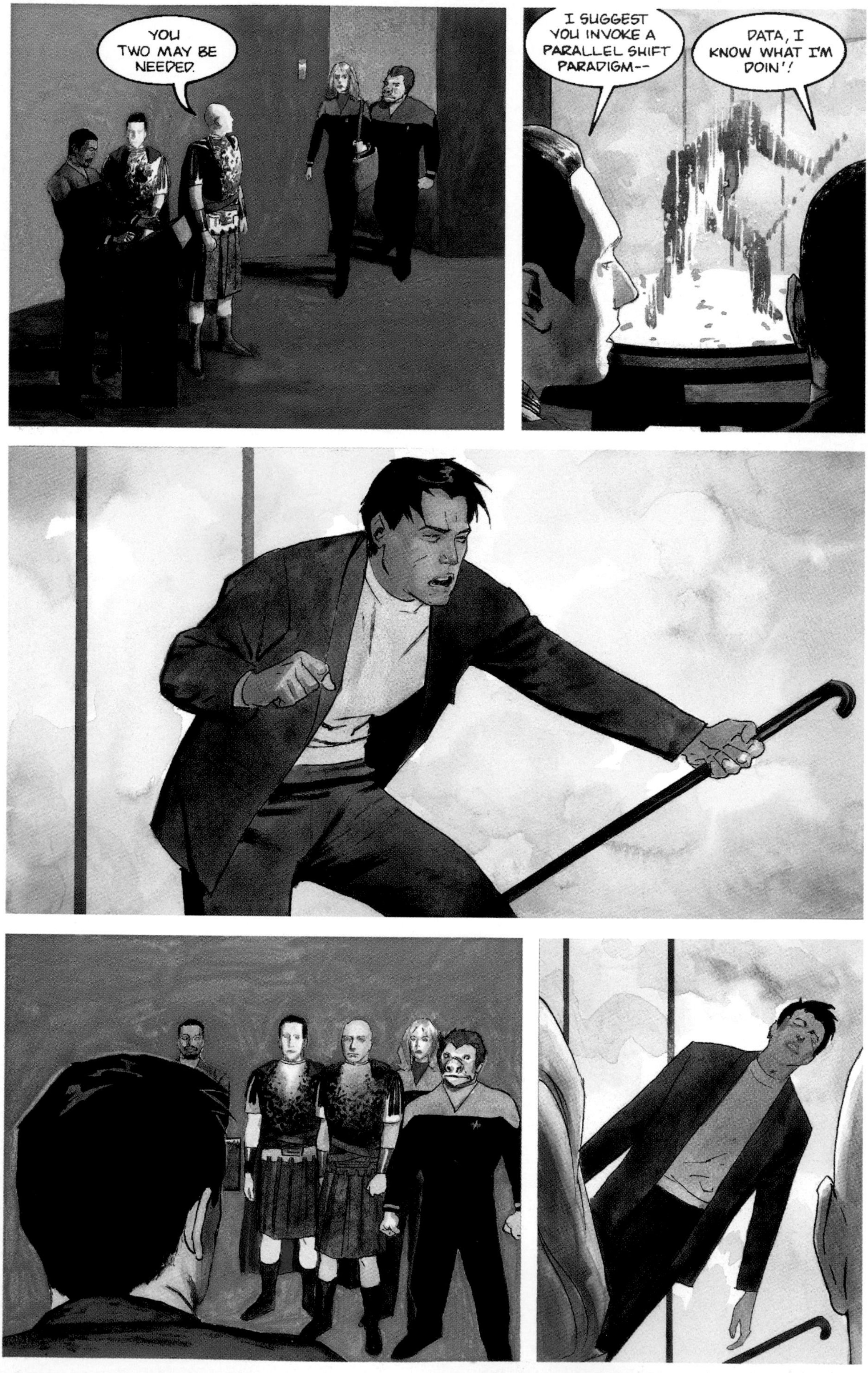
YOU TWO MAY BE NEEDED.
I SUGGEST YOU INVOKE A PARALLEL SHIFT PARADIGM--
DATA, I KNOW WHAT I'M DOIN'!

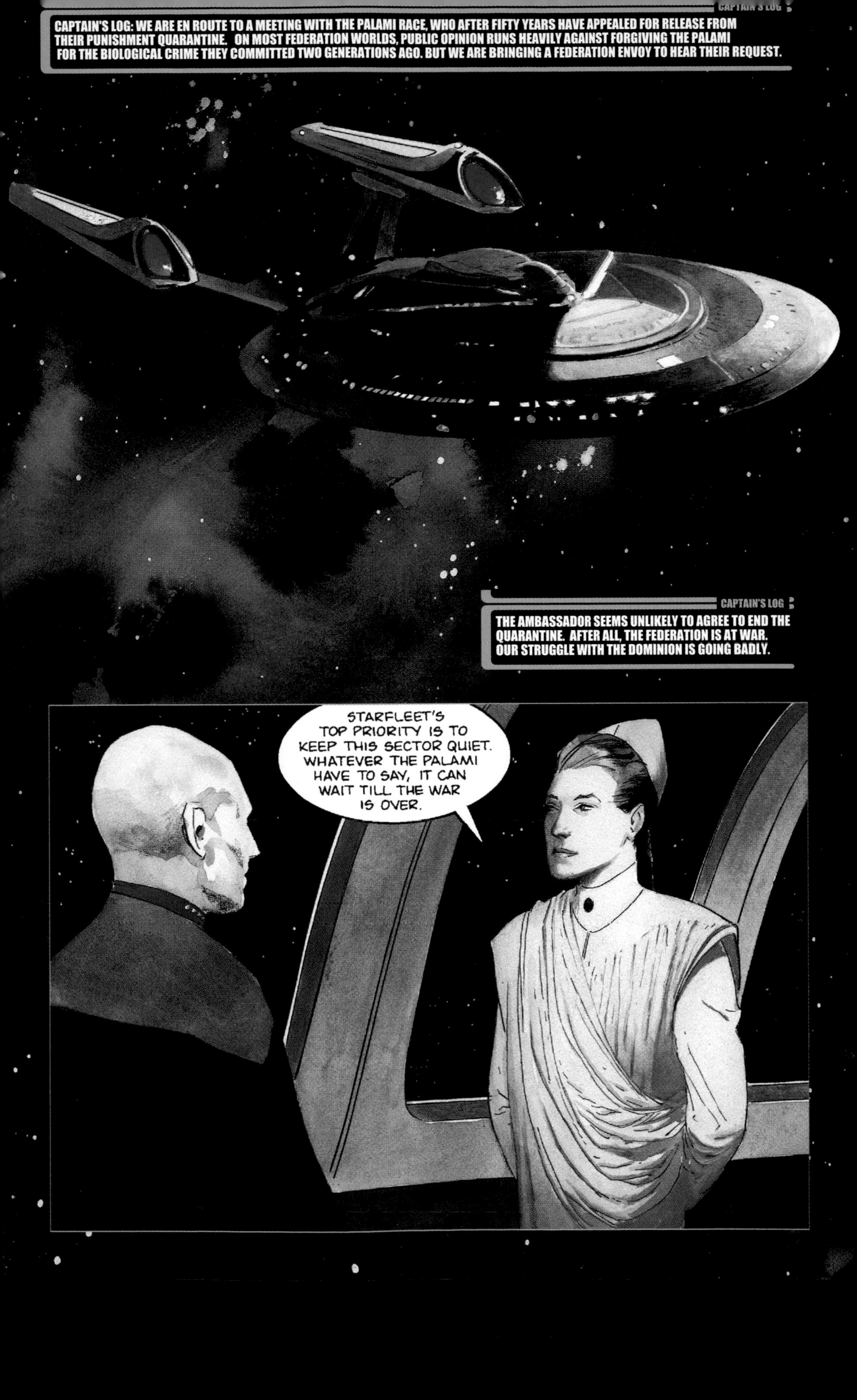
CAPTAIN'S LOG: WE ARE EN ROUTE TO A MEETING WITH THE PALAMI RACE, WHO AFTER FIFTY YEARS HAVE APPEALED FOR RELEASE FROM THEIR PUNISHMENT QUARANTINE. ON MOST FEDERATION WORLDS, PUBLIC OPINION RUNS HEAVILY AGAINST FORGIVING THE PALAMI FOR THE BIOLOGICAL CRIME THEY COMMITTED TWO GENERATIONS AGO. BUT WE ARE BRINGING A FEDERATION ENVOY TO HEAR THEIR REQUEST.
CAPTAIN'S LOG
THE AMBASSADOR SEEMS UNLIKELY TO AGREE TO END THE QUARANTINE. AFTER ALL, THE FEDERATION IS AT WAR. OUR STRUGGLE WITH THE DOMINION IS GOING BADLY.
STARFLEET'S TOP PRIORITY IS TO KEEP THIS SECTOR QUIET. WHATEVER THE PALAMI HAVE TO SAY, IT CAN WAIT TILL THE WAR IS OVER.

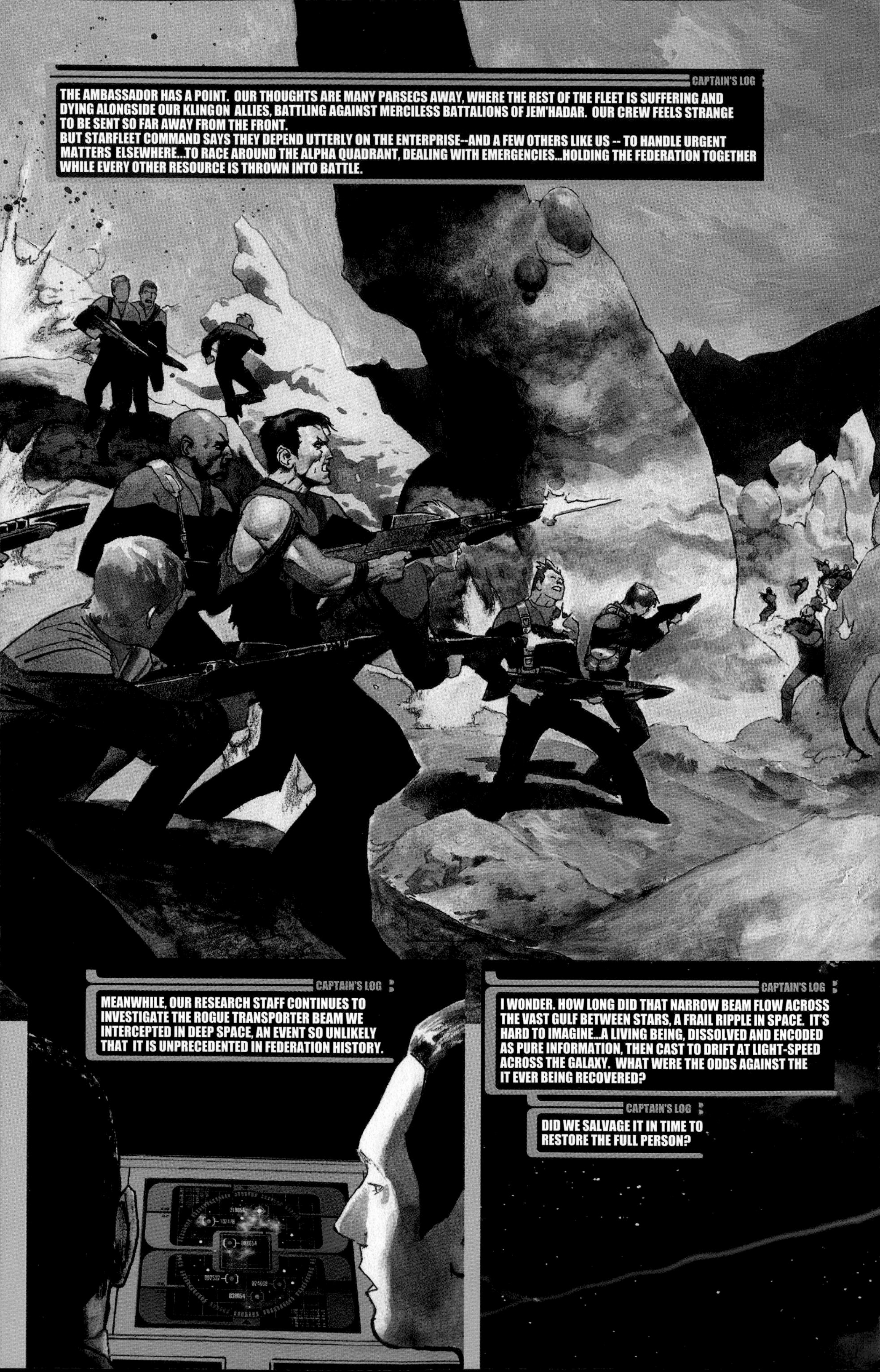
CAPTAIN'S LOG
THE AMBASSADOR HAS A POINT. OUR THOUGHTS ARE MANY PARSECS AWAY, WHERE THE REST OF THE FLEET IS SUFFERING AND DYING ALONGSIDE OUR KLINGON ALLIES, BATTLING AGAINST MERCILESS BATTALIONS OF JEM'HADAR. OUR CREW FEELS STRANGE TO BE SENT SO FAR AWAY FROM THE FRONT.
BUT STARFLEET COMMAND SAYS THEY DEPEND UTTERLY ON THE ENTERPRISE--AND A FEW OTHERS LIKE US -- TO HANDLE URGENT MATTERS ELSEWHERE...TO RACE AROUND THE ALPHA QUADRANT, DEALING WITH EMERGENCIES...HOLDING THE FEDERATION TOGETHER WHILE EVERY OTHER RESOURCE IS THROWN INTO BATTLE.
CAPTAIN'S LOG
MEANWHILE, OUR RESEARCH STAFF CONTINUES TO INVESTIGATE THE ROGUE TRANSPORTER BEAM WE INTERCEPTED IN DEEP SPACE, AN EVENT SO UNLIKELY THAT IT IS UNPRECEDENTED IN FEDERATION HISTORY.
CAPTAIN'S LOG
I WONDER. HOW LONG DID THAT NARROW BEAM FLOW ACROSS THE VAST GULF BETWEEN STARS, A FRAIL RIPPLE IN SPACE. IT'S HARD TO IMAGINE...A LIVING BEING, DISSOLVED AND ENCODED AS PURE INFORMATION, THEN CAST TO DRIFT AT LIGHT-SPEED ACROSS THE GALAXY. WHAT WERE THE ODDS AGAINST THE IT EVER BEING RECOVERED?
CAPTAIN'S LOG
DID WE SALVAGE IT IN TIME TO RESTORE THE FULL PERSON?

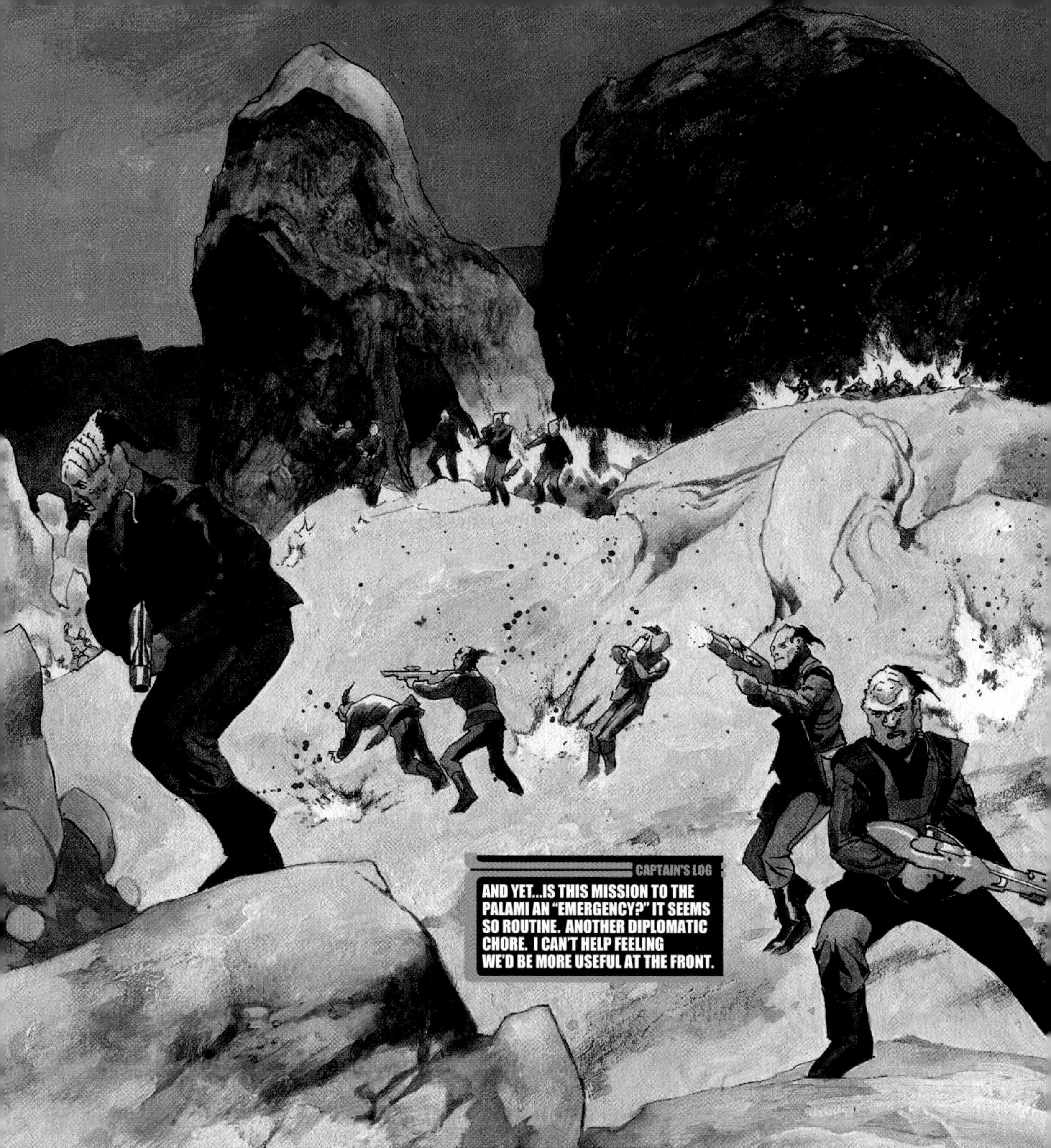
CAPTAIN'S LOG
AND YET...IS THIS MISSION TO THE PALAMI AN "EMERGENCY?" IT SEEMS SO ROUTINE. ANOTHER DIPLOMATIC CHORE. I CAN'T HELP FEELING WE'D BE MORE USEFUL AT THE FRONT.

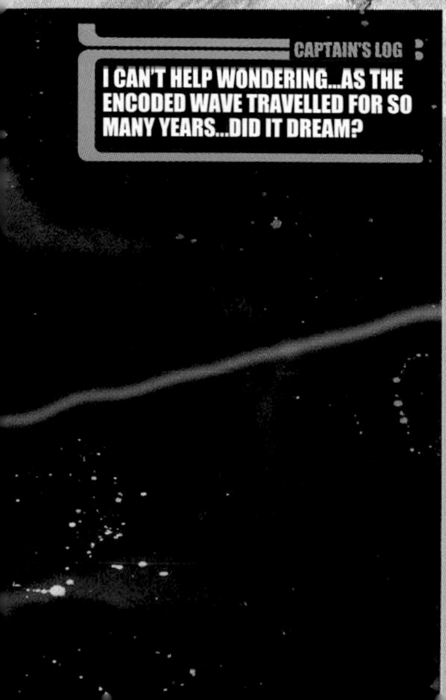
CAPTAIN'S LOG
I CAN'T HELP WONDERING...AS THE ENCODED WAVE TRAVELLED FOR SO MANY YEARS...DID IT DREAM?

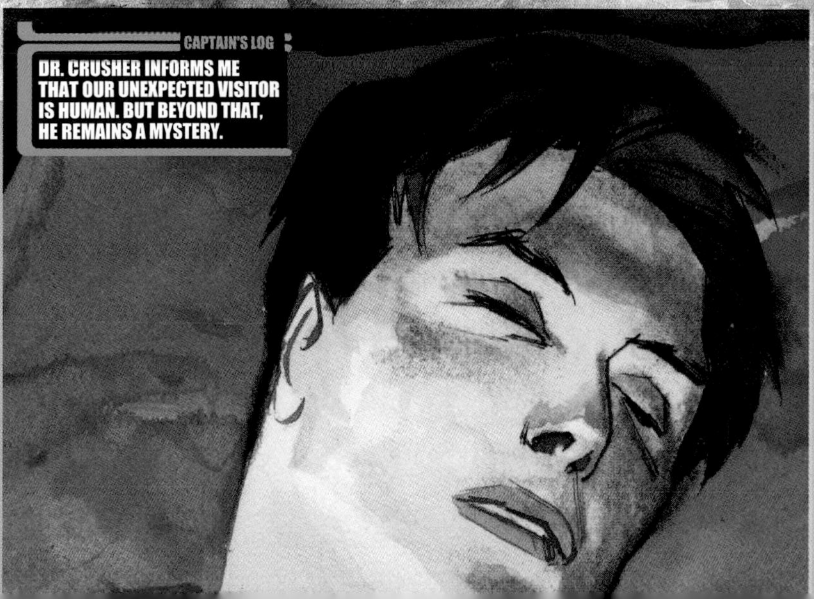
CAPTAIN'S LOG
DR. CRUSHER INFORMS ME THAT OUR UNEXPECTED VISITOR IS HUMAN. BUT BEYOND THAT, HE REMAINS A MYSTERY.

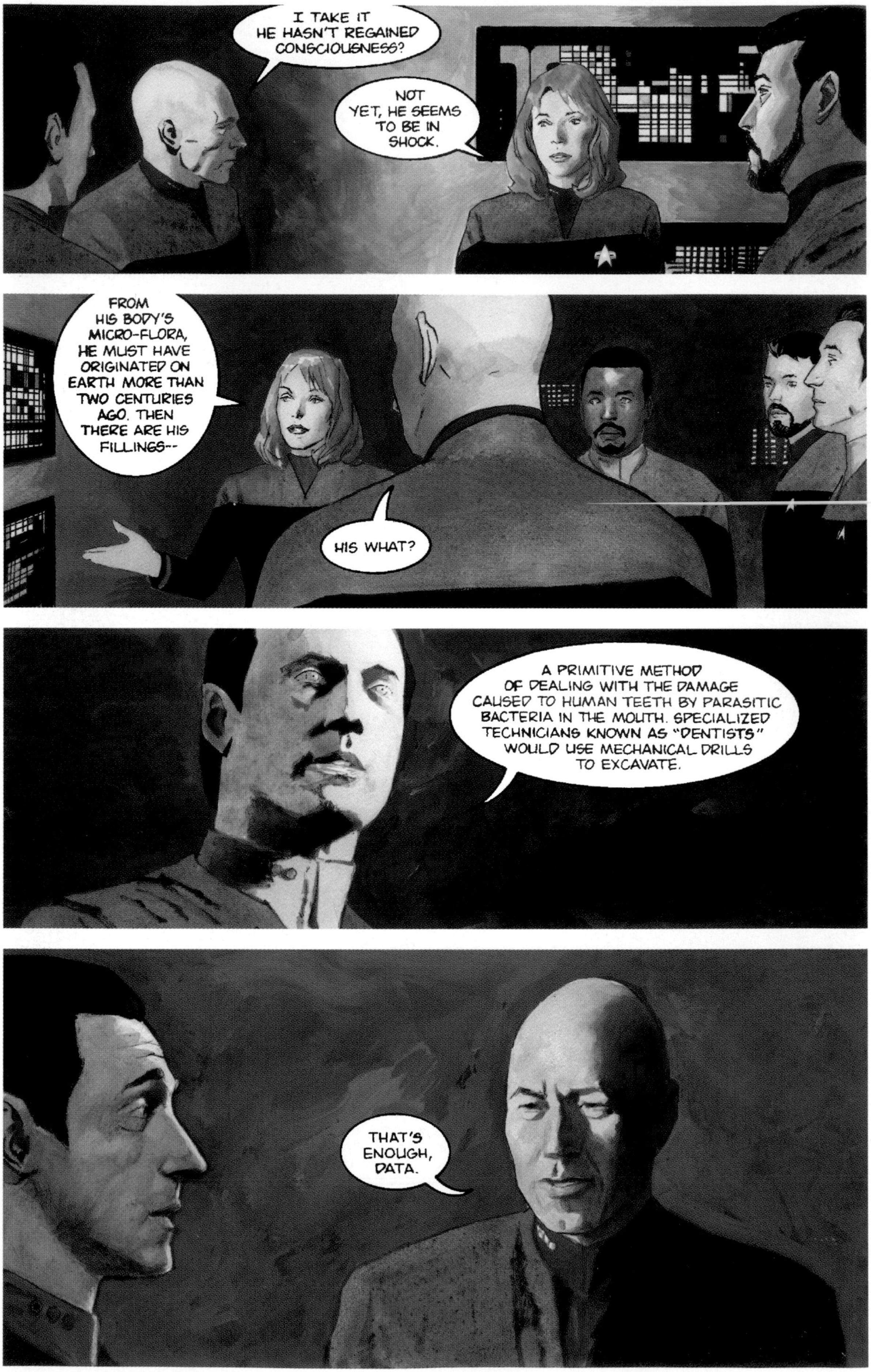
I TAKE IT HE HASN'T REGAINED CONSCIOUSNESS?
NOT YET, HE SEEMS TO BE IN SHOCK.
FROM HIS BODY'S MICRO-FLORA, HE MUST HAVE ORIGINATED ON EARTH MORE THAN TWO CENTURIES AGO. THEN THERE ARE HIS FILLINGS--
HIS WHAT?
A PRIMITIVE METHOD OF DEALING WITH THE DAMAGE CAUSED TO HUMAN TEETH BY PARASITIC BACTERIA IN THE MOUTH. SPECIALIZED TECHNICIANS KNOWN AS "DENTISTS" WOULD USE MECHANICAL DRILLS TO EXCAVATE.
THAT'S ENOUGH, DATA.

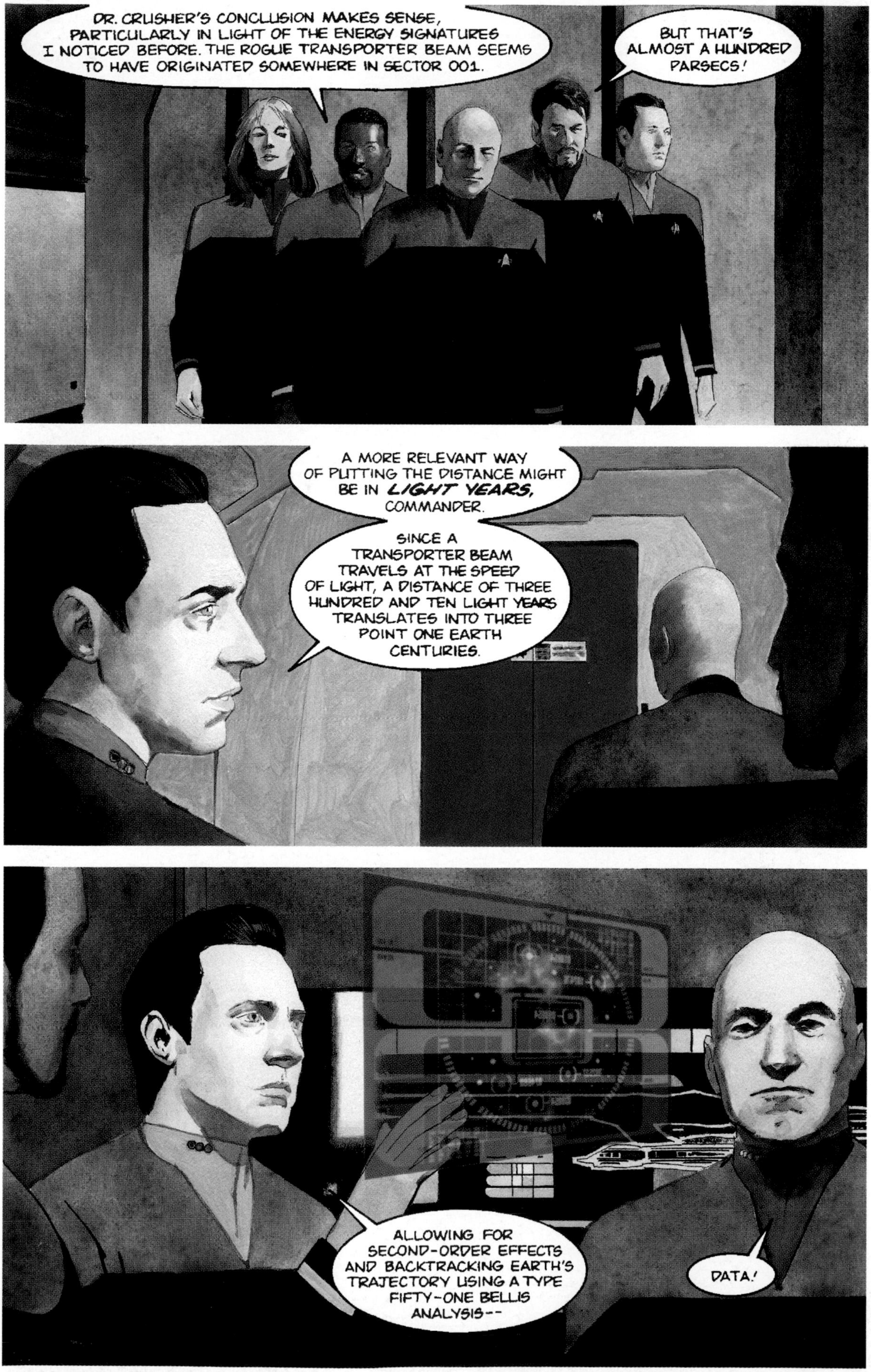
DR. CRUSHER'S CONCLUSION MAKES SENSE, PARTICULARLY IN LIGHT OF THE ENERGY SIGNATURES I NOTICED BEFORE. THE ROGUE TRANSPORTER BEAM SEEMS TO HAVE ORIGINATED SOMEWHERE IN SECTOR 001.
BUT THAT'S ALMOST A HUNDRED PARSECS!
A MORE RELEVANT WAY OF PUTTING THE DISTANCE MIGHT BE IN LIGHT YEARS, COMMANDER.
SINCE A TRANSPORTER BEAM TRAVELS AT THE SPEED OF LIGHT, A DISTANCE OF THREE HUNDRED AND TEN LIGHT YEARS TRANSLATES INTO THREE POINT ONE EARTH CENTURIES.
ALLOWING FOR SECOND-ORDER EFFECTS AND BACKTRACKING EARTH'S TRAJECTORY USING A TYPE FIFTY-ONE BELLIS ANALYSIS--
DATA!

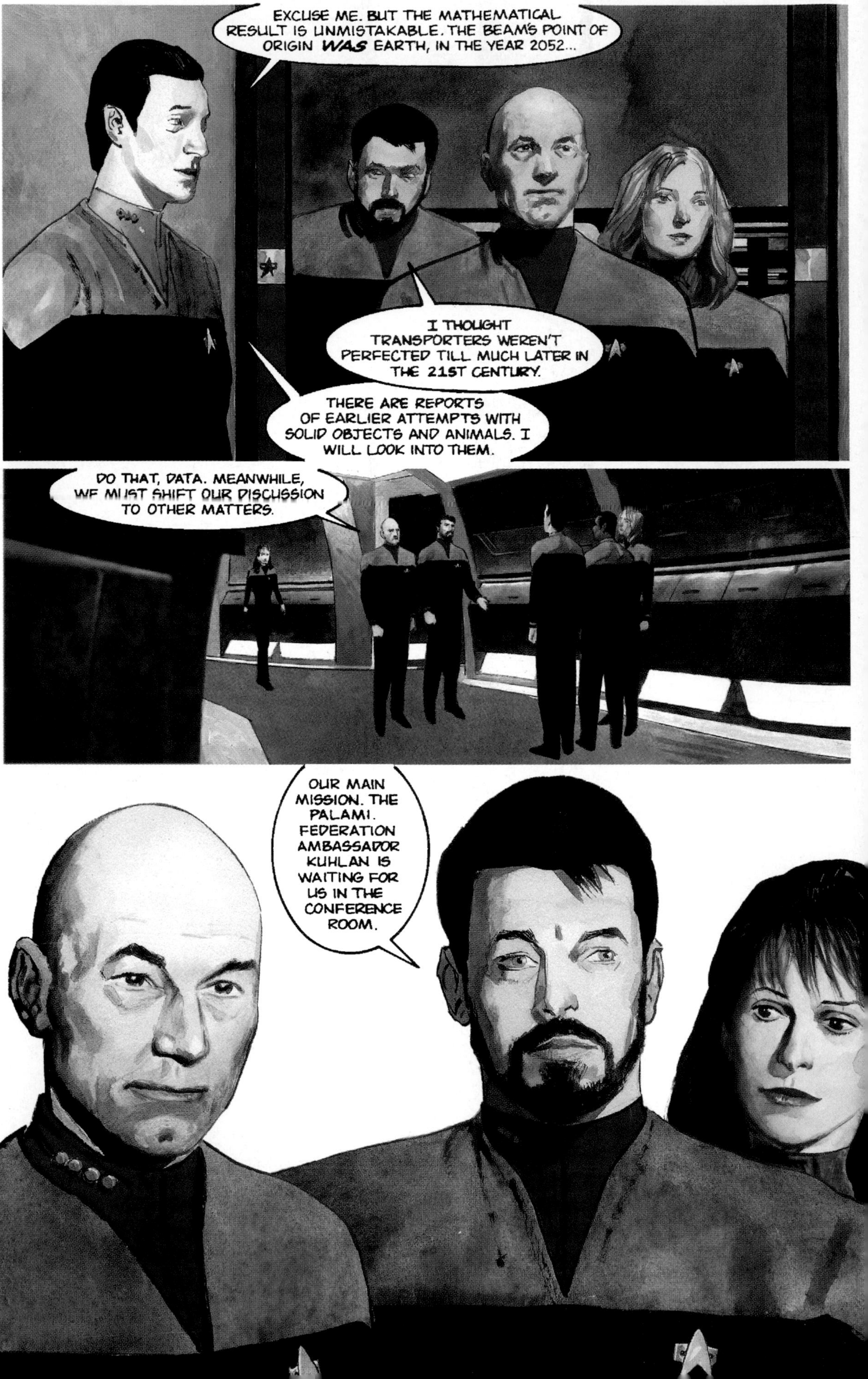
EXCUSE ME. BUT THE MATHEMATICAL RESULT IS UNMISTAKABLE. THE BEAM'S POINT OF ORIGIN WAS EARTH, IN THE YEAR 2052...
I THOUGHT TRANSPORTERS WEREN'T PERFECTED TILL MUCH LATER IN THE 21ST CENTURY.
THERE ARE REPORTS OF EARLIER ATTEMPTS WITH SOLID OBJECTS AND ANIMALS. I WILL LOOK INTO THEM.
DO THAT, DATA. MEANWHILE, WE MUST SHIFT OUR DISCUSSION TO OTHER MATTERS.
OUR MAIN MISSION. THE PALAMI. FEDERATION AMBASSADOR KUHLAN IS WAITING FOR US IN THE CONFERENCE ROOM.

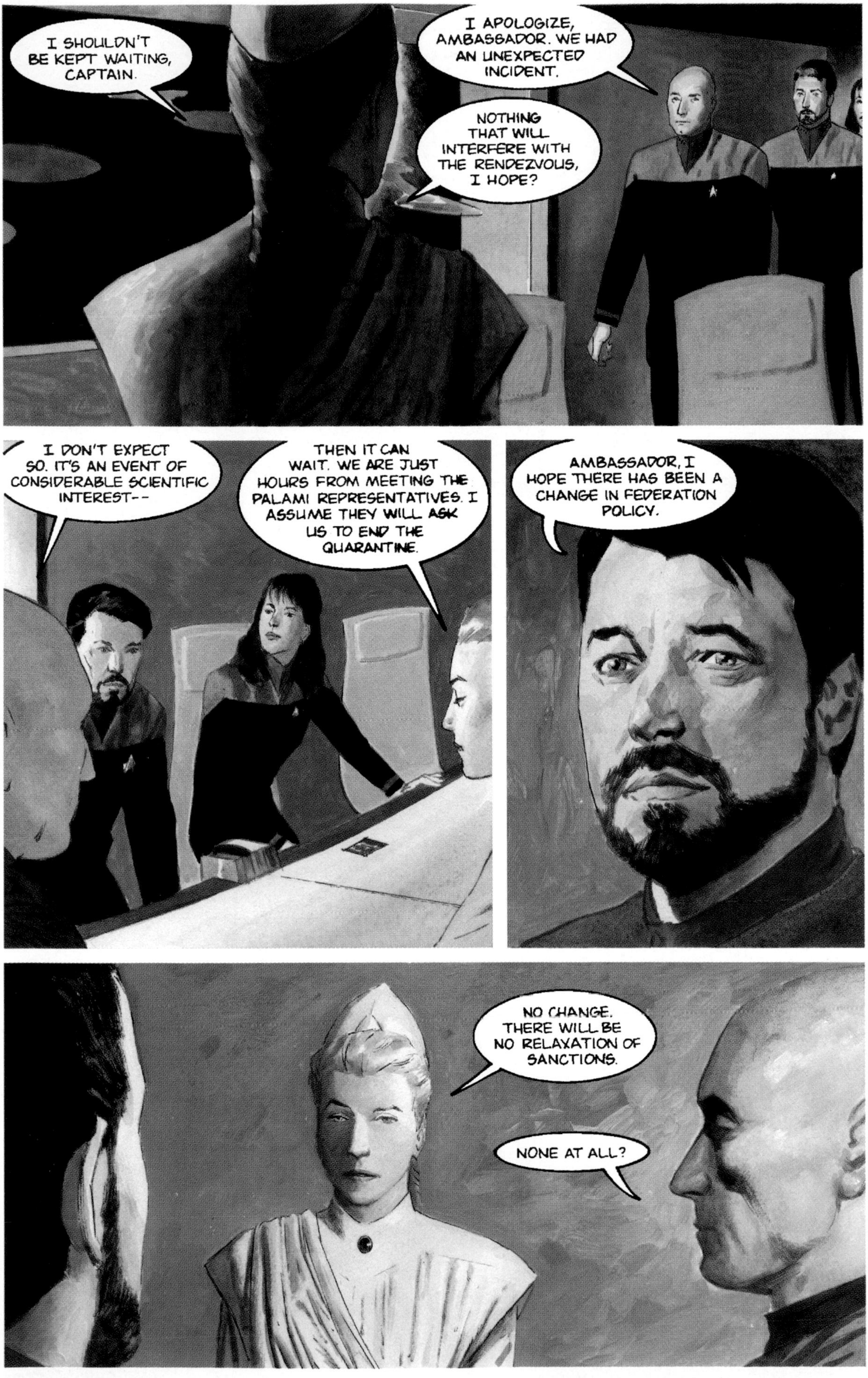
I SHOULDN'T BE KEPT WAITING, CAPTAIN.
I APOLOGIZE, AMBASSADOR. WE HAD AN UNEXPECTED INCIDENT.
NOTHING THAT WILL INTERFERE WITH THE RENDEZVOUS, I HOPE?
I DON'T EXPECT SO. IT'S AN EVENT OF CONSIDERABLE SCIENTIFIC INTEREST--
THEN IT CAN WAIT. WE ARE JUST HOURS FROM MEETING THE PALAMI REPRESENTATIVES. I ASSUME THEY WILL ASK US TO END THE QUARANTINE.
AMBASSADOR, I HOPE THERE HAS BEEN A CHANGE IN FEDERATION POLICY.
NO CHANGE. THERE WILL BE NO RELAXATION OF SANCTIONS.
NONE AT ALL?

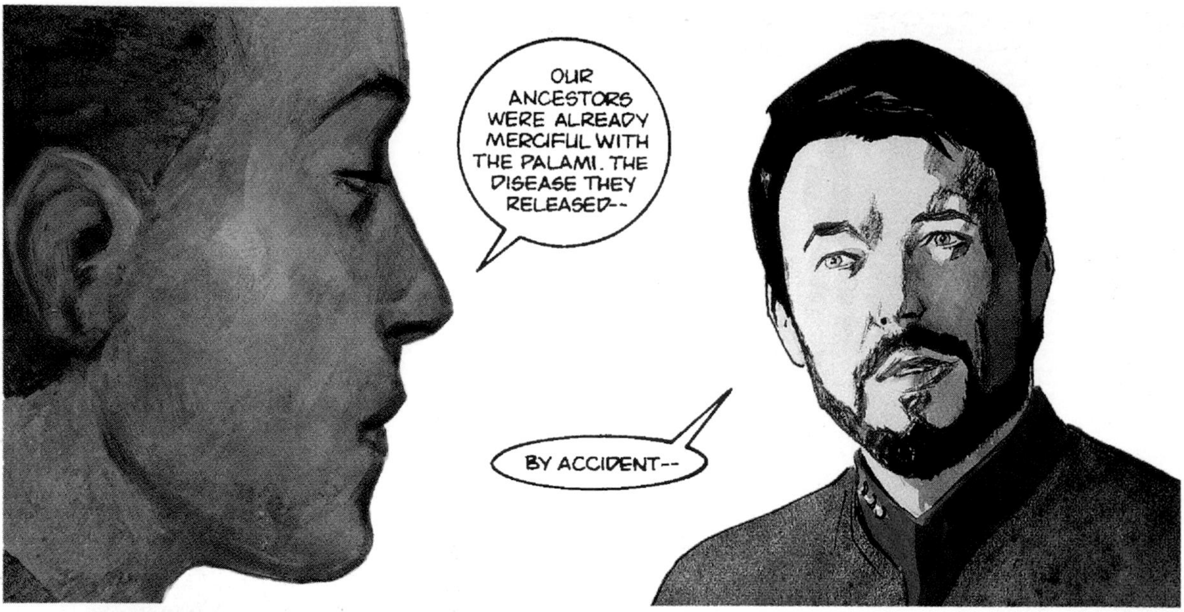
OUR ANCESTORS WERE ALREADY MERCIFUL WITH THE PALAMI. THE DISEASE THEY RELEASED--
BY ACCIDENT--

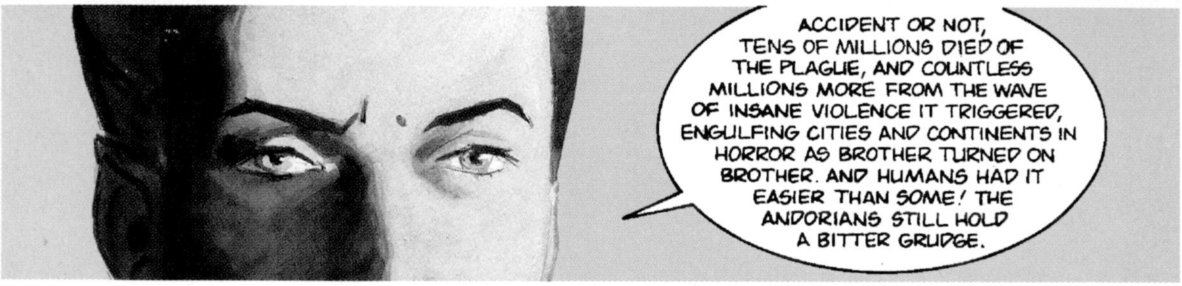
ACCIDENT OR NOT, TENS OF MILLIONS DIED OF THE PLAGUE, AND COUNTLESS MILLIONS MORE FROM THE WAVE OF INSANE VIOLENCE IT TRIGGERED, ENGULFING CITIES AND CONTINENTS IN HORROR AS BROTHER TURNED ON BROTHER. AND HUMANS HAD IT EASIER THAN SOME! THE ANDORIANS STILL HOLD A BITTER GRUDGE.

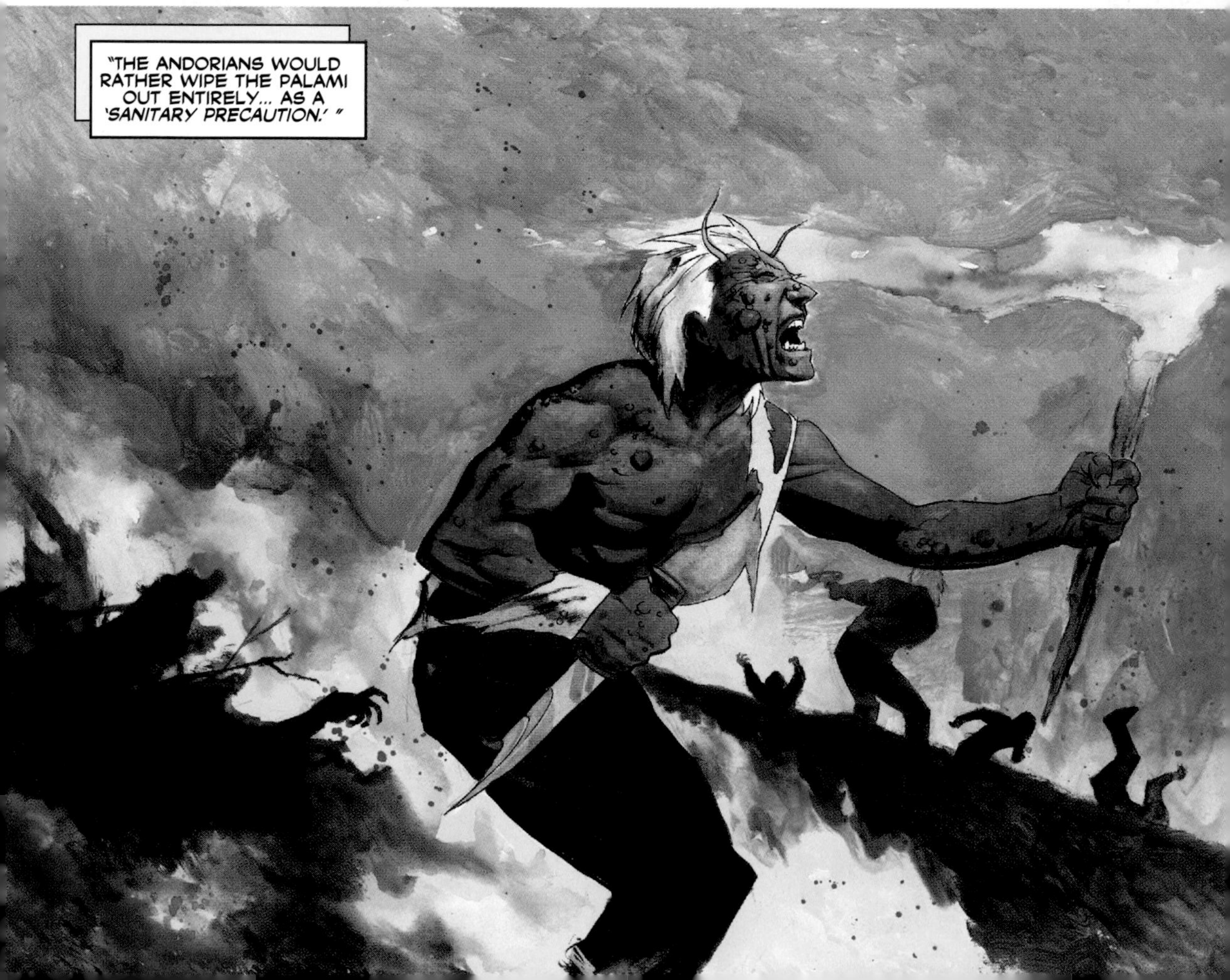
"THE ANDORIANS WOULD RATHER WIPE THE PALAMI OUT ENTIRELY... AS A '*SANITARY PRECAUTION.*' "

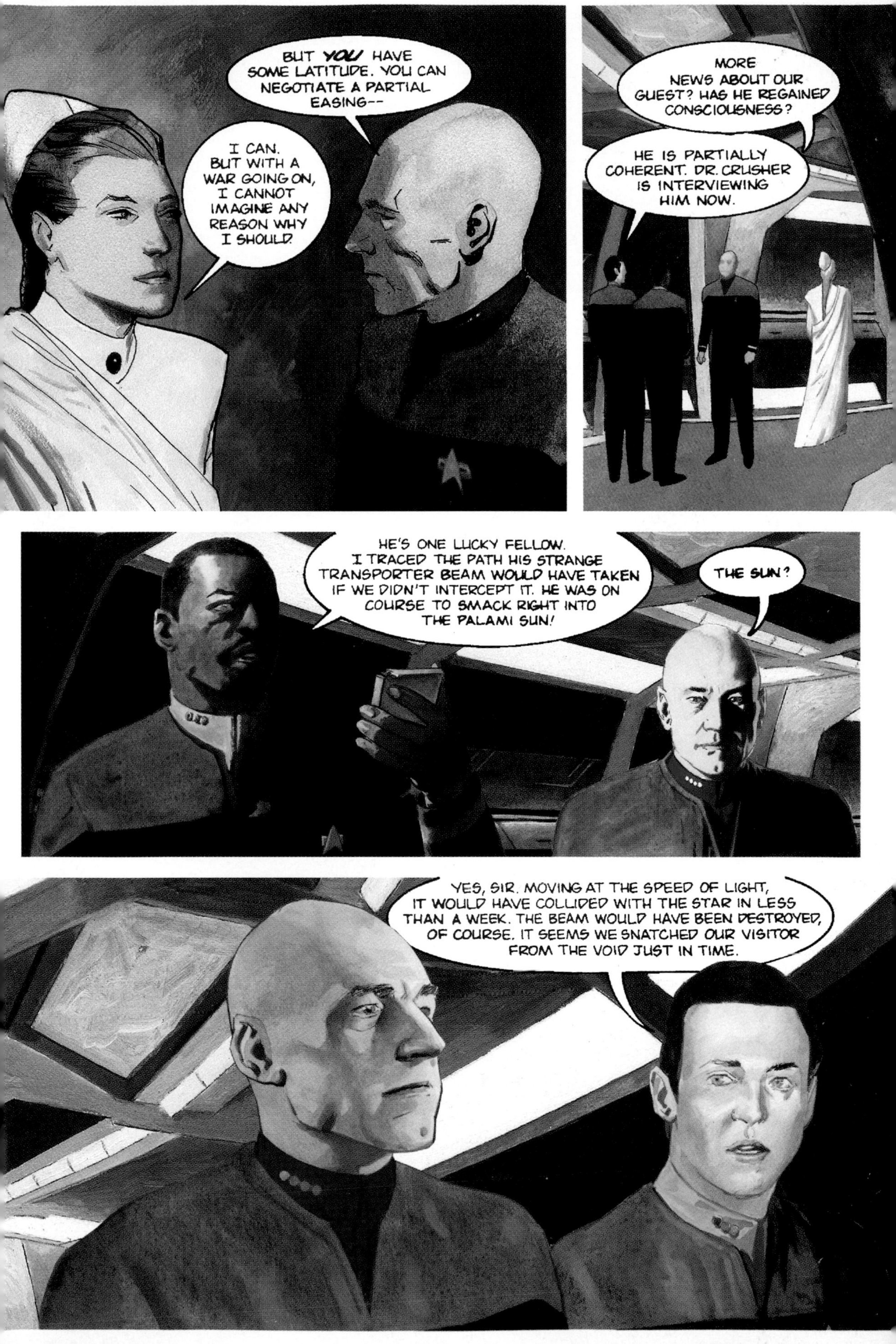
BUT YOU HAVE SOME LATITUDE. YOU CAN NEGOTIATE A PARTIAL EASING--
I CAN. BUT WITH A WAR GOING ON, I CANNOT IMAGINE ANY REASON WHY I SHOULD.
MORE NEWS ABOUT OUR GUEST? HAS HE REGAINED CONSCIOUSNESS?
HE IS PARTIALLY COHERENT. DR. CRUSHER IS INTERVIEWING HIM NOW.
HE'S ONE LUCKY FELLOW. I TRACED THE PATH HIS STRANGE TRANSPORTER BEAM WOULD HAVE TAKEN IF WE DIDN'T INTERCEPT IT. HE WAS ON COURSE TO SMACK RIGHT INTO THE PALAMI SUN!
THE SUN?
YES, SIR. MOVING AT THE SPEED OF LIGHT, IT WOULD HAVE COLLIDED WITH THE STAR IN LESS THAN A WEEK. THE BEAM WOULD HAVE BEEN DESTROYED, OF COURSE. IT SEEMS WE SNATCHED OUR VISITOR FROM THE VOID JUST IN TIME.

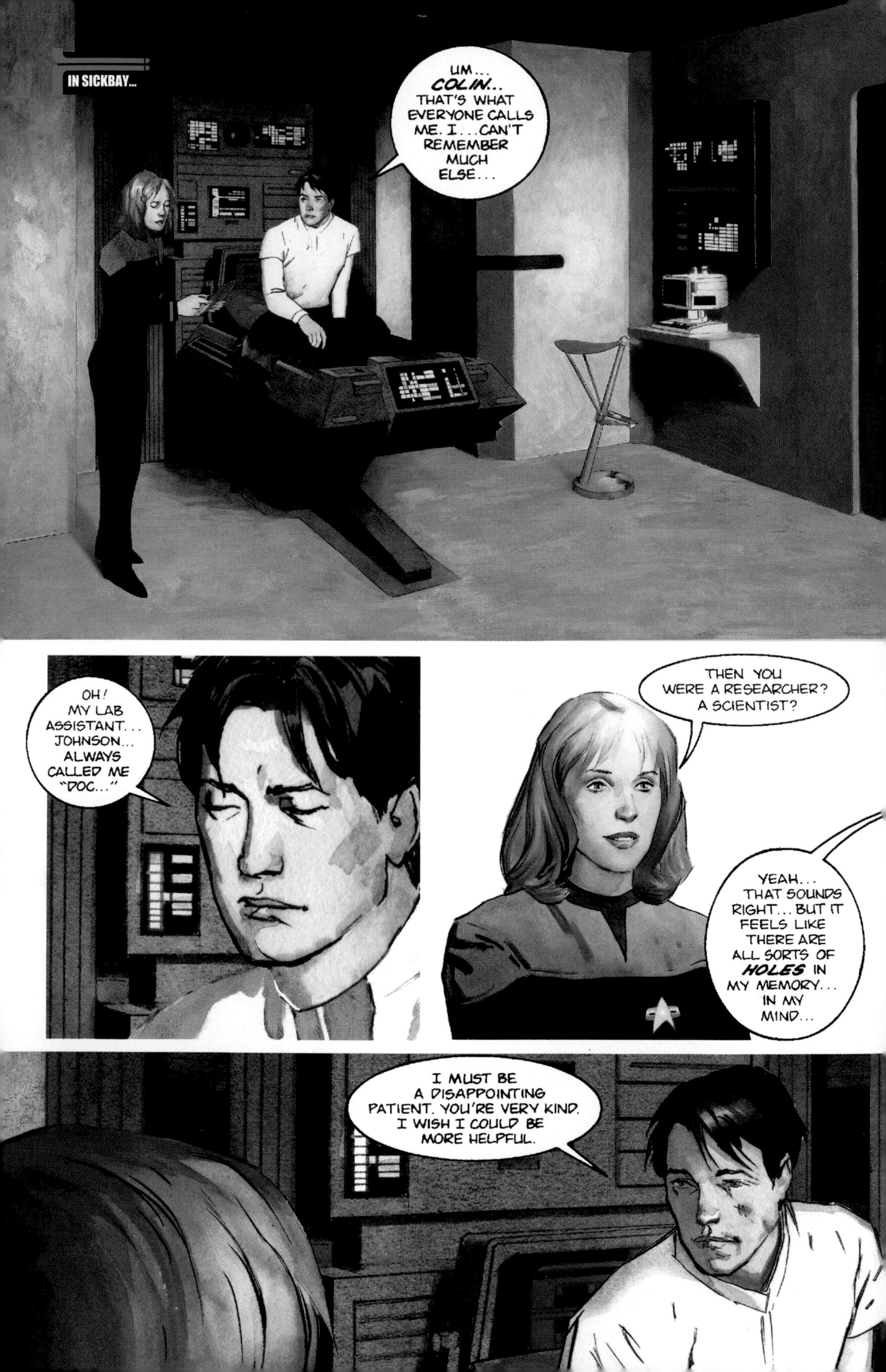
IN SICKBAY...
UM... COLIN... THAT'S WHAT EVERYONE CALLS ME. I...CAN'T REMEMBER MUCH ELSE...
OH! MY LAB ASSISTANT... JOHNSON... ALWAYS CALLED ME "DOC..."
THEN YOU WERE A RESEARCHER? A SCIENTIST?
YEAH... THAT SOUNDS RIGHT... BUT IT FEELS LIKE THERE ARE ALL SORTS OF HOLES IN MY MEMORY... IN MY MIND...
I MUST BE A DISAPPOINTING PATIENT. YOU'RE VERY KIND. I WISH I COULD BE MORE HELPFUL.

THESE ITEMS WERE ON YOUR PERSON WHEN YOU BEAMED...WHEN YOU ARRIVED. DO THEY LOOK FAMILIAR?

YEAH...MY LAB COAT...AND I USED A CANE BECAUSE OF MY LEG--

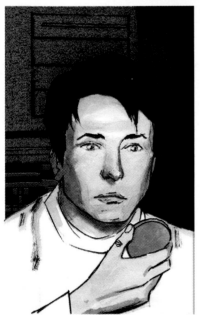

MARIA AND STEVIE...MY WIFE AND SON...WE'RE HEADING OFF TOGETHER FOR HOLIDAY...I'M SUPPOSED TO GO PICK THEM UP IN--

OHHH...

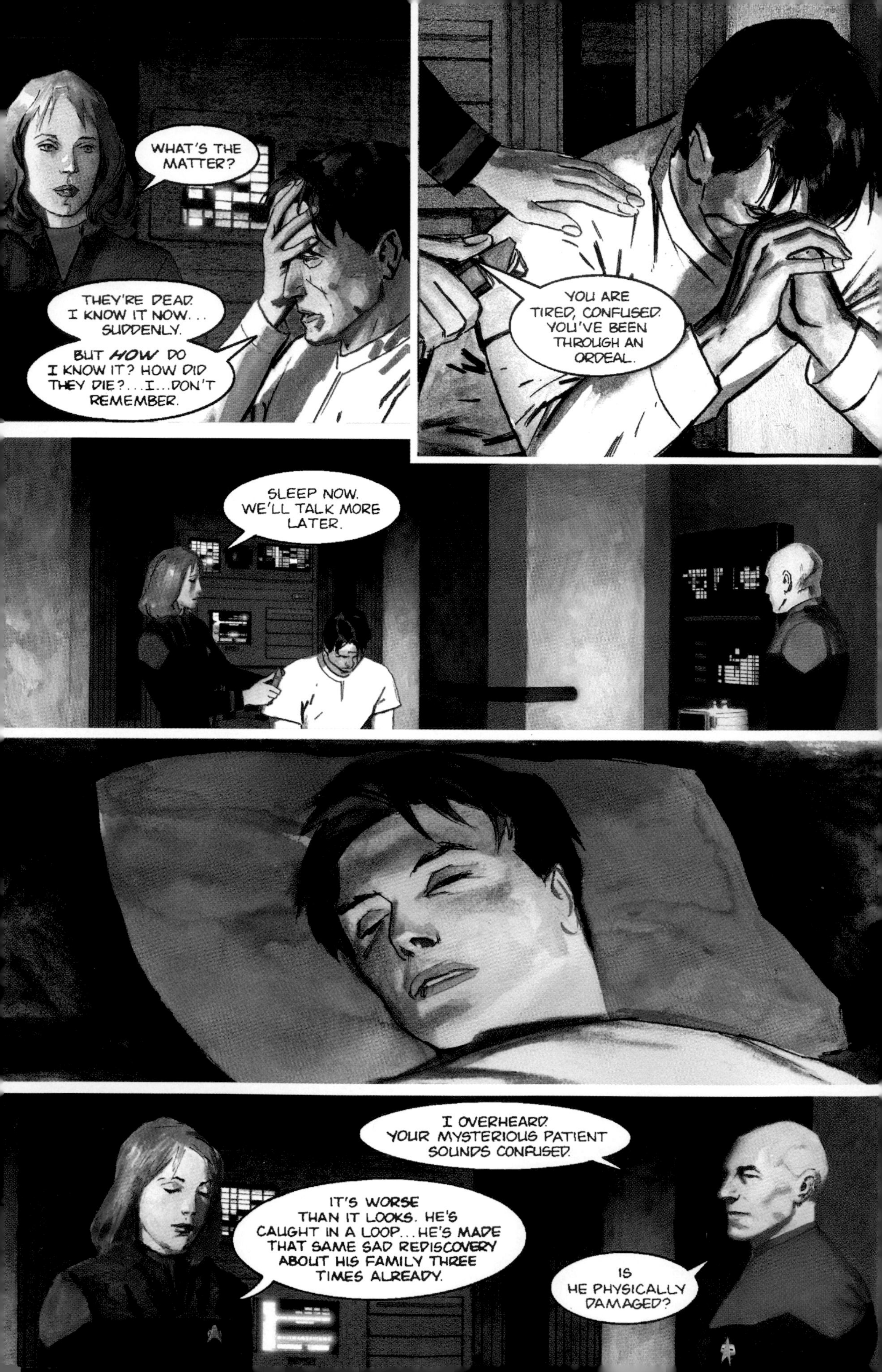
WHAT'S THE MATTER?
THEY'RE DEAD. I KNOW IT NOW... SUDDENLY.
BUT HOW DO I KNOW IT? HOW DID THEY DIE?...I...DON'T REMEMBER.
YOU ARE TIRED, CONFUSED. YOU'VE BEEN THROUGH AN ORDEAL.
SLEEP NOW. WE'LL TALK MORE LATER.
I OVERHEARD. YOUR MYSTERIOUS PATIENT SOUNDS CONFUSED.
IT'S WORSE THAN IT LOOKS. HE'S CAUGHT IN A LOOP...HE'S MADE THAT SAME SAD REDISCOVERY ABOUT HIS FAMILY THREE TIMES ALREADY.
IS HE PHYSICALLY DAMAGED?

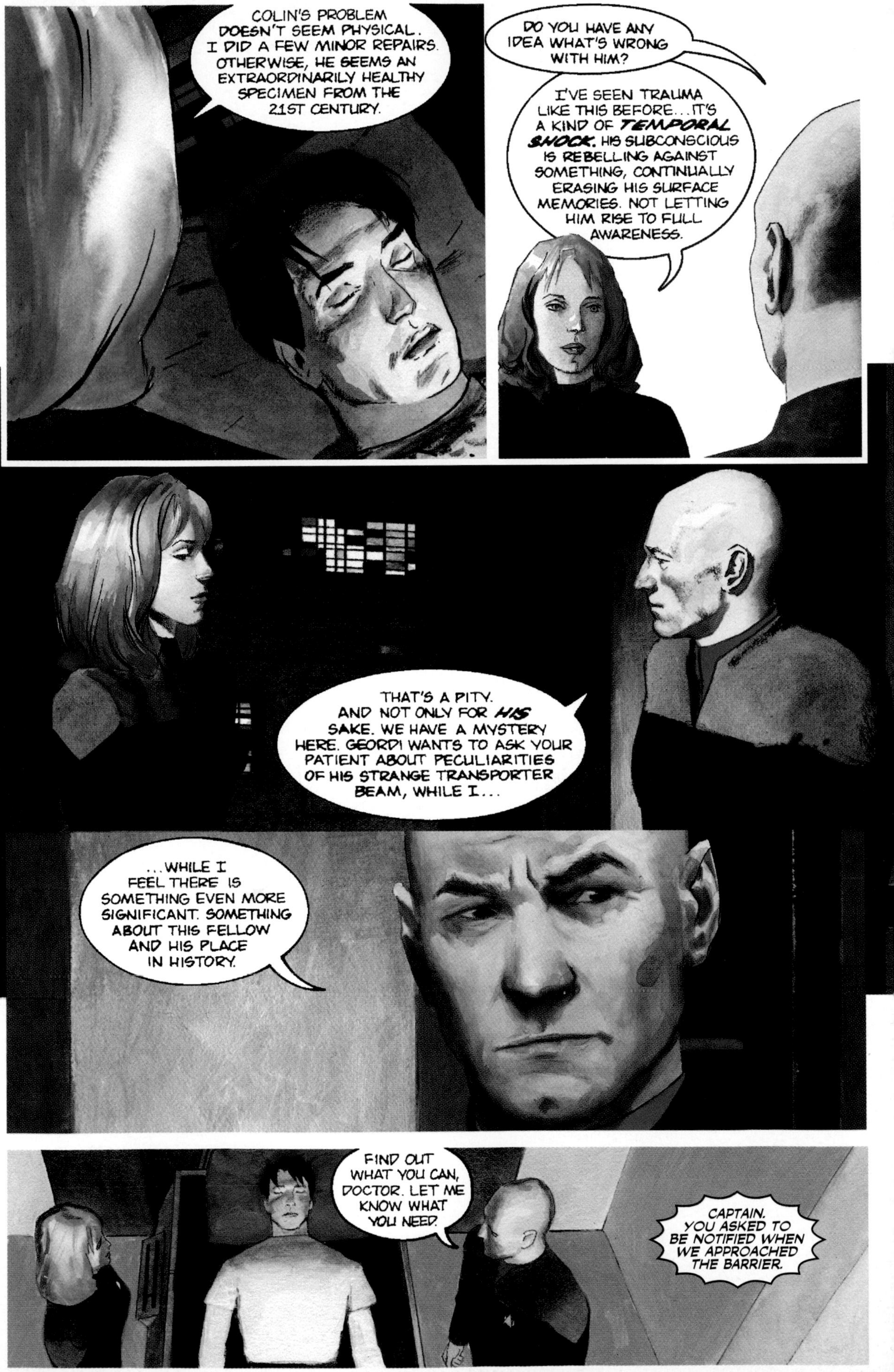
COLIN'S PROBLEM DOESN'T SEEM PHYSICAL. I DID A FEW MINOR REPAIRS. OTHERWISE, HE SEEMS AN EXTRAORDINARILY HEALTHY SPECIMEN FROM THE 21ST CENTURY.
DO YOU HAVE ANY IDEA WHAT'S WRONG WITH HIM?
I'VE SEEN TRAUMA LIKE THIS BEFORE... IT'S A KIND OF *TEMPORAL SHOCK.* HIS SUBCONSCIOUS IS REBELLING AGAINST SOMETHING, CONTINUALLY ERASING HIS SURFACE MEMORIES. NOT LETTING HIM RISE TO FULL AWARENESS.
THAT'S A PITY. AND NOT ONLY FOR *HIS* SAKE. WE HAVE A MYSTERY HERE. GEORDI WANTS TO ASK YOUR PATIENT ABOUT PECULIARITIES OF HIS STRANGE TRANSPORTER BEAM, WHILE I...
...WHILE I FEEL THERE IS SOMETHING EVEN MORE SIGNIFICANT. SOMETHING ABOUT THIS FELLOW AND HIS PLACE IN HISTORY.
FIND OUT WHAT YOU CAN, DOCTOR. LET ME KNOW WHAT YOU NEED.
CAPTAIN. YOU ASKED TO BE NOTIFIED WHEN WE APPROACHED THE BARRIER.

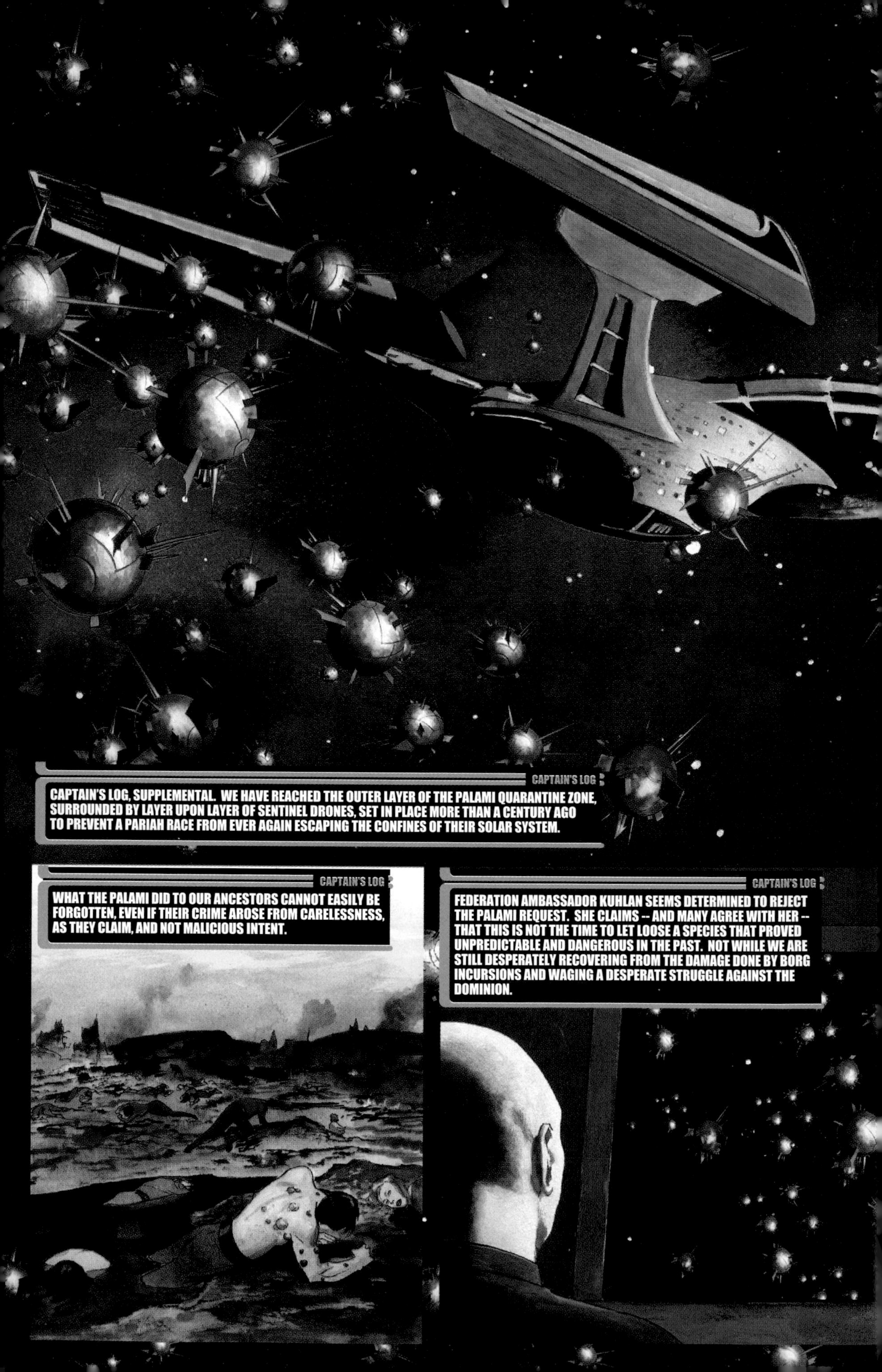
CAPTAIN'S LOG
CAPTAIN'S LOG, SUPPLEMENTAL. WE HAVE REACHED THE OUTER LAYER OF THE PALAMI QUARANTINE ZONE, SURROUNDED BY LAYER UPON LAYER OF SENTINEL DRONES, SET IN PLACE MORE THAN A CENTURY AGO TO PREVENT A PARIAH RACE FROM EVER AGAIN ESCAPING THE CONFINES OF THEIR SOLAR SYSTEM.
CAPTAIN'S LOG
WHAT THE PALAMI DID TO OUR ANCESTORS CANNOT EASILY BE FORGOTTEN, EVEN IF THEIR CRIME AROSE FROM CARELESSNESS, AS THEY CLAIM, AND NOT MALICIOUS INTENT.
CAPTAIN'S LOG
FEDERATION AMBASSADOR KUHLAN SEEMS DETERMINED TO REJECT THE PALAMI REQUEST. SHE CLAIMS -- AND MANY AGREE WITH HER -- THAT THIS IS NOT THE TIME TO LET LOOSE A SPECIES THAT PROVED UNPREDICTABLE AND DANGEROUS IN THE PAST. NOT WHILE WE ARE STILL DESPERATELY RECOVERING FROM THE DAMAGE DONE BY BORG INCURSIONS AND WAGING A DESPERATE STRUGGLE AGAINST THE DOMINION.

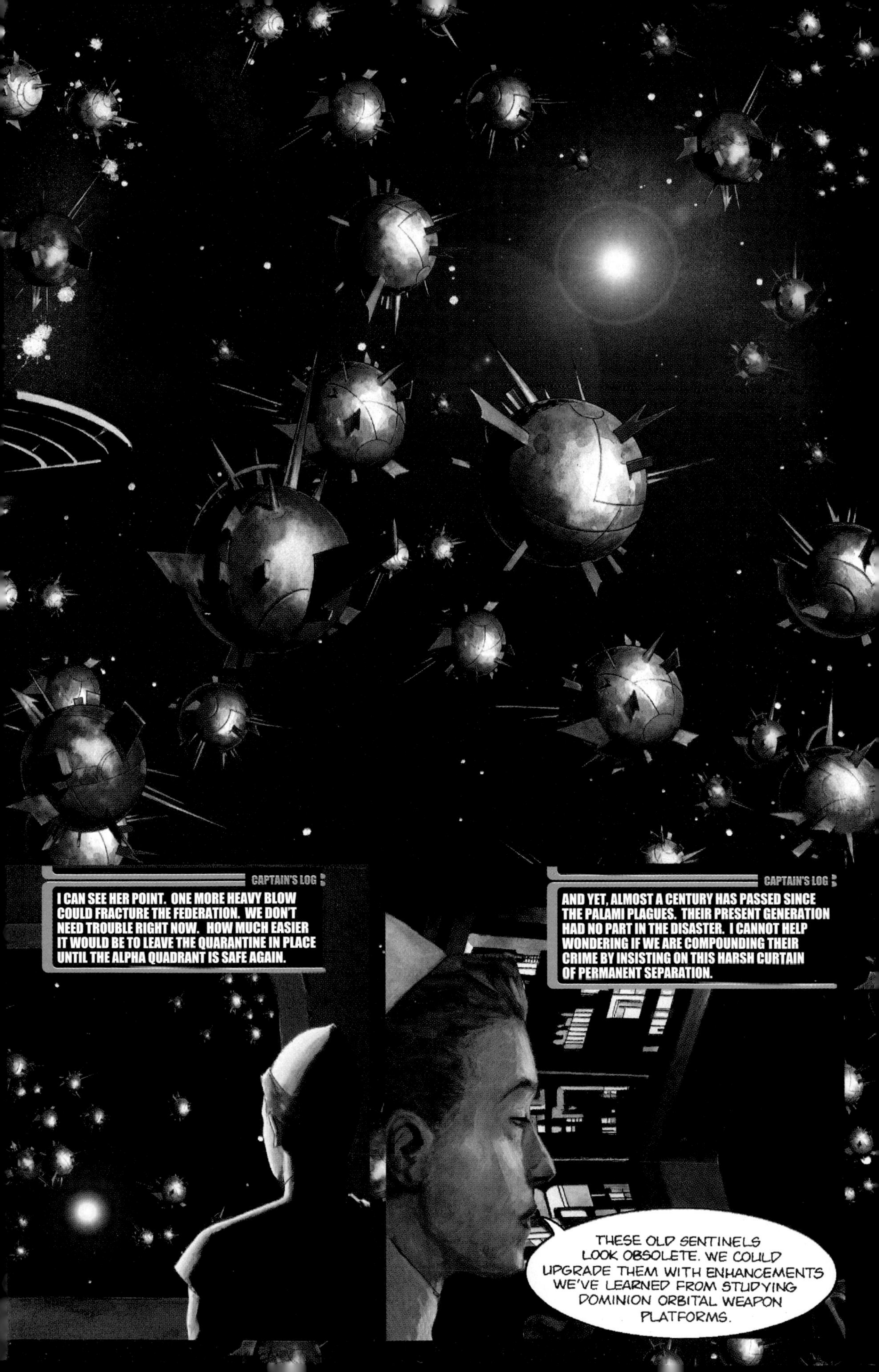
CAPTAIN'S LOG
I CAN SEE HER POINT. ONE MORE HEAVY BLOW COULD FRACTURE THE FEDERATION. WE DON'T NEED TROUBLE RIGHT NOW. HOW MUCH EASIER IT WOULD BE TO LEAVE THE QUARANTINE IN PLACE UNTIL THE ALPHA QUADRANT IS SAFE AGAIN.
CAPTAIN'S LOG
AND YET, ALMOST A CENTURY HAS PASSED SINCE THE PALAMI PLAGUES. THEIR PRESENT GENERATION HAD NO PART IN THE DISASTER. I CANNOT HELP WONDERING IF WE ARE COMPOUNDING THEIR CRIME BY INSISTING ON THIS HARSH CURTAIN OF PERMANENT SEPARATION.
THESE OLD SENTINELS LOOK OBSOLETE. WE COULD UPGRADE THEM WITH ENHANCEMENTS WE'VE LEARNED FROM STUDYING DOMINION ORBITAL WEAPON PLATFORMS.

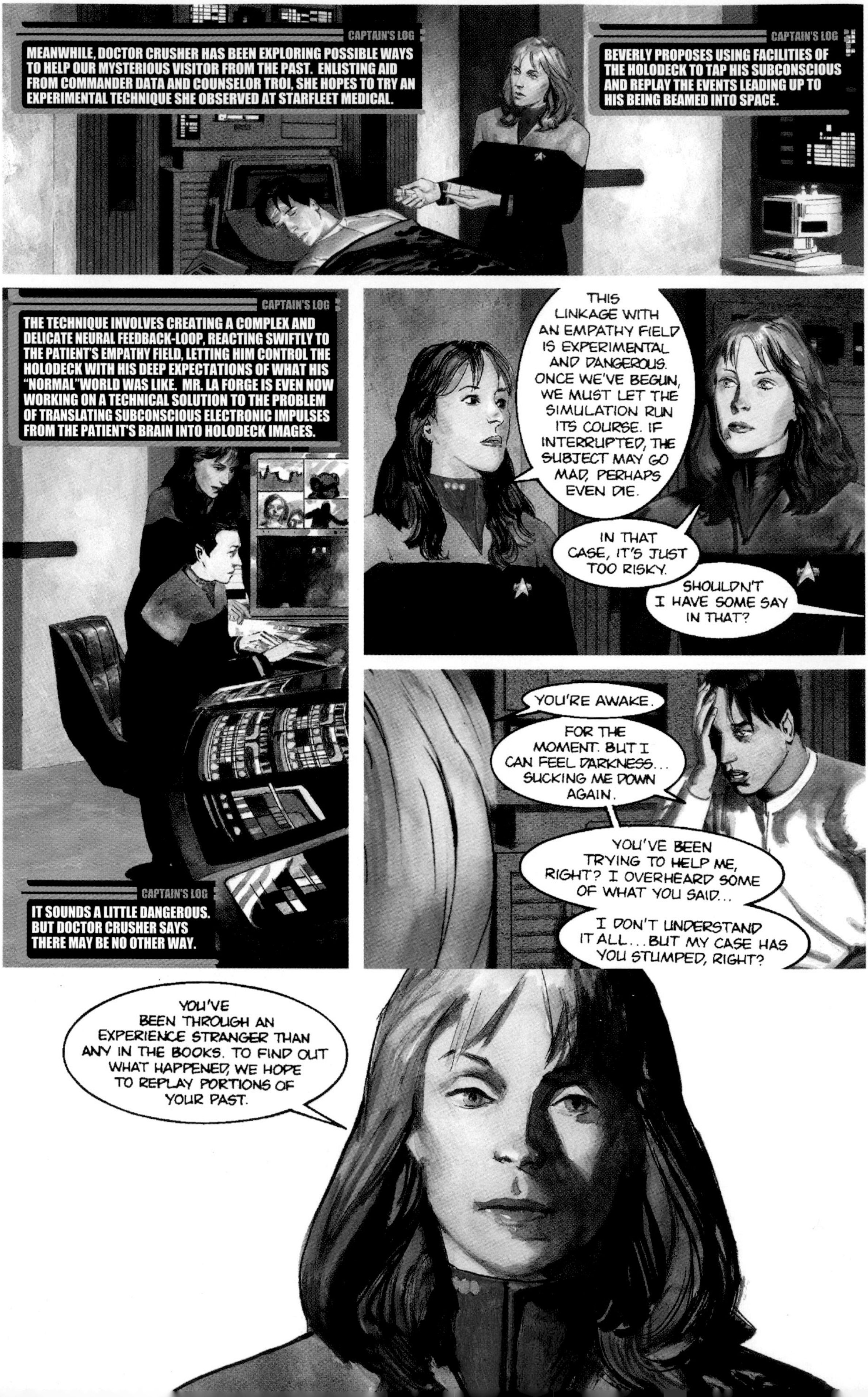
CAPTAIN'S LOG
MEANWHILE, DOCTOR CRUSHER HAS BEEN EXPLORING POSSIBLE WAYS TO HELP OUR MYSTERIOUS VISITOR FROM THE PAST. ENLISTING AID FROM COMMANDER DATA AND COUNSELOR TROI, SHE HOPES TO TRY AN EXPERIMENTAL TECHNIQUE SHE OBSERVED AT STARFLEET MEDICAL.
CAPTAIN'S LOG
BEVERLY PROPOSES USING FACILITIES OF THE HOLODECK TO TAP HIS SUBCONSCIOUS AND REPLAY THE EVENTS LEADING UP TO HIS BEING BEAMED INTO SPACE.
CAPTAIN'S LOG
THE TECHNIQUE INVOLVES CREATING A COMPLEX AND DELICATE NEURAL FEEDBACK-LOOP, REACTING SWIFTLY TO THE PATIENT'S EMPATHY FIELD, LETTING HIM CONTROL THE HOLODECK WITH HIS DEEP EXPECTATIONS OF WHAT HIS "NORMAL"WORLD WAS LIKE. MR. LA FORGE IS EVEN NOW WORKING ON A TECHNICAL SOLUTION TO THE PROBLEM OF TRANSLATING SUBCONSCIOUS ELECTRONIC IMPULSES FROM THE PATIENT'S BRAIN INTO HOLODECK IMAGES.
CAPTAIN'S LOG
IT SOUNDS A LITTLE DANGEROUS. BUT DOCTOR CRUSHER SAYS THERE MAY BE NO OTHER WAY.
THIS LINKAGE WITH AN EMPATHY FIELD IS EXPERIMENTAL AND DANGEROUS. ONCE WE'VE BEGUN, WE MUST LET THE SIMULATION RUN ITS COURSE. IF INTERRUPTED, THE SUBJECT MAY GO MAD, PERHAPS EVEN DIE.
IN THAT CASE, IT'S JUST TOO RISKY.
SHOULDN'T I HAVE SOME SAY IN THAT?
YOU'RE AWAKE.
FOR THE MOMENT. BUT I CAN FEEL DARKNESS... SUCKING ME DOWN AGAIN.
YOU'VE BEEN TRYING TO HELP ME, RIGHT? I OVERHEARD SOME OF WHAT YOU SAID...
I DON'T UNDERSTAND IT ALL... BUT MY CASE HAS YOU STUMPED, RIGHT?
YOU'VE BEEN THROUGH AN EXPERIENCE STRANGER THAN ANY IN THE BOOKS. TO FIND OUT WHAT HAPPENED, WE HOPE TO REPLAY PORTIONS OF YOUR PAST.

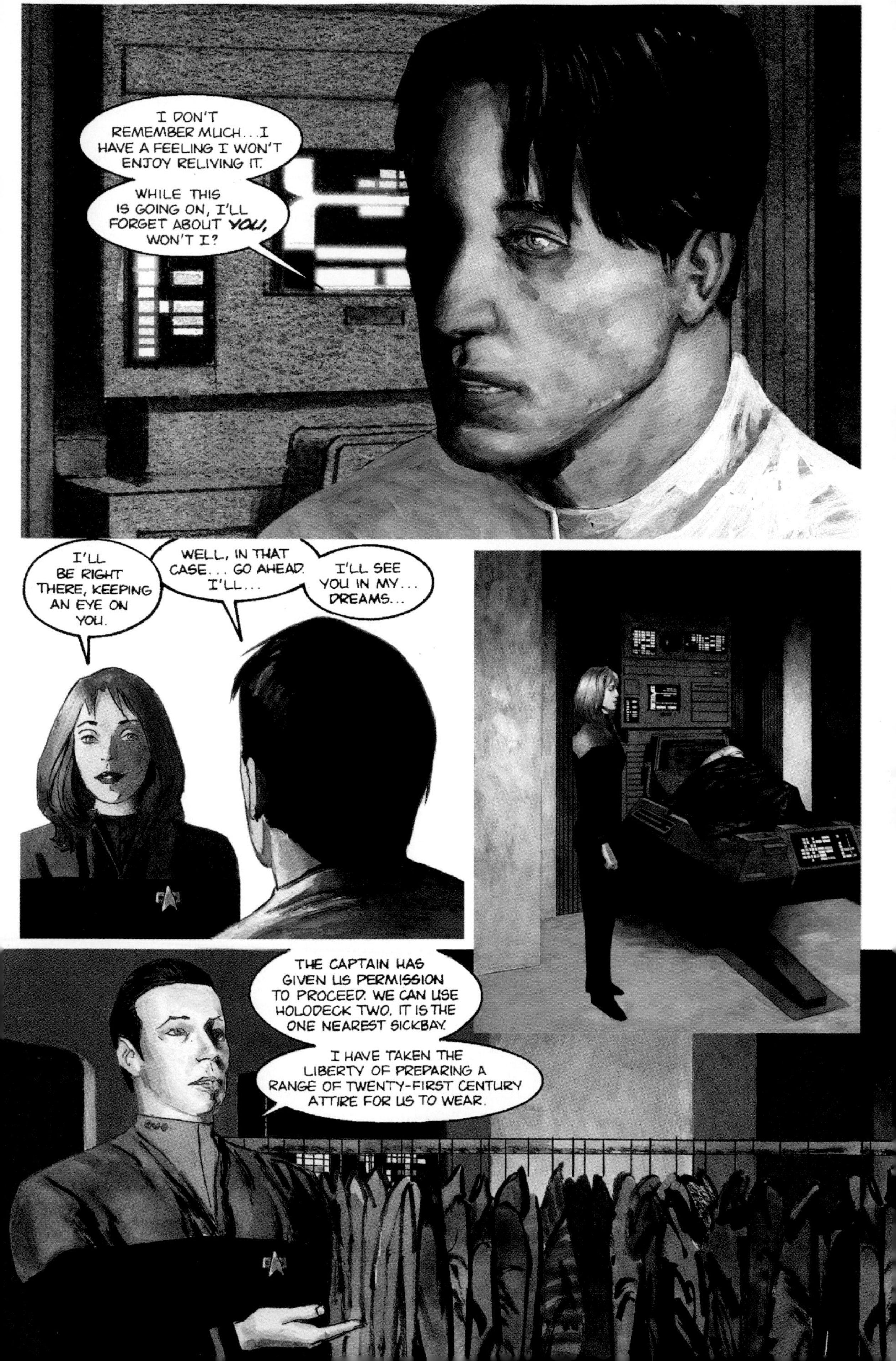
I DON'T REMEMBER MUCH... I HAVE A FEELING I WON'T ENJOY RELIVING IT.
WHILE THIS IS GOING ON, I'LL FORGET ABOUT *YOU,* WON'T I?
I'LL BE RIGHT THERE, KEEPING AN EYE ON YOU.
WELL, IN THAT CASE... GO AHEAD. I'LL...
I'LL SEE YOU IN MY... DREAMS...
THE CAPTAIN HAS GIVEN US **PERMISSION** TO PROCEED. WE CAN USE HOLODECK TWO. IT IS THE ONE NEAREST SICKBAY.
I HAVE TAKEN THE LIBERTY OF PREPARING A RANGE OF TWENTY-FIRST CENTURY ATTIRE FOR US TO WEAR.

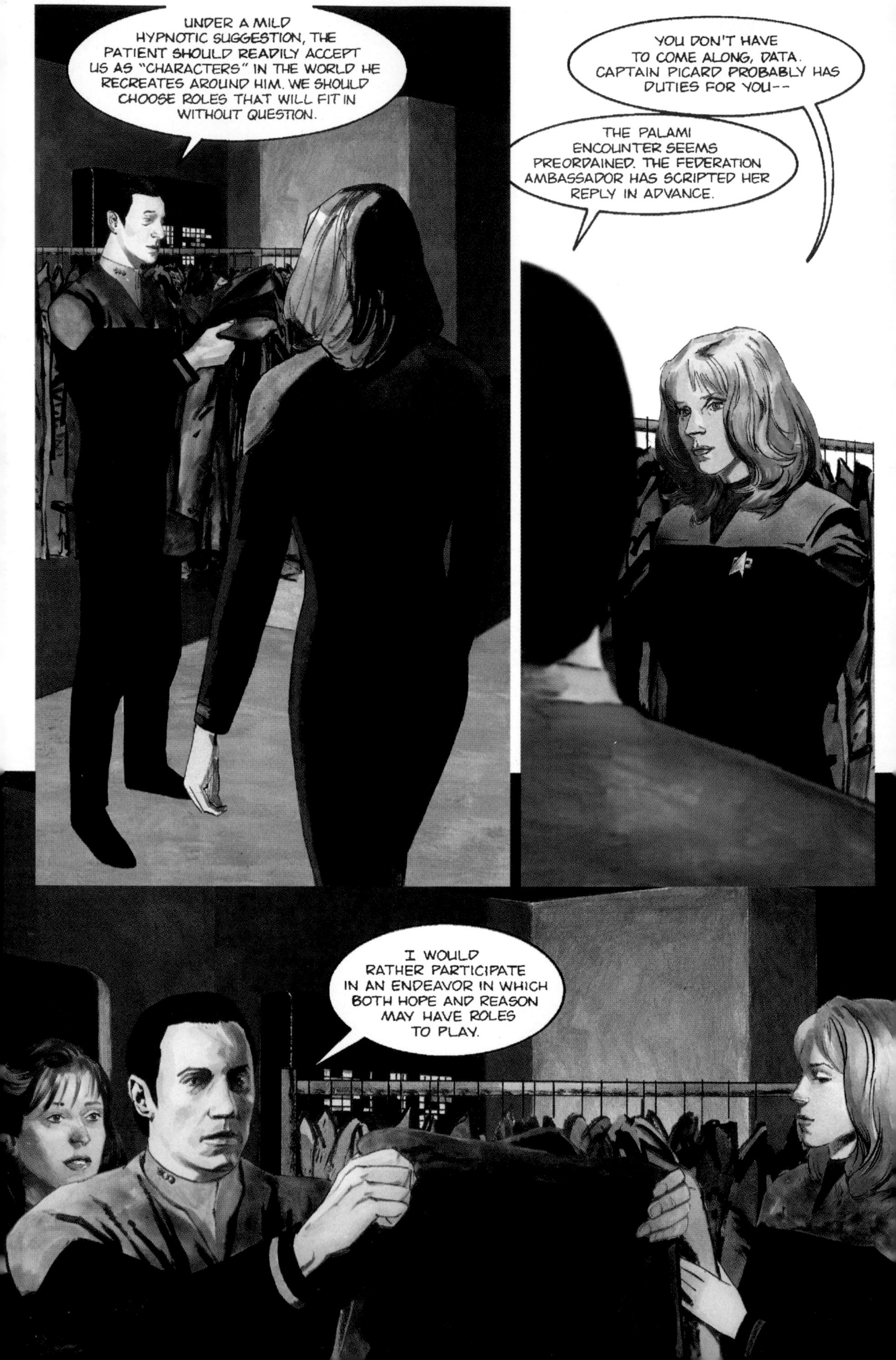
UNDER A MILD HYPNOTIC SUGGESTION, THE PATIENT SHOULD READILY ACCEPT US AS "CHARACTERS" IN THE WORLD HE RECREATES AROUND HIM. WE SHOULD CHOOSE ROLES THAT WILL FIT IN WITHOUT QUESTION.
YOU DON'T HAVE TO COME ALONG, DATA. CAPTAIN PICARD PROBABLY HAS DUTIES FOR YOU--
THE PALAMI ENCOUNTER SEEMS PREORDAINED. THE FEDERATION AMBASSADOR HAS SCRIPTED HER REPLY IN ADVANCE.
I WOULD RATHER PARTICIPATE IN AN ENDEAVOR IN WHICH BOTH HOPE AND REASON MAY HAVE ROLES TO PLAY.

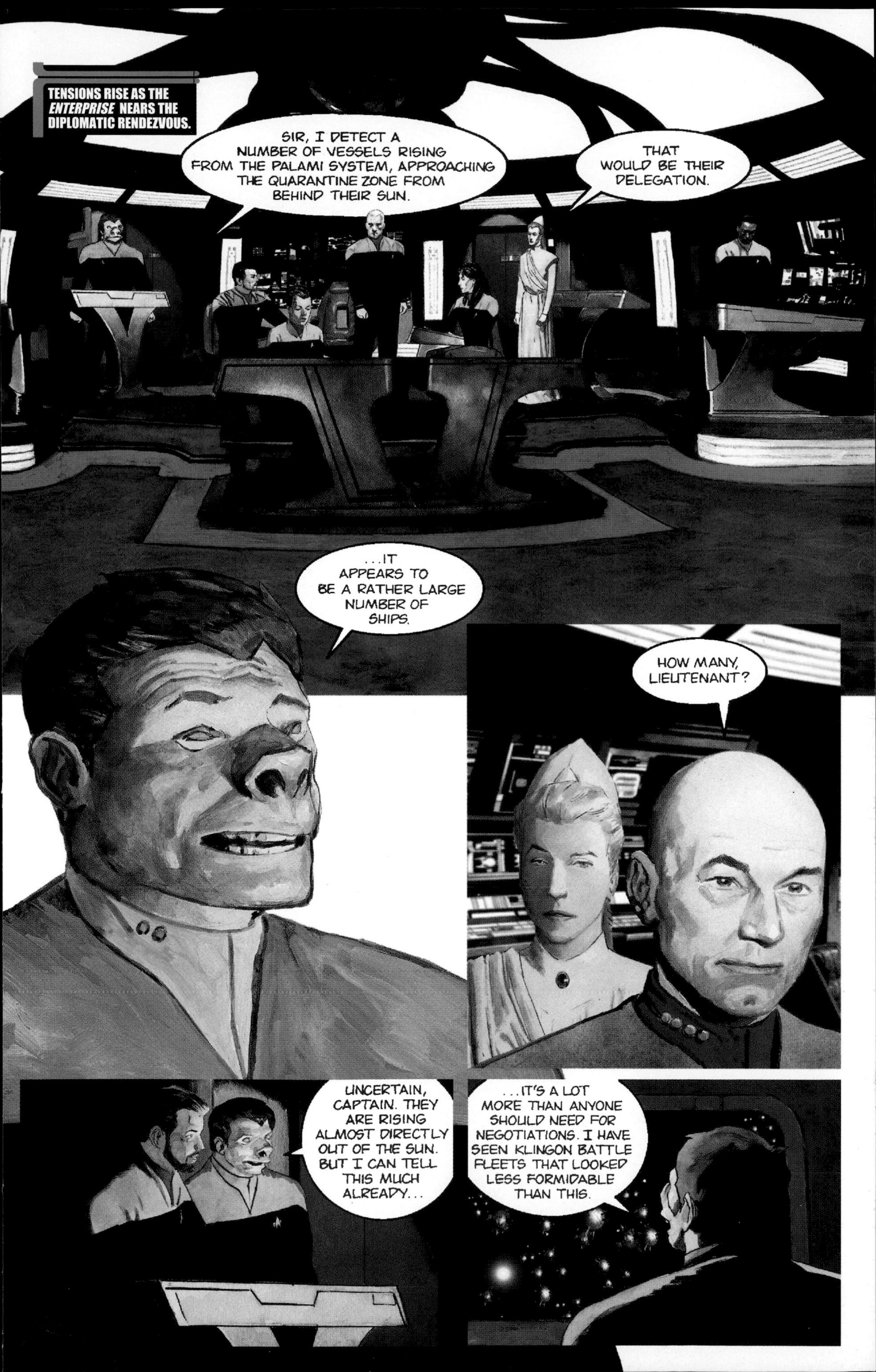
TENSIONS RISE AS THE *ENTERPRISE* NEARS THE DIPLOMATIC RENDEZVOUS.
SIR, I DETECT A NUMBER OF VESSELS RISING FROM THE PALAMI SYSTEM, APPROACHING THE QUARANTINE ZONE FROM BEHIND THEIR SUN.
THAT WOULD BE THEIR DELEGATION.
...IT APPEARS TO BE A RATHER LARGE NUMBER OF SHIPS.
HOW MANY, LIEUTENANT?
UNCERTAIN, CAPTAIN. THEY ARE RISING ALMOST DIRECTLY OUT OF THE SUN. BUT I CAN TELL THIS MUCH ALREADY...
...IT'S A LOT MORE THAN ANYONE SHOULD NEED FOR NEGOTIATIONS. I HAVE SEEN KLINGON BATTLE FLEETS THAT LOOKED LESS FORMIDABLE THAN THIS.

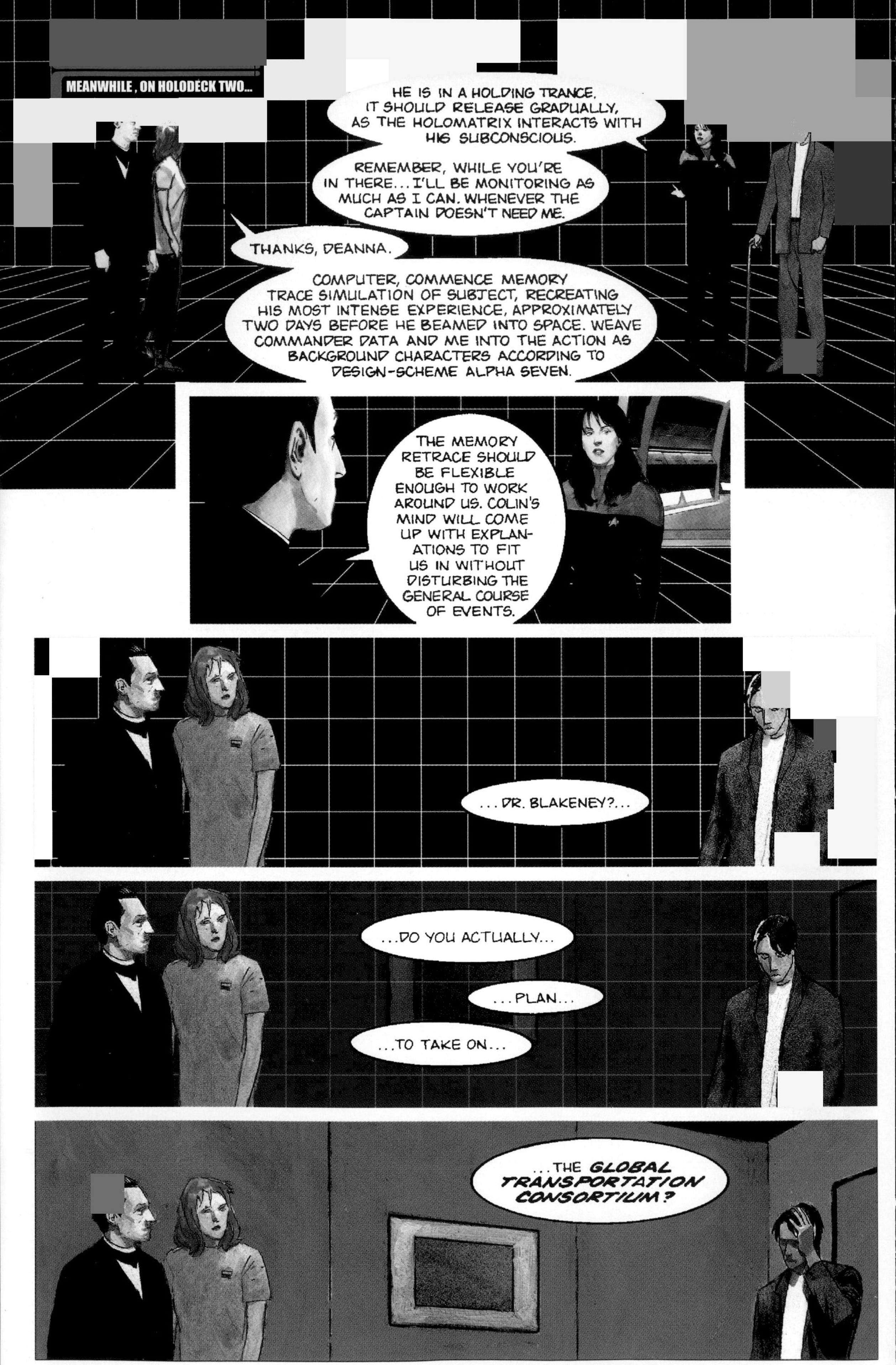
MEANWHILE, ON HOLODECK TWO...
HE IS IN A HOLDING TRANCE. IT SHOULD RELEASE GRADUALLY, AS THE HOLOMATRIX INTERACTS WITH HIS SUBCONSCIOUS.
REMEMBER, WHILE YOU'RE IN THERE... I'LL BE MONITORING AS MUCH AS I CAN. WHENEVER THE CAPTAIN DOESN'T NEED ME.
THANKS, DEANNA.
COMPUTER, COMMENCE MEMORY TRACE SIMULATION OF SUBJECT, RECREATING HIS MOST INTENSE EXPERIENCE, APPROXIMATELY TWO DAYS BEFORE HE BEAMED INTO SPACE. WEAVE COMMANDER DATA AND ME INTO THE ACTION AS BACKGROUND CHARACTERS ACCORDING TO DESIGN-SCHEME ALPHA SEVEN.
THE MEMORY RETRACE SHOULD BE FLEXIBLE ENOUGH TO WORK AROUND US. COLIN'S MIND WILL COME UP WITH EXPLAN-ATIONS TO FIT US IN WITHOUT DISTURBING THE GENERAL COURSE OF EVENTS.
...DR. BLAKENEY?...
...DO YOU ACTUALLY...
...PLAN...
...TO TAKE ON...
...THE GLOBAL TRANSPORTATION CONSORTIUM?

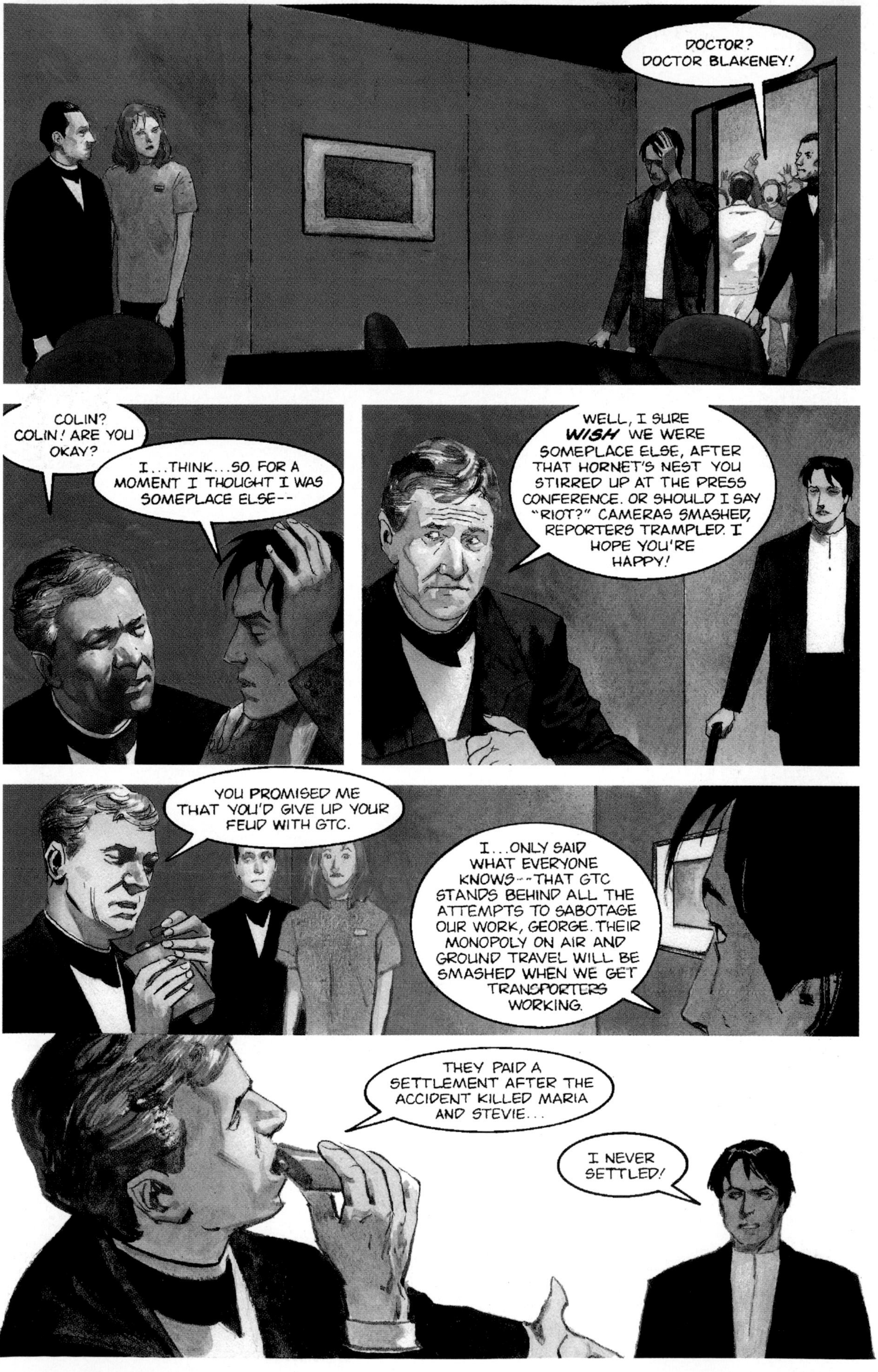

DOCTOR? DOCTOR BLAKENEY!
COLIN? COLIN! ARE YOU OKAY?
I...THINK...SO. FOR A MOMENT I THOUGHT I WAS SOMEPLACE ELSE--
WELL, I SURE WISH WE WERE SOMEPLACE ELSE, AFTER THAT HORNET'S NEST YOU STIRRED UP AT THE PRESS CONFERENCE. OR SHOULD I SAY "RIOT?" CAMERAS SMASHED, REPORTERS TRAMPLED. I HOPE YOU'RE HAPPY!
YOU PROMISED ME THAT YOU'D GIVE UP YOUR FEUD WITH GTC.
I...ONLY SAID WHAT EVERYONE KNOWS--THAT GTC STANDS BEHIND ALL THE ATTEMPTS TO SABOTAGE OUR WORK, GEORGE. THEIR MONOPOLY ON AIR AND GROUND TRAVEL WILL BE SMASHED WHEN WE GET TRANSPORTERS WORKING.
THEY PAID A SETTLEMENT AFTER THE ACCIDENT KILLED MARIA AND STEVIE...
I NEVER SETTLED!

LOOK, COLIN, I'M WITH YOU, BUT OUR INVESTORS ARE WORRIED. THIS PASCAL LEIGHT CHARACTER AND HIS PSYCHOTIC HARANGUES HAVE GOT THE PUBLIC SPOOKED.

MAYBE WE SHOULD CONCENTRATE ON HIGH-VALUE CARGO FOR NOW--

WE'LL NEVER BREAK EVEN WITH CARGO, GEORGE. PASSENGERS! LET FOLKS FLIT IN AN INSTANT FROM TOKYO TO PARIS. THEY'LL HAPPILY COVER OUR DEVELOPMENT COSTS. THEN WE'LL CUT PRICES...USE THE TRANSPORTER TO REVISIT THE MOON...OPEN UP SPACE...

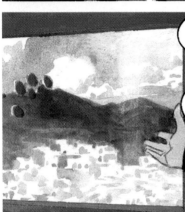

SPACE! COLIN, I'VE TOLD YOU BEFORE, WE ALREADY HAVE AN IMAGE PROBLEM WITHOUT CONFUSING IT WITH BUCK ROGERS STUFF.

ANYWAY, SPACE HAS BEEN A DEAD-END FOR DECADES. LET'S BE HAPPY WE GOT APPROVAL TO EXPERIMENT WITH TRANSPORTING CARGO--

"-- TO UNIT B ON MOUNT THUNDER AND THEN BACK AGAIN."

THAT'S ONLY THE BEGINNING, GEORGE...

DREAM ON, BLAKENEY!

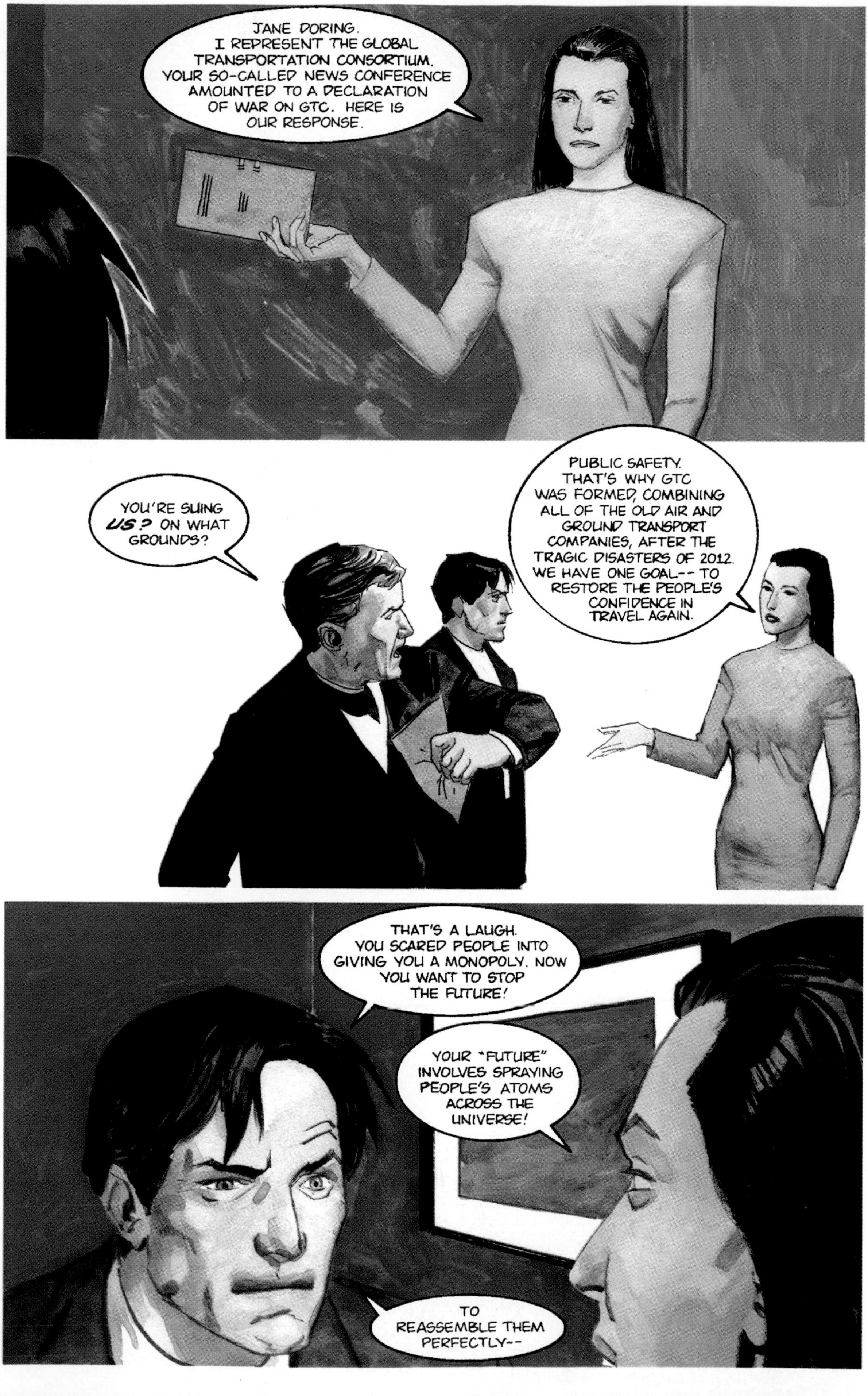
JANE DORING. I REPRESENT THE GLOBAL TRANSPORTATION CONSORTIUM. YOUR SO-CALLED NEWS CONFERENCE AMOUNTED TO A DECLARATION OF WAR ON GTC. HERE IS OUR RESPONSE.
YOU'RE SUING US? ON WHAT GROUNDS?
PUBLIC SAFETY. THAT'S WHY GTC WAS FORMED, COMBINING ALL OF THE OLD AIR AND GROUND TRANSPORT COMPANIES, AFTER THE TRAGIC DISASTERS OF 2012. WE HAVE ONE GOAL-- TO RESTORE THE PEOPLE'S CONFIDENCE IN TRAVEL AGAIN.
THAT'S A LAUGH. YOU SCARED PEOPLE INTO GIVING YOU A MONOPOLY. NOW YOU WANT TO STOP THE FUTURE!
YOUR "FUTURE" INVOLVES SPRAYING PEOPLE'S ATOMS ACROSS THE UNIVERSE!
TO REASSEMBLE THEM PERFECTLY--

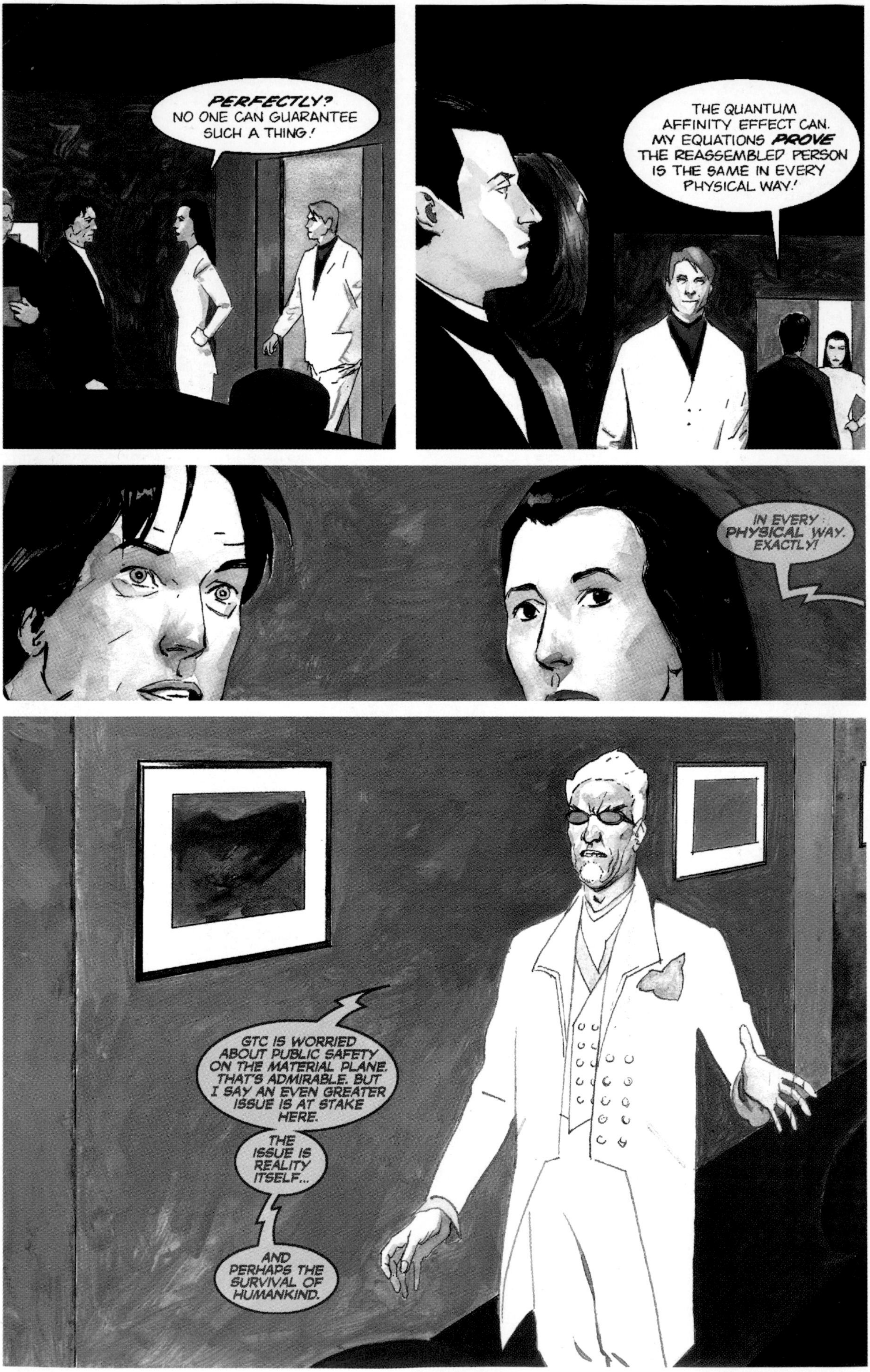
PERFECTLY? NO ONE CAN GUARANTEE SUCH A THING!
THE QUANTUM AFFINITY EFFECT CAN. MY EQUATIONS PROVE THE REASSEMBLED PERSON IS THE SAME IN EVERY PHYSICAL WAY!
IN EVERY PHYSICAL WAY. EXACTLY!
GTC IS WORRIED ABOUT PUBLIC SAFETY ON THE MATERIAL PLANE. THAT'S ADMIRABLE. BUT I SAY AN EVEN GREATER ISSUE IS AT STAKE HERE.
THE ISSUE IS REALITY ITSELF...
AND PERHAPS THE SURVIVAL OF HUMANKIND.

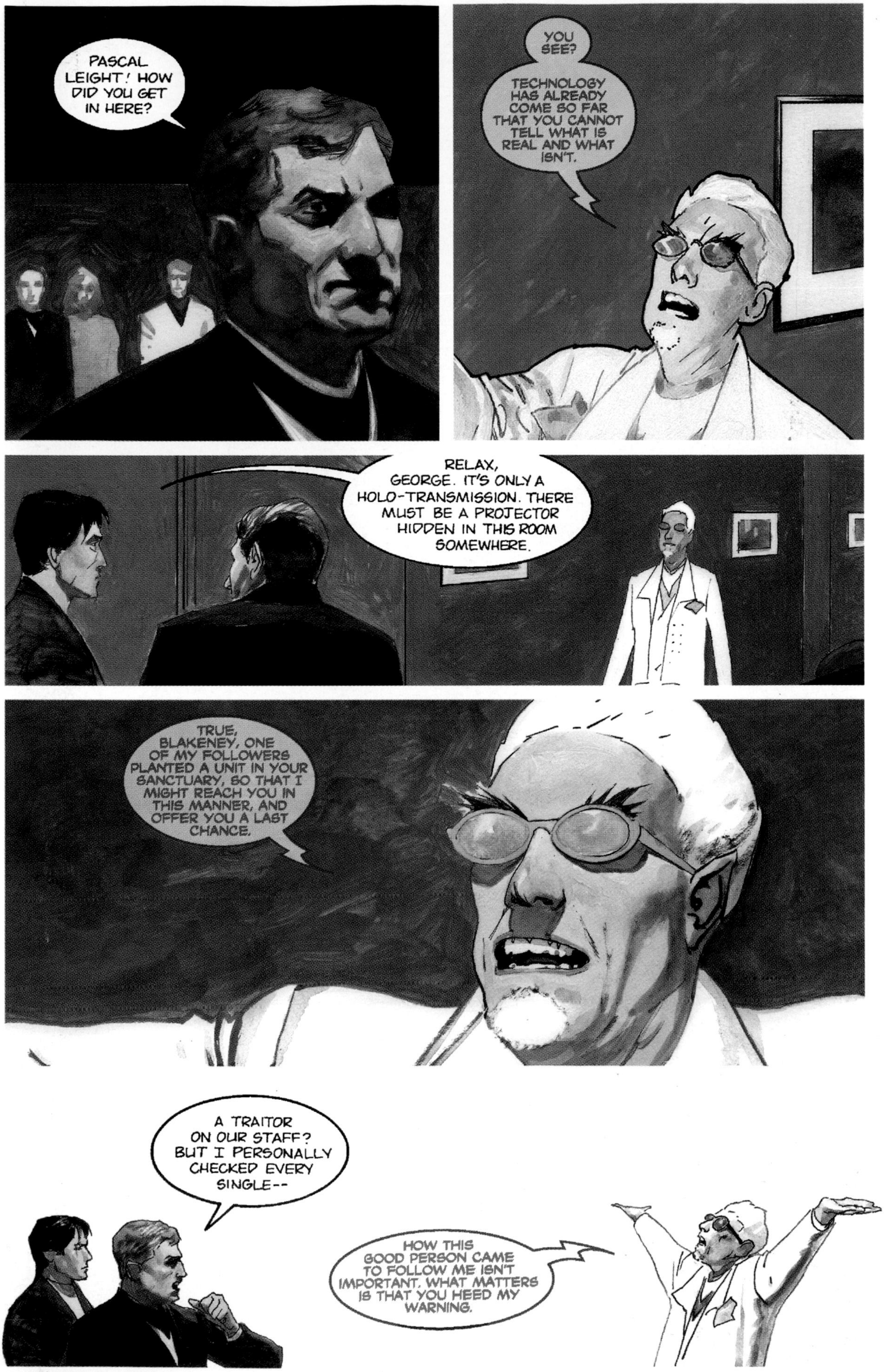
PASCAL LEIGHT! HOW DID YOU GET IN HERE?
YOU SEE?
TECHNOLOGY HAS ALREADY COME SO FAR THAT YOU CANNOT TELL WHAT IS REAL AND WHAT ISN'T.
RELAX, GEORGE. IT'S ONLY A HOLO-TRANSMISSION. THERE MUST BE A PROJECTOR HIDDEN IN THIS ROOM SOMEWHERE.
TRUE, BLAKENEY. ONE OF MY FOLLOWERS PLANTED A UNIT IN YOUR SANCTUARY, SO THAT I MIGHT REACH YOU IN THIS MANNER, AND OFFER YOU A LAST CHANCE.
A TRAITOR ON OUR STAFF? BUT I PERSONALLY CHECKED EVERY SINGLE--
HOW THIS GOOD PERSON CAME TO FOLLOW ME ISN'T IMPORTANT. WHAT MATTERS IS THAT YOU HEED MY WARNING.

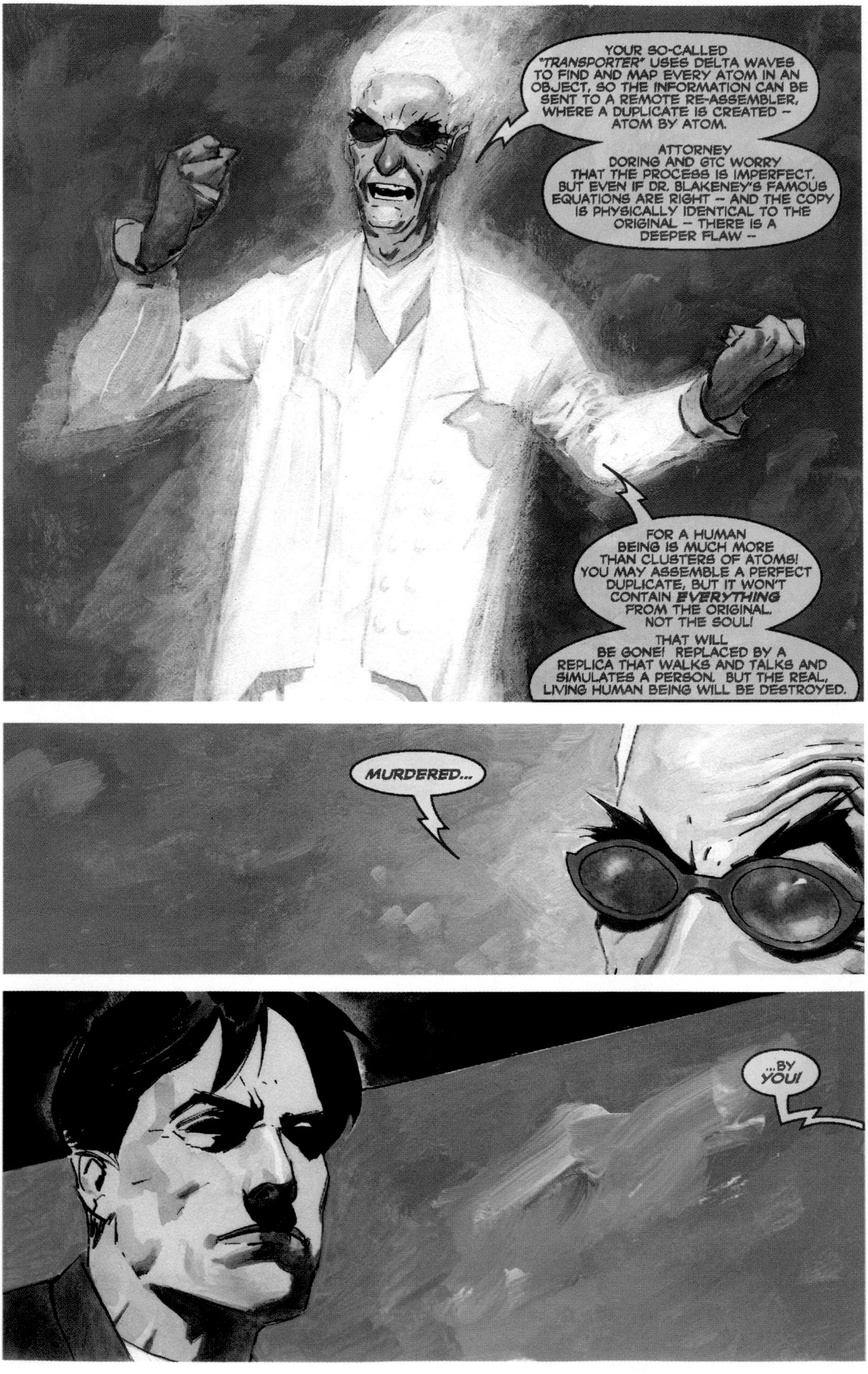
YOUR SO-CALLED "TRANSPORTER" USES DELTA WAVES TO FIND AND MAP EVERY ATOM IN AN OBJECT, SO THE INFORMATION CAN BE SENT TO A REMOTE RE-ASSEMBLER, WHERE A DUPLICATE IS CREATED -- ATOM BY ATOM.
ATTORNEY DORING AND GTC WORRY THAT THE PROCESS IS IMPERFECT, BUT EVEN IF DR. BLAKENEY'S FAMOUS EQUATIONS ARE RIGHT -- AND THE COPY IS PHYSICALLY IDENTICAL TO THE ORIGINAL -- THERE IS A DEEPER FLAW --
FOR A HUMAN BEING IS MUCH MORE THAN CLUSTERS OF ATOMS! YOU MAY ASSEMBLE A PERFECT DUPLICATE, BUT IT WON'T CONTAIN EVERYTHING FROM THE ORIGINAL. NOT THE SOUL!
THAT WILL BE GONE! REPLACED BY A REPLICA THAT WALKS AND TALKS AND SIMULATES A PERSON. BUT THE REAL, LIVING HUMAN BEING WILL BE DESTROYED.
MURDERED...
...BY YOU!

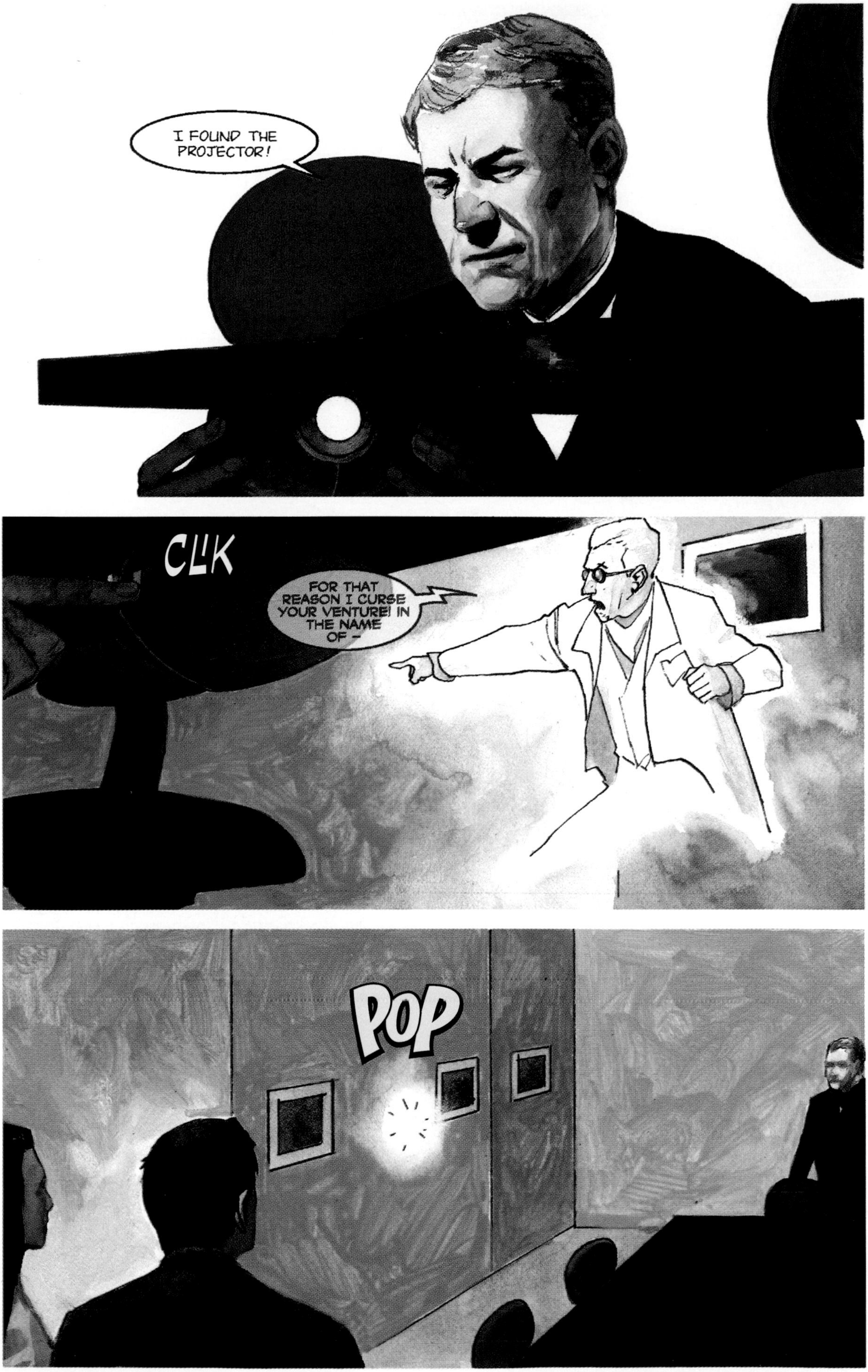
I FOUND THE PROJECTOR!
CLIK
FOR THAT REASON I CURSE YOUR VENTURE! IN THE NAME OF –
POP

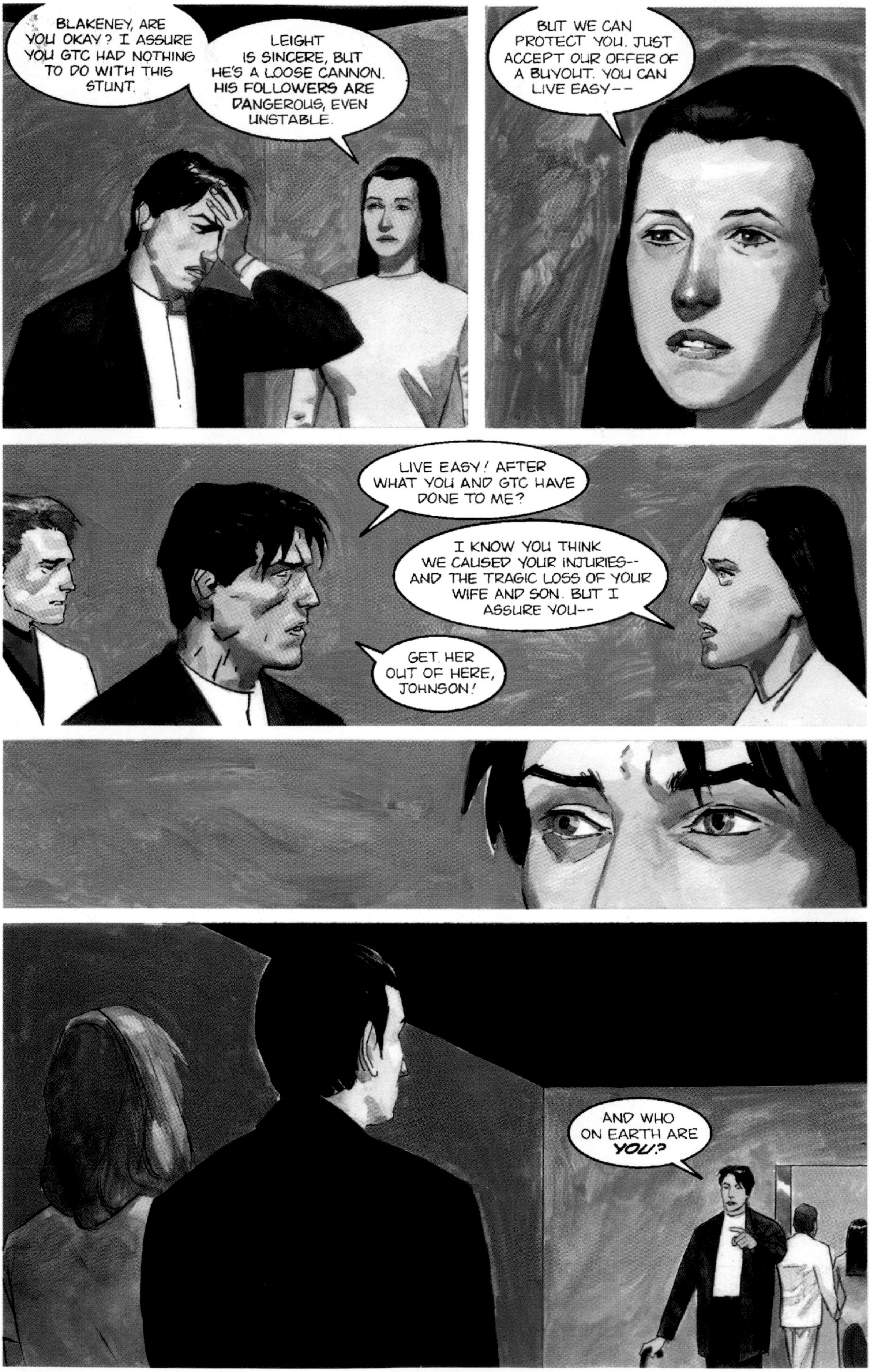
BLAKENEY, ARE YOU OKAY? I ASSURE YOU GTC HAD NOTHING TO DO WITH THIS STUNT.
LEIGHT IS SINCERE, BUT HE'S A LOOSE CANNON. HIS FOLLOWERS ARE DANGEROUS, EVEN UNSTABLE.
BUT WE CAN PROTECT YOU. JUST ACCEPT OUR OFFER OF A BUYOUT. YOU CAN LIVE EASY--
LIVE EASY! AFTER WHAT YOU AND GTC HAVE DONE TO ME?
I KNOW YOU THINK WE CAUSED YOUR INJURIES-- AND THE TRAGIC LOSS OF YOUR WIFE AND SON. BUT I ASSURE YOU--
GET HER OUT OF HERE, JOHNSON!
AND WHO ON EARTH ARE ***YOU***?

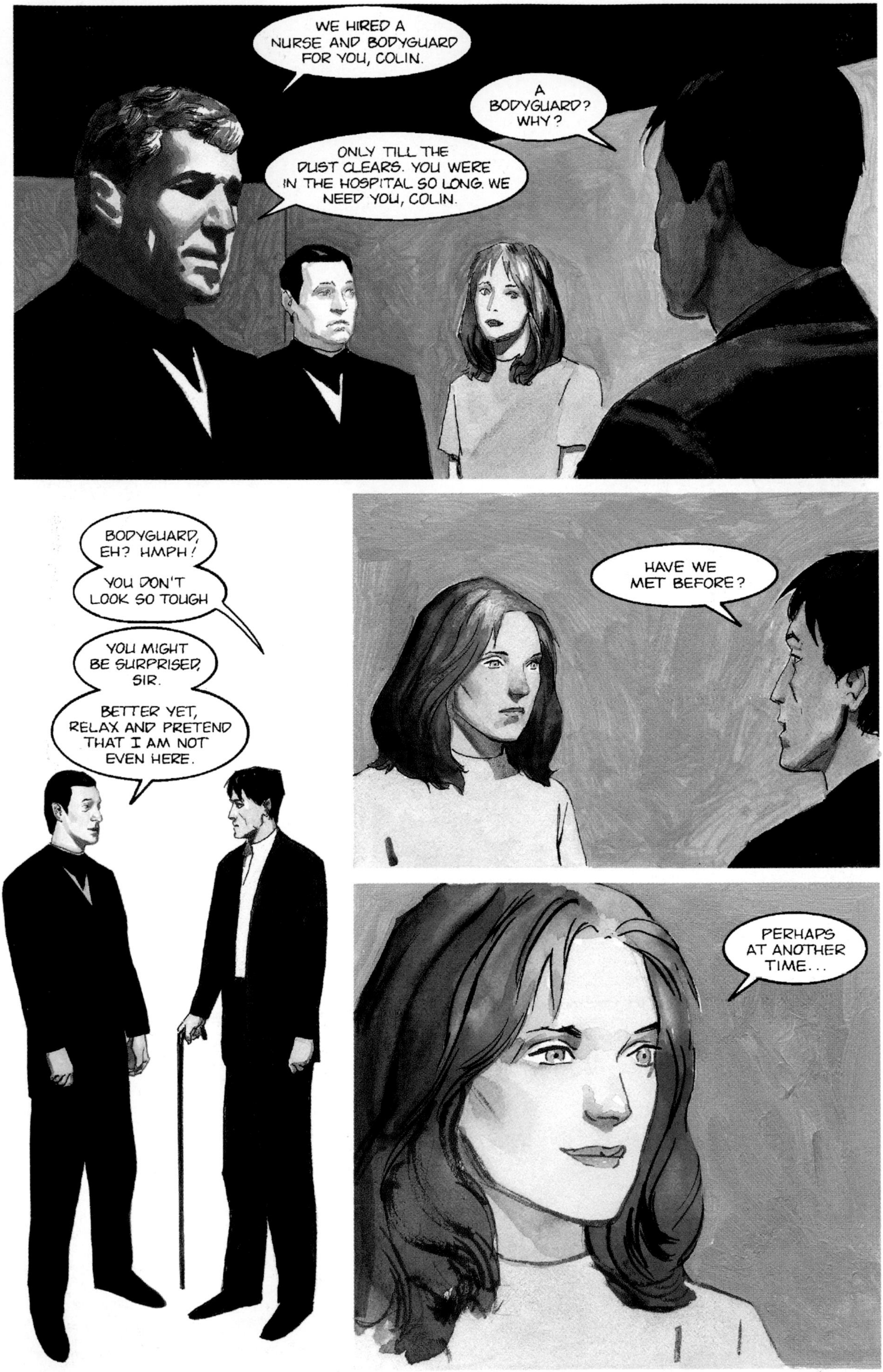
WE HIRED A NURSE AND BODYGUARD FOR YOU, COLIN.
A BODYGUARD? WHY?
ONLY TILL THE DUST CLEARS. YOU WERE IN THE HOSPITAL SO LONG. WE NEED YOU, COLIN.
BODYGUARD, EH? HMPH!
YOU DON'T LOOK SO TOUGH
YOU MIGHT BE SURPRISED, SIR.
BETTER YET, RELAX AND PRETEND THAT I AM NOT EVEN HERE.
HAVE WE MET BEFORE?
PERHAPS AT ANOTHER TIME...

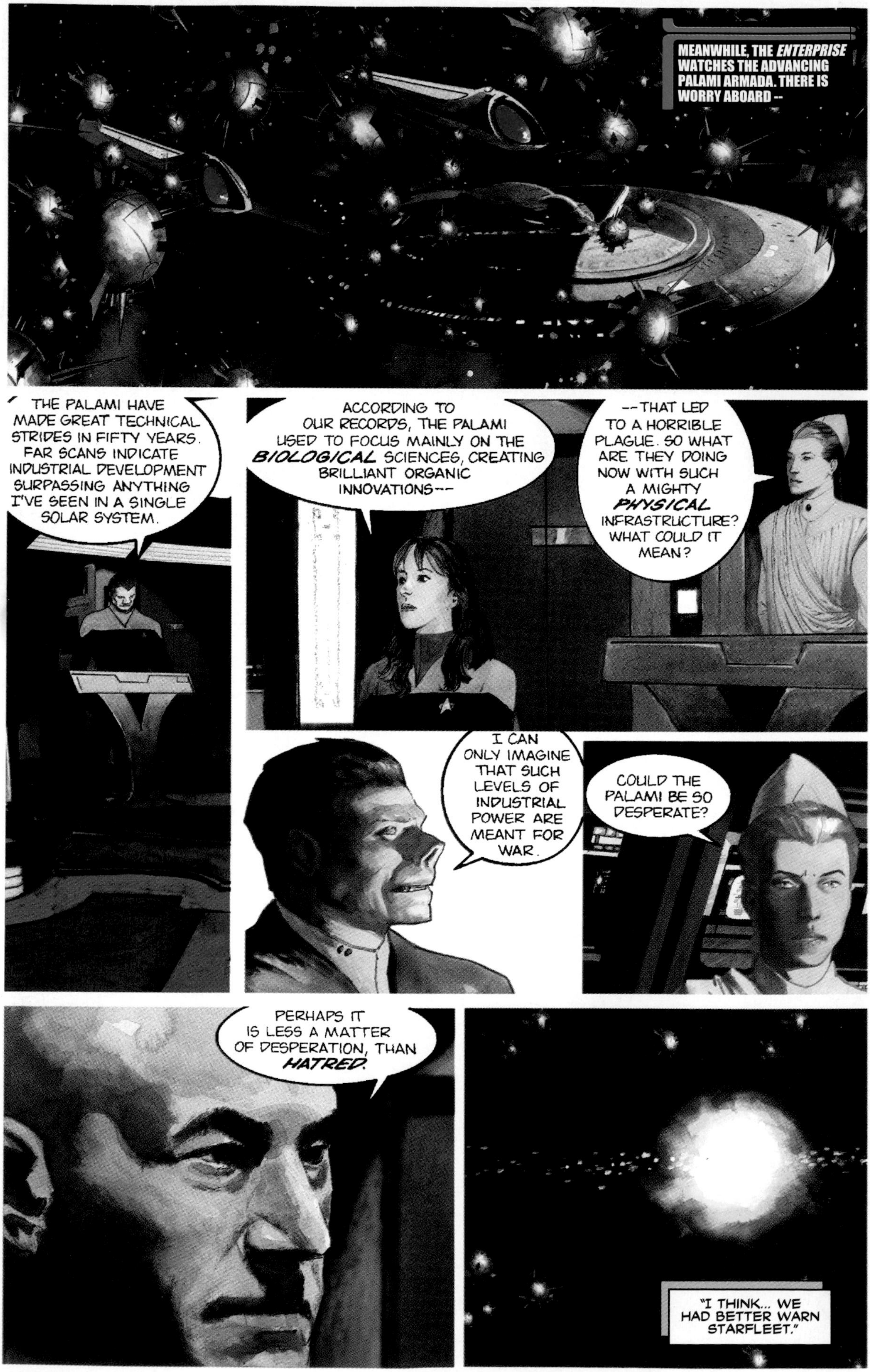
MEANWHILE, THE *ENTERPRISE* WATCHES THE ADVANCING PALAMI ARMADA. THERE IS WORRY ABOARD --
THE PALAMI HAVE MADE GREAT TECHNICAL STRIDES IN FIFTY YEARS. FAR SCANS INDICATE INDUSTRIAL DEVELOPMENT SURPASSING ANYTHING I'VE SEEN IN A SINGLE SOLAR SYSTEM.
ACCORDING TO OUR RECORDS, THE PALAMI USED TO FOCUS MAINLY ON THE *BIOLOGICAL* SCIENCES, CREATING BRILLIANT ORGANIC INNOVATIONS--
--THAT LED TO A HORRIBLE PLAGUE. SO WHAT ARE THEY DOING NOW WITH SUCH A MIGHTY *PHYSICAL* INFRASTRUCTURE? WHAT COULD IT MEAN?
I CAN ONLY IMAGINE THAT SUCH LEVELS OF INDUSTRIAL POWER ARE MEANT FOR WAR.
COULD THE PALAMI BE SO DESPERATE?
PERHAPS IT IS LESS A MATTER OF DESPERATION, THAN *HATRED.*
"I THINK... WE HAD BETTER WARN STARFLEET."

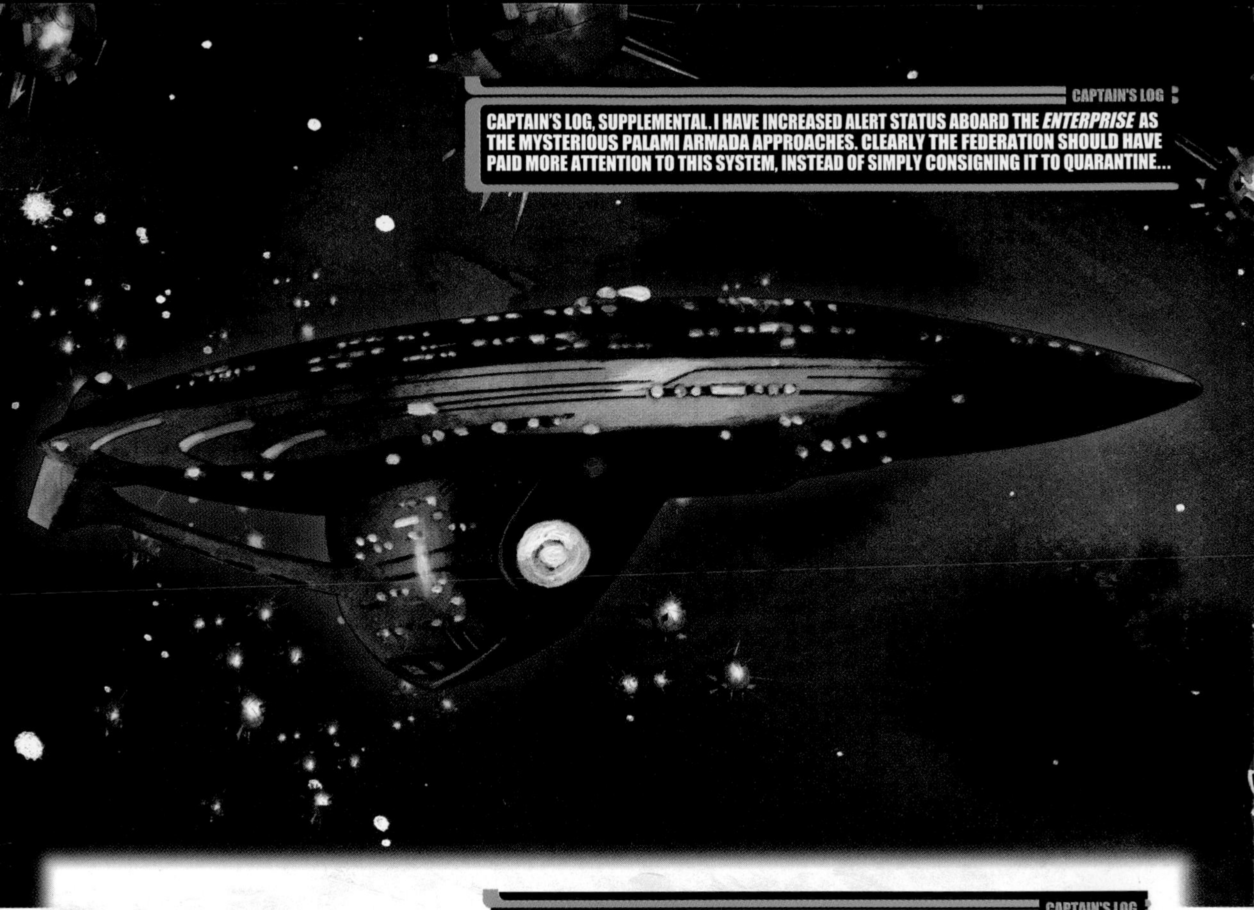
CAPTAIN'S LOG
CAPTAIN'S LOG, SUPPLEMENTAL. I HAVE INCREASED ALERT STATUS ABOARD THE *ENTERPRISE* AS THE MYSTERIOUS PALAMI ARMADA APPROACHES. CLEARLY THE FEDERATION SHOULD HAVE PAID MORE ATTENTION TO THIS SYSTEM, INSTEAD OF SIMPLY CONSIGNING IT TO QUARANTINE...

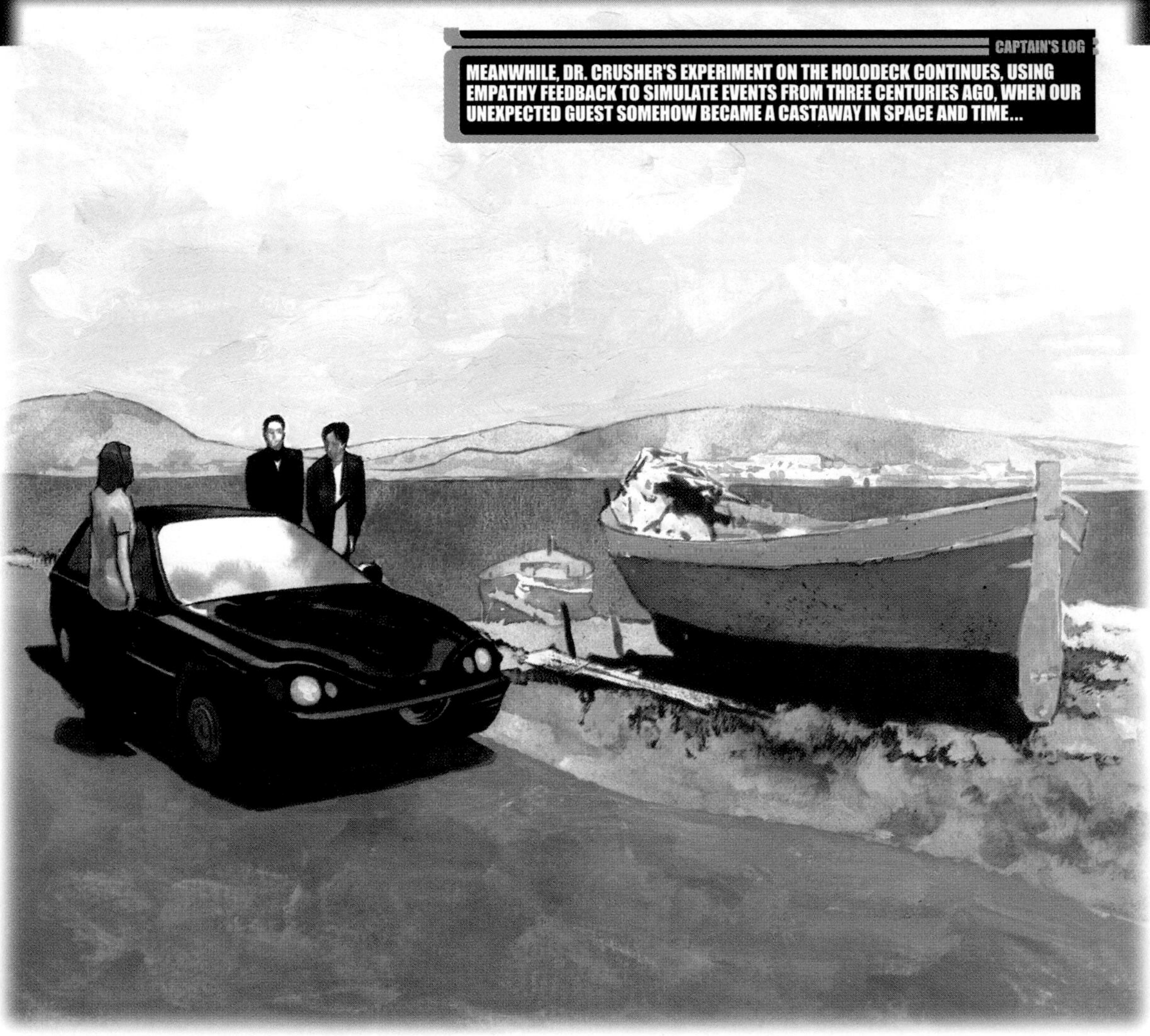
CAPTAIN'S LOG
MEANWHILE, DR. CRUSHER'S EXPERIMENT ON THE HOLODECK CONTINUES, USING EMPATHY FEEDBACK TO SIMULATE EVENTS FROM THREE CENTURIES AGO, WHEN OUR UNEXPECTED GUEST SOMEHOW BECAME A CASTAWAY IN SPACE AND TIME...

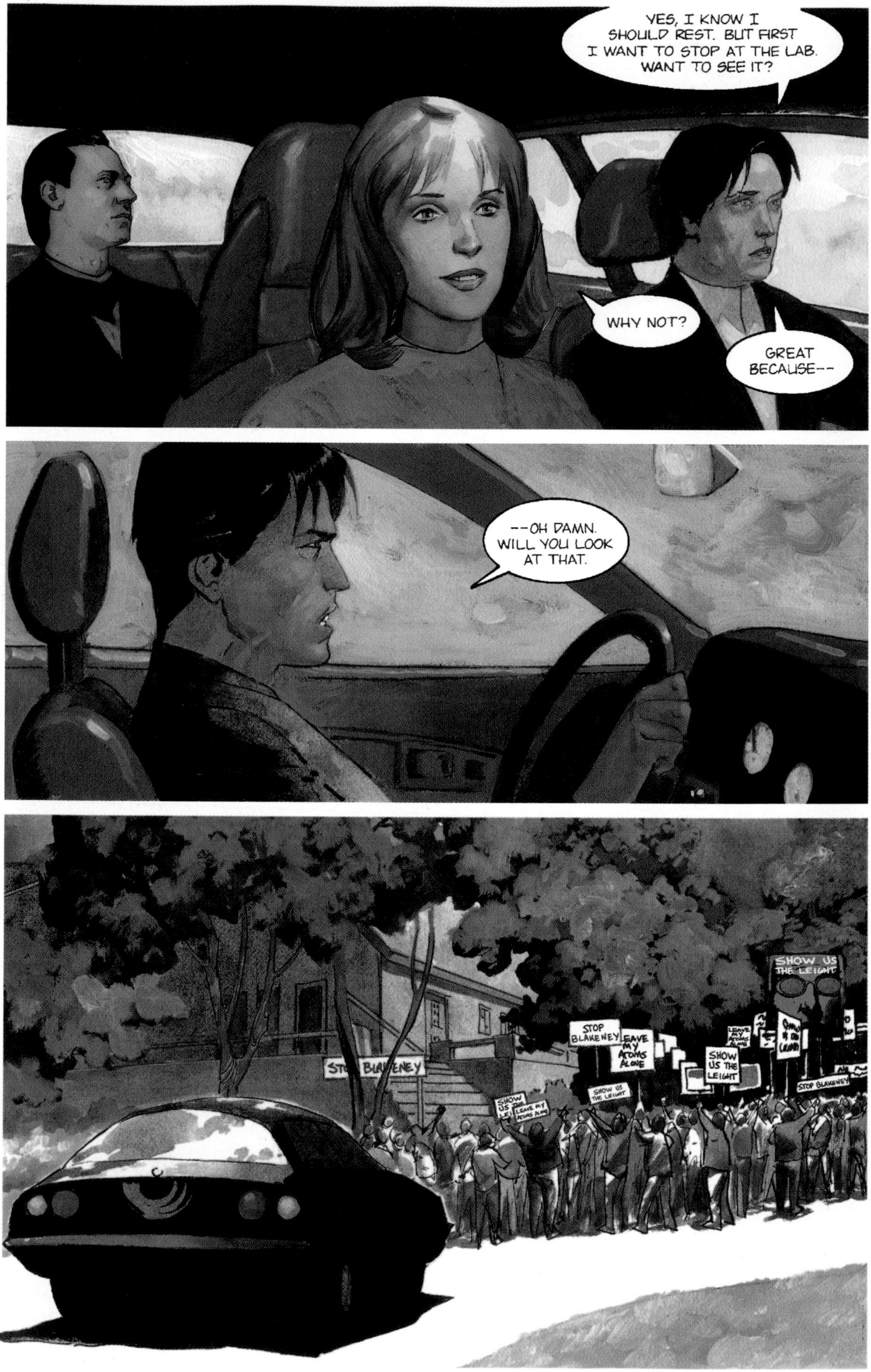
YES, I KNOW I SHOULD REST. BUT FIRST I WANT TO STOP AT THE LAB. WANT TO SEE IT?
WHY NOT?
GREAT BECAUSE--
--OH DAMN. WILL YOU LOOK AT THAT.
STOP BLAKENEY
SHOW US THE LEIGHT
STOP BLAKENEY
LEAVE MY ATOMS ALONE
SHOW US THE LEIGHT
STOP BLAKENEY

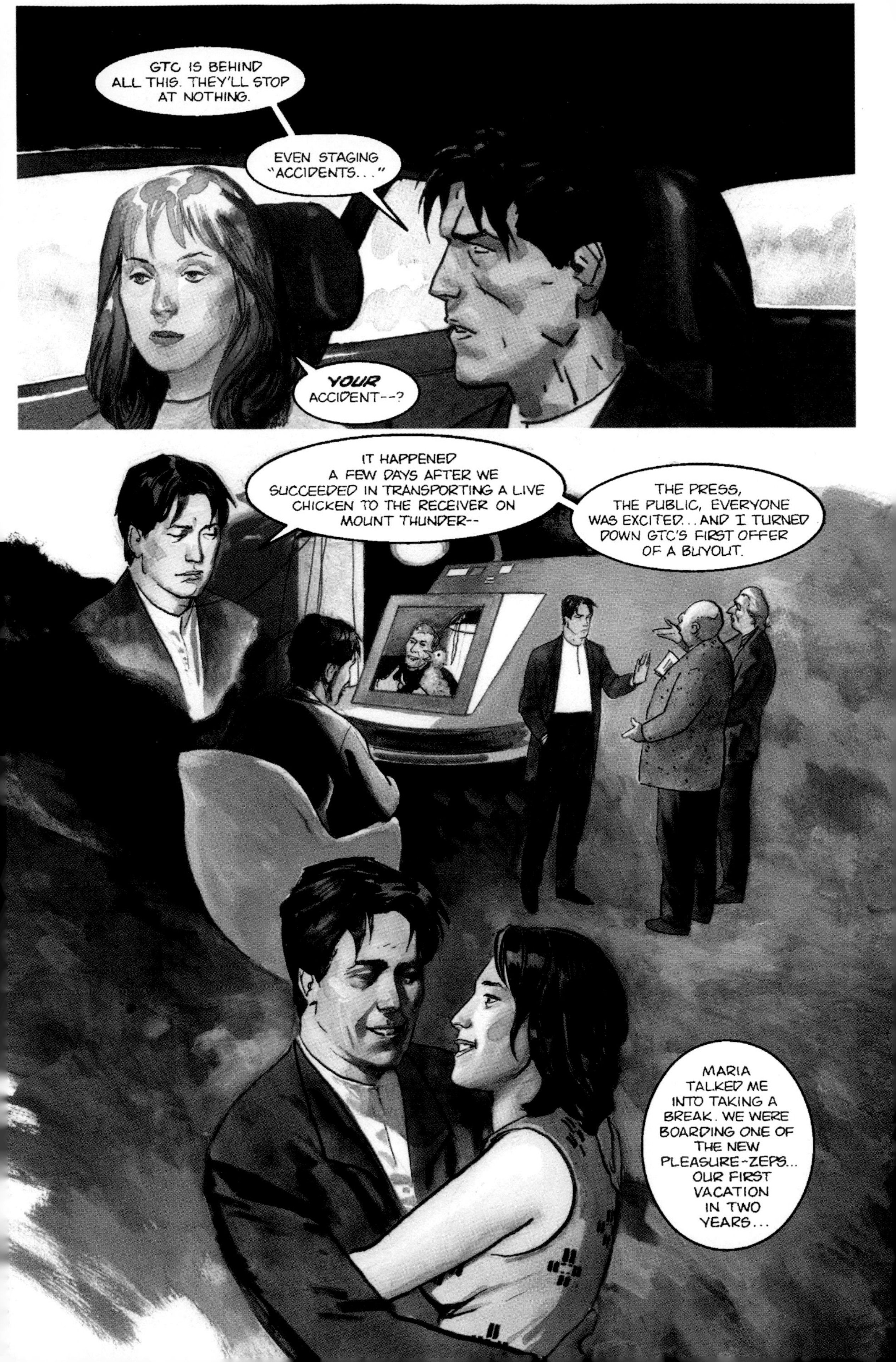
GTC IS BEHIND ALL THIS. THEY'LL STOP AT NOTHING.
EVEN STAGING "ACCIDENTS..."
YOUR ACCIDENT--?
IT HAPPENED A FEW DAYS AFTER WE SUCCEEDED IN TRANSPORTING A LIVE CHICKEN TO THE RECEIVER ON MOUNT THUNDER--
THE PRESS, THE PUBLIC, EVERYONE WAS EXCITED... AND I TURNED DOWN GTC'S FIRST OFFER OF A BUYOUT.
MARIA TALKED ME INTO TAKING A BREAK. WE WERE BOARDING ONE OF THE NEW PLEASURE-ZEPS... OUR FIRST VACATION IN TWO YEARS...

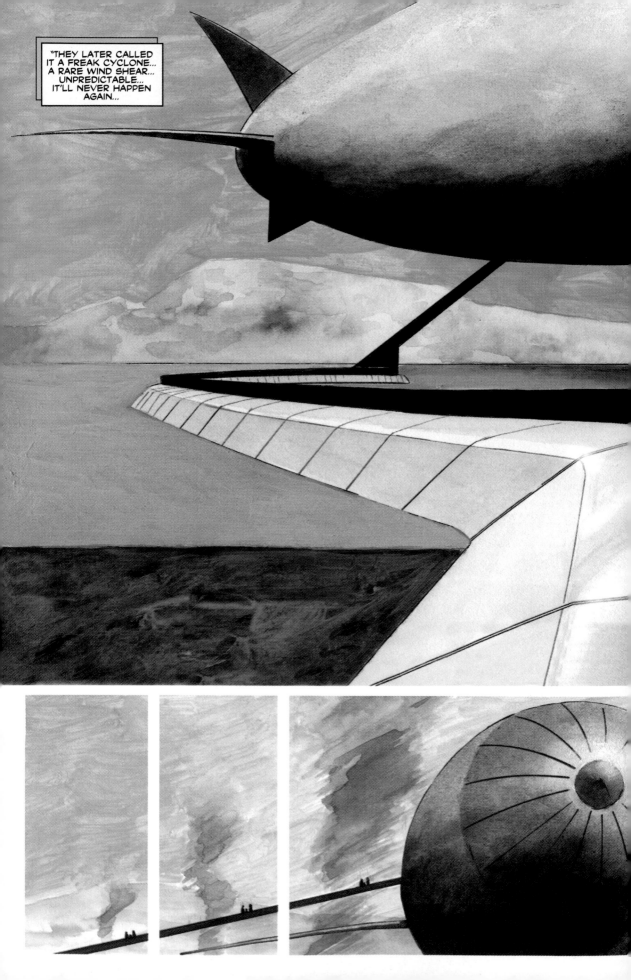

"THEY LATER CALLED IT A FREAK CYCLONE... A RARE WIND SHEAR... UNPREDICTABLE... IT'LL NEVER HAPPEN AGAIN...

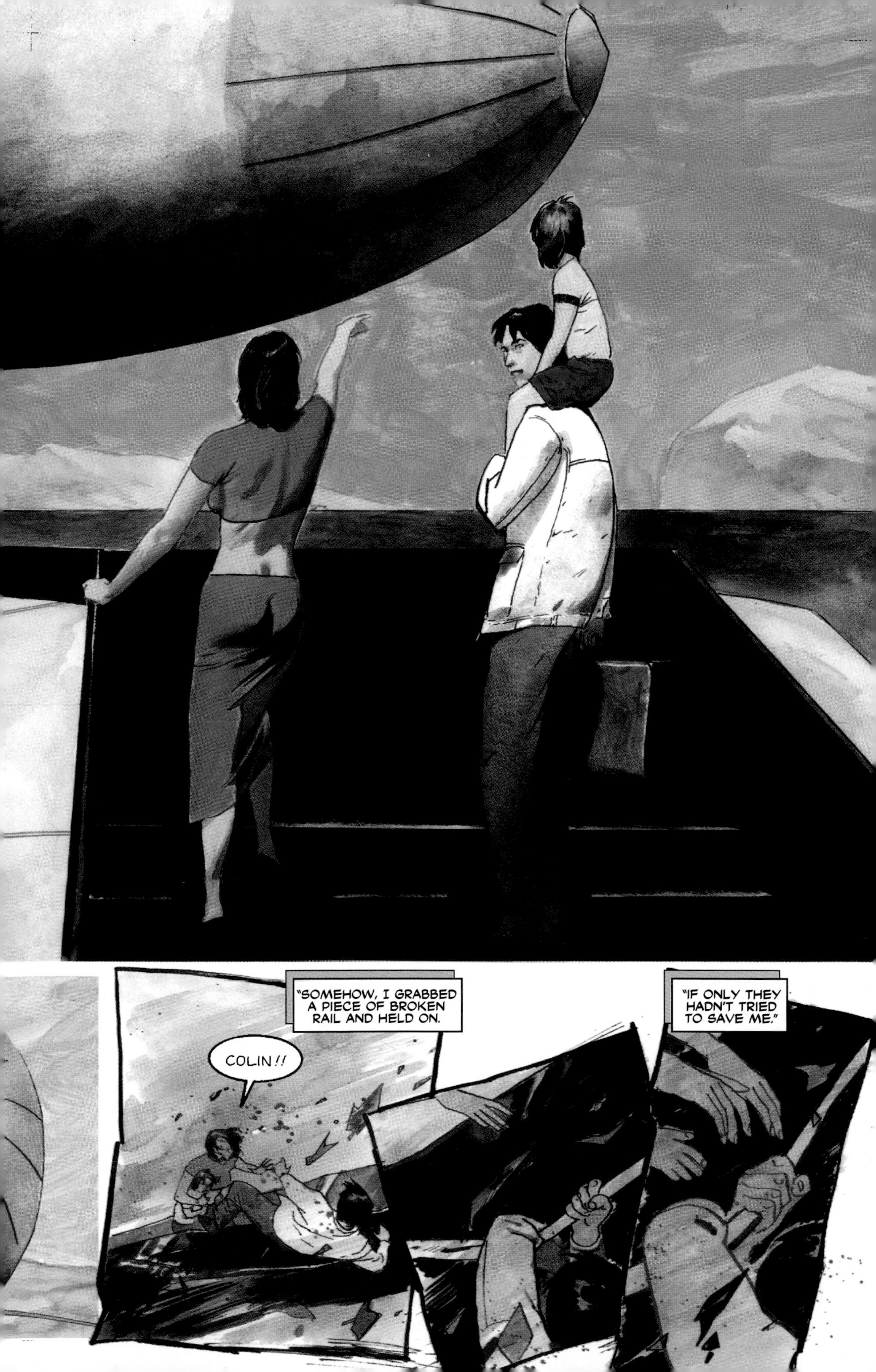
"SOMEHOW, I GRABBED A PIECE OF BROKEN RAIL AND HELD ON.
COLIN!!
"IF ONLY THEY HADN'T TRIED TO SAVE ME."

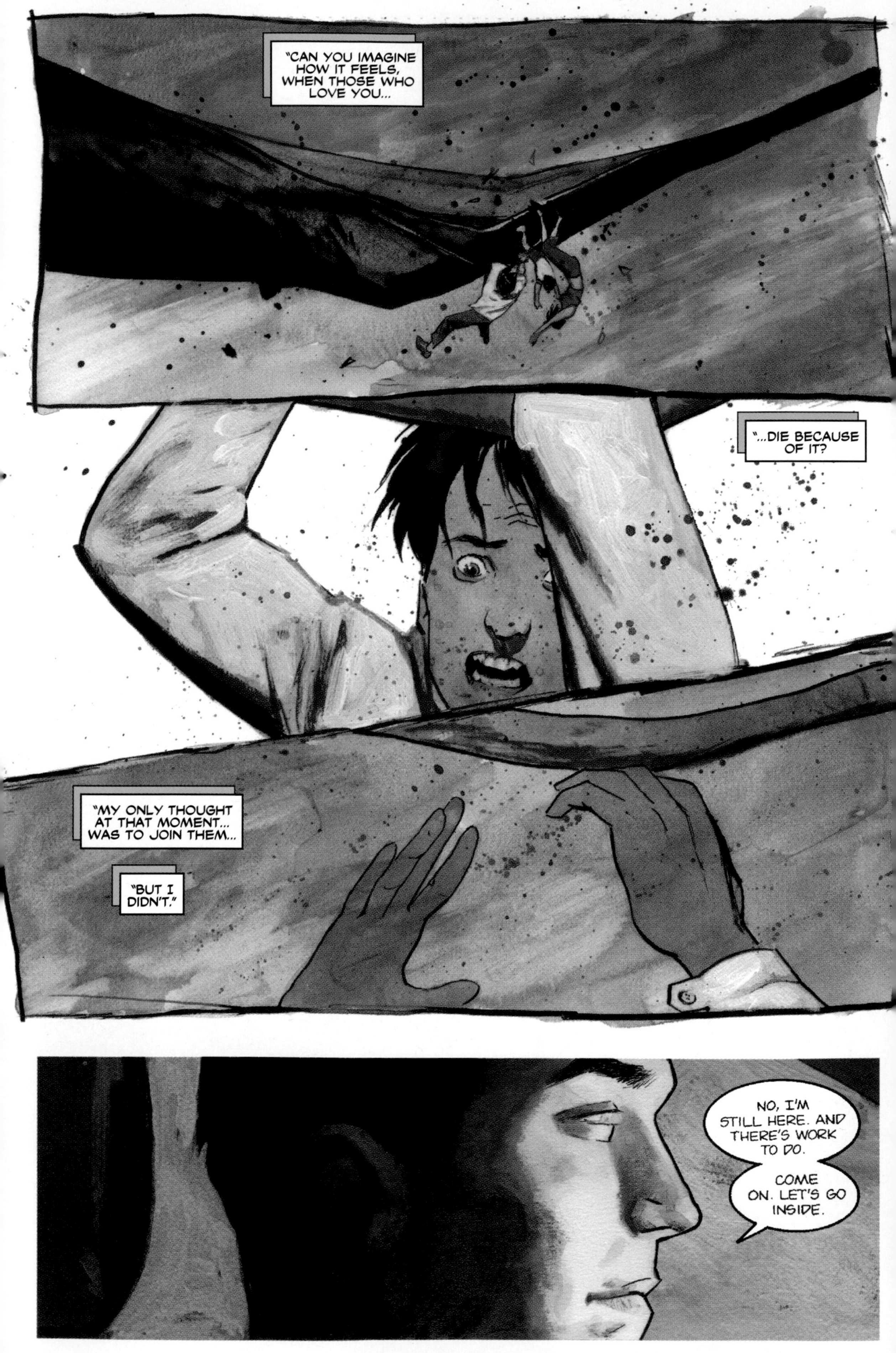
"CAN YOU IMAGINE HOW IT FEELS, WHEN THOSE WHO LOVE YOU...
"...DIE BECAUSE OF IT?
"MY ONLY THOUGHT AT THAT MOMENT... WAS TO JOIN THEM...
"BUT I DIDN'T."
NO, I'M STILL HERE. AND THERE'S WORK TO DO.
COME ON. LET'S GO INSIDE.

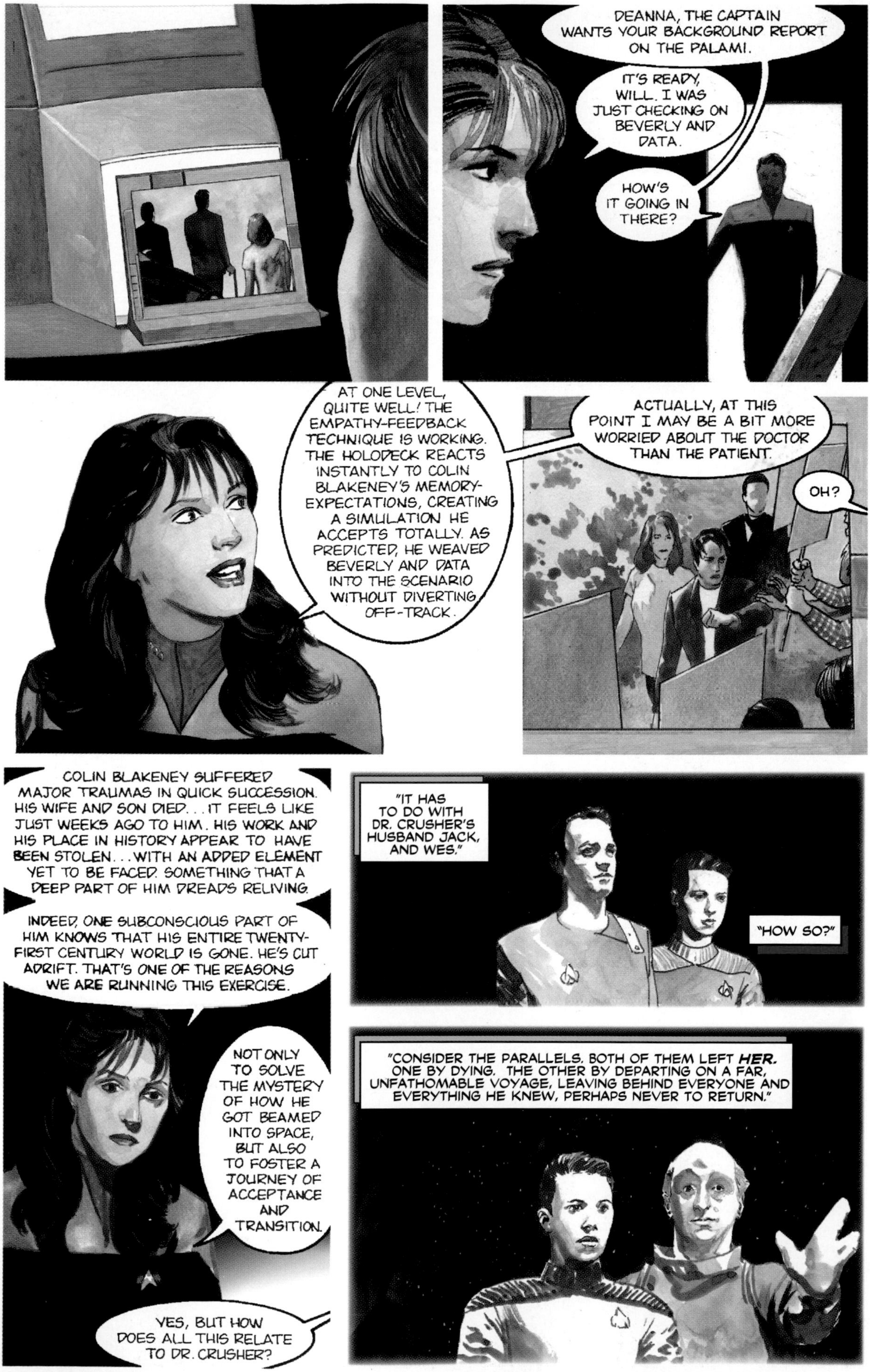

DEANNA, THE CAPTAIN WANTS YOUR BACKGROUND REPORT ON THE PALAMI.
IT'S READY, WILL. I WAS JUST CHECKING ON BEVERLY AND DATA.
HOW'S IT GOING IN THERE?
AT ONE LEVEL, QUITE WELL! THE EMPATHY-FEEDBACK TECHNIQUE IS WORKING. THE HOLODECK REACTS INSTANTLY TO COLIN BLAKENEY'S MEMORY-EXPECTATIONS, CREATING A SIMULATION HE ACCEPTS TOTALLY. AS PREDICTED, HE WEAVED BEVERLY AND DATA INTO THE SCENARIO WITHOUT DIVERTING OFF-TRACK.
ACTUALLY, AT THIS POINT I MAY BE A BIT MORE WORRIED ABOUT THE DOCTOR THAN THE PATIENT.
OH?
COLIN BLAKENEY SUFFERED MAJOR TRAUMAS IN QUICK SUCCESSION. HIS WIFE AND SON DIED. . . IT FEELS LIKE JUST WEEKS AGO TO HIM. HIS WORK AND HIS PLACE IN HISTORY APPEAR TO HAVE BEEN STOLEN. . . WITH AN ADDED ELEMENT YET TO BE FACED. SOMETHING THAT A DEEP PART OF HIM DREADS RELIVING.
INDEED, ONE SUBCONSCIOUS PART OF HIM KNOWS THAT HIS ENTIRE TWENTY-FIRST CENTURY WORLD IS GONE. HE'S CUT ADRIFT. THAT'S ONE OF THE REASONS WE ARE RUNNING THIS EXERCISE.
NOT ONLY TO SOLVE THE MYSTERY OF HOW HE GOT BEAMED INTO SPACE, BUT ALSO TO FOSTER A JOURNEY OF ACCEPTANCE AND TRANSITION.
YES, BUT HOW DOES ALL THIS RELATE TO DR. CRUSHER?
"IT HAS TO DO WITH DR. CRUSHER'S HUSBAND JACK, AND WES."
"HOW SO?"
"CONSIDER THE PARALLELS. BOTH OF THEM LEFT HER. ONE BY DYING. THE OTHER BY DEPARTING ON A FAR, UNFATHOMABLE VOYAGE, LEAVING BEHIND EVERYONE AND EVERYTHING HE KNEW, PERHAPS NEVER TO RETURN."

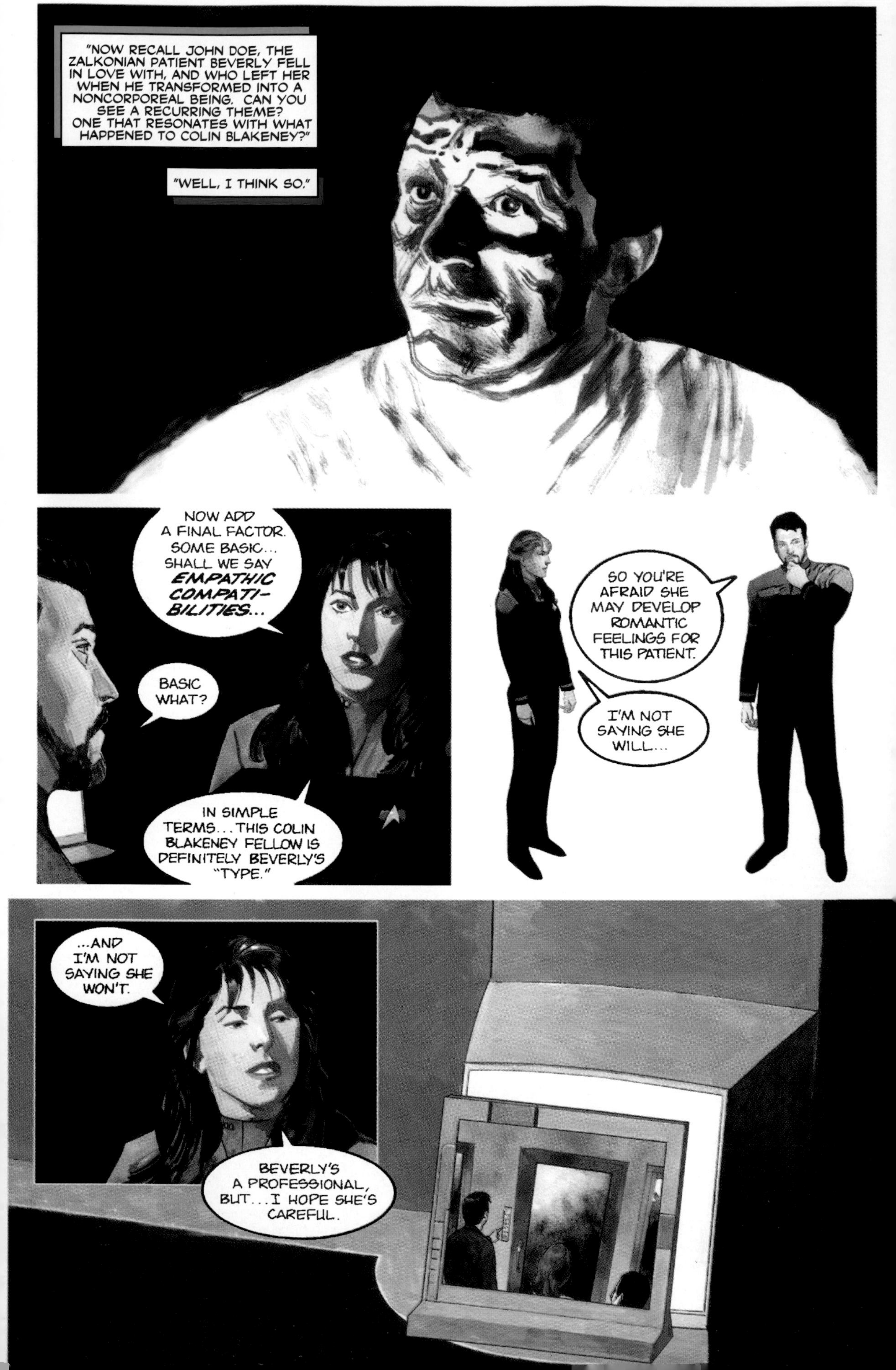
"NOW RECALL JOHN DOE, THE ZALKONIAN PATIENT BEVERLY FELL IN LOVE WITH, AND WHO LEFT HER WHEN HE TRANSFORMED INTO A NONCORPOREAL BEING. CAN YOU SEE A RECURRING THEME? ONE THAT RESONATES WITH WHAT HAPPENED TO COLIN BLAKENEY?"
"WELL, I THINK SO."
NOW ADD A FINAL FACTOR. SOME BASIC... SHALL WE SAY *EMPATHIC COMPATI-BILITIES*...
BASIC WHAT?
IN SIMPLE TERMS... THIS COLIN BLAKENEY FELLOW IS DEFINITELY BEVERLY'S "TYPE."
SO YOU'RE AFRAID SHE MAY DEVELOP ROMANTIC FEELINGS FOR THIS PATIENT.
I'M NOT SAYING SHE WILL...
...AND I'M NOT SAYING SHE WON'T.
BEVERLY'S A PROFESSIONAL, BUT... I HOPE SHE'S CAREFUL.

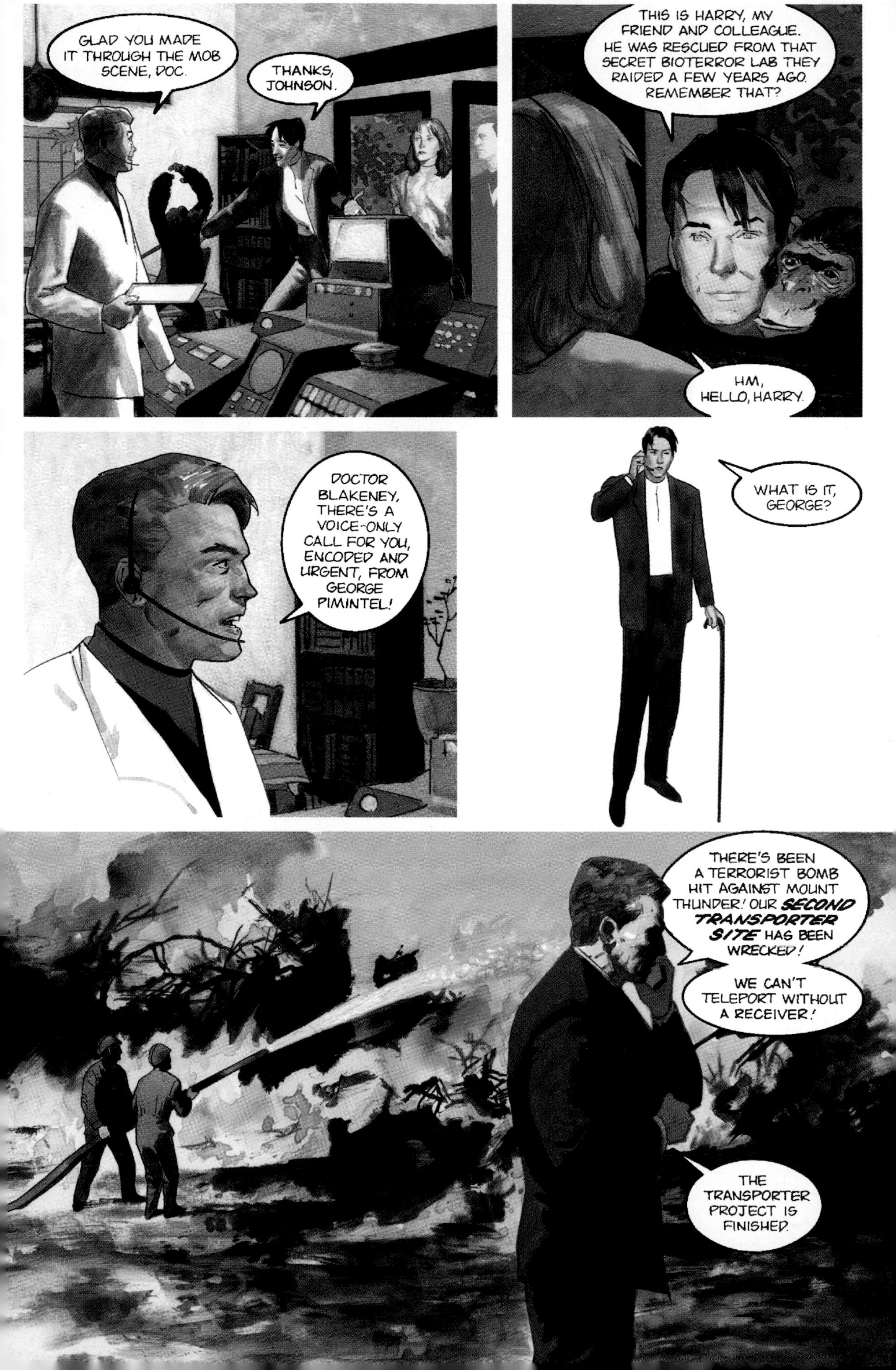
GLAD YOU MADE IT THROUGH THE MOB SCENE, DOC.
THANKS, JOHNSON.
THIS IS HARRY, MY FRIEND AND COLLEAGUE. HE WAS RESCUED FROM THAT SECRET BIOTERROR LAB THEY RAIDED A FEW YEARS AGO. REMEMBER THAT?
HM, HELLO, HARRY.
DOCTOR BLAKENEY, THERE'S A VOICE-ONLY CALL FOR YOU, ENCODED AND URGENT, FROM GEORGE PIMINTEL!
WHAT IS IT, GEORGE?
THERE'S BEEN A TERRORIST BOMB HIT AGAINST MOUNT THUNDER! OUR ***SECOND TRANSPORTER SITE*** HAS BEEN WRECKED!
WE CAN'T TELEPORT WITHOUT A RECEIVER!
THE TRANSPORTER PROJECT IS FINISHED.

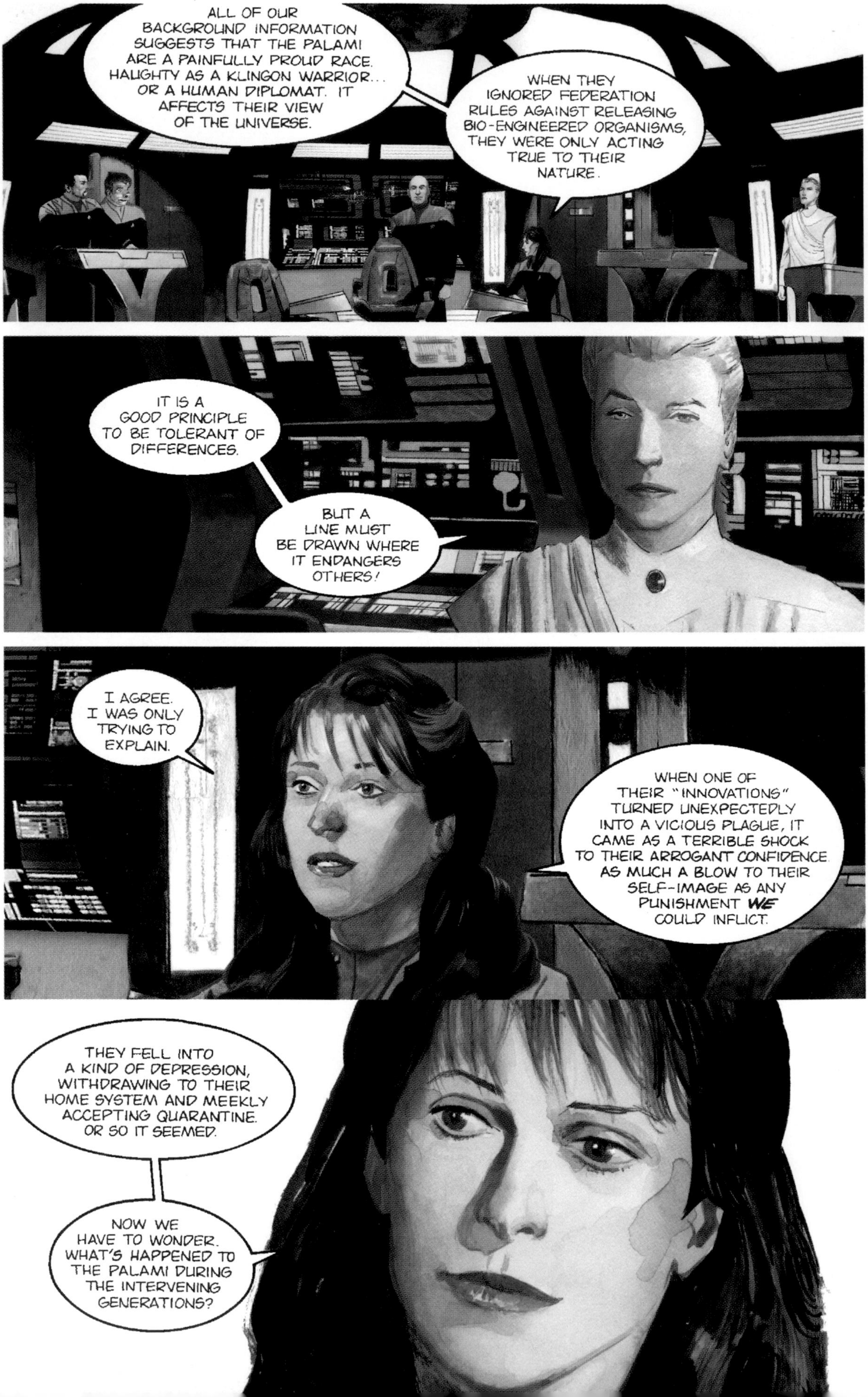
ALL OF OUR BACKGROUND INFORMATION SUGGESTS THAT THE PALAMI ARE A PAINFULLY PROUD RACE. HAUGHTY AS A KLINGON WARRIOR... OR A HUMAN DIPLOMAT. IT AFFECTS THEIR VIEW OF THE UNIVERSE.
WHEN THEY IGNORED FEDERATION RULES AGAINST RELEASING BIO-ENGINEERED ORGANISMS, THEY WERE ONLY ACTING TRUE TO THEIR NATURE.
IT IS A GOOD PRINCIPLE TO BE TOLERANT OF DIFFERENCES.
BUT A LINE MUST BE DRAWN WHERE IT ENDANGERS OTHERS!
I AGREE. I WAS ONLY TRYING TO EXPLAIN.
WHEN ONE OF THEIR "INNOVATIONS" TURNED UNEXPECTEDLY INTO A VICIOUS PLAGUE, IT CAME AS A TERRIBLE SHOCK TO THEIR ARROGANT CONFIDENCE. AS MUCH A BLOW TO THEIR SELF-IMAGE AS ANY PUNISHMENT WE COULD INFLICT.
THEY FELL INTO A KIND OF DEPRESSION, WITHDRAWING TO THEIR HOME SYSTEM AND MEEKLY ACCEPTING QUARANTINE. OR SO IT SEEMED.
NOW WE HAVE TO WONDER. WHAT'S HAPPENED TO THE PALAMI DURING THE INTERVENING GENERATIONS?

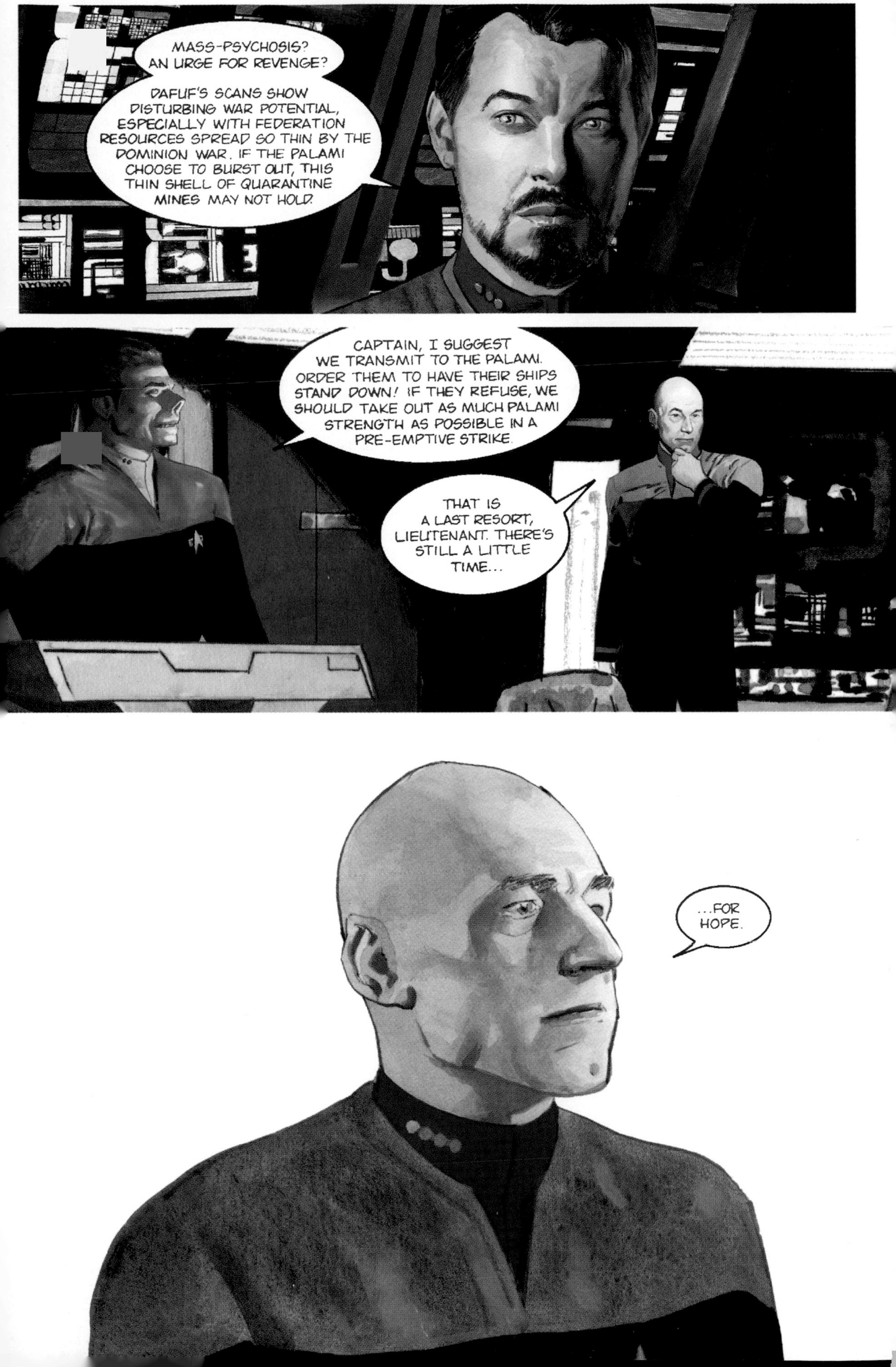
MASS-PSYCHOSIS? AN URGE FOR REVENGE?
DAFUF'S SCANS SHOW DISTURBING WAR POTENTIAL, ESPECIALLY WITH FEDERATION RESOURCES SPREAD SO THIN BY THE DOMINION WAR. IF THE PALAMI CHOOSE TO BURST OUT, THIS THIN SHELL OF QUARANTINE MINES MAY NOT HOLD.
CAPTAIN, I SUGGEST WE TRANSMIT TO THE PALAMI. ORDER THEM TO HAVE THEIR SHIPS STAND DOWN! IF THEY REFUSE, WE SHOULD TAKE OUT AS MUCH PALAMI STRENGTH AS POSSIBLE IN A PRE-EMPTIVE STRIKE.
THAT IS A LAST RESORT, LIEUTENANT. THERE'S STILL A LITTLE TIME...
...FOR HOPE.

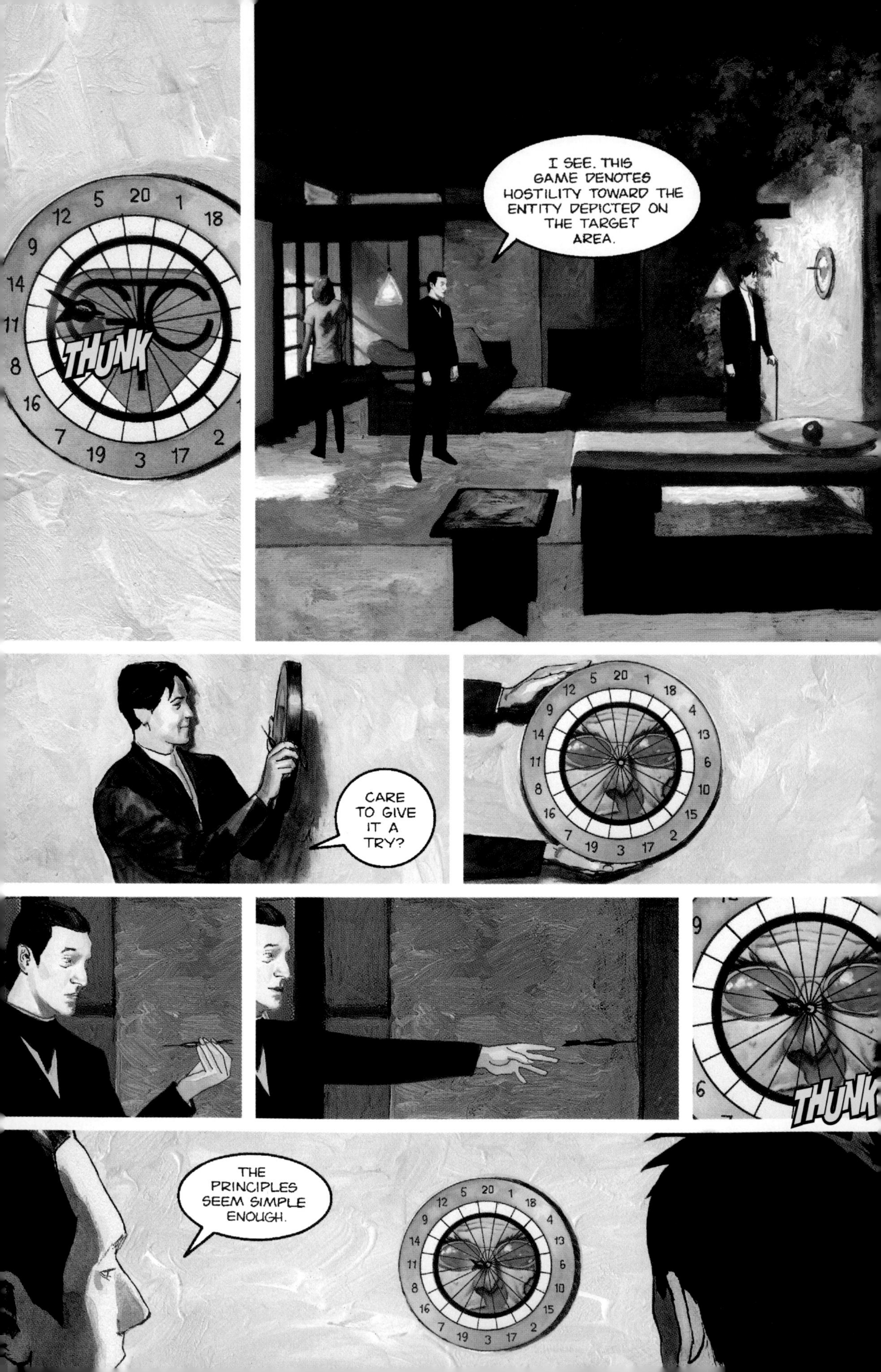
THUNK
I SEE. THIS GAME DENOTES HOSTILITY TOWARD THE ENTITY DEPICTED ON THE TARGET AREA.
CARE TO GIVE IT A TRY?
THUNK
THE PRINCIPLES SEEM SIMPLE ENOUGH.

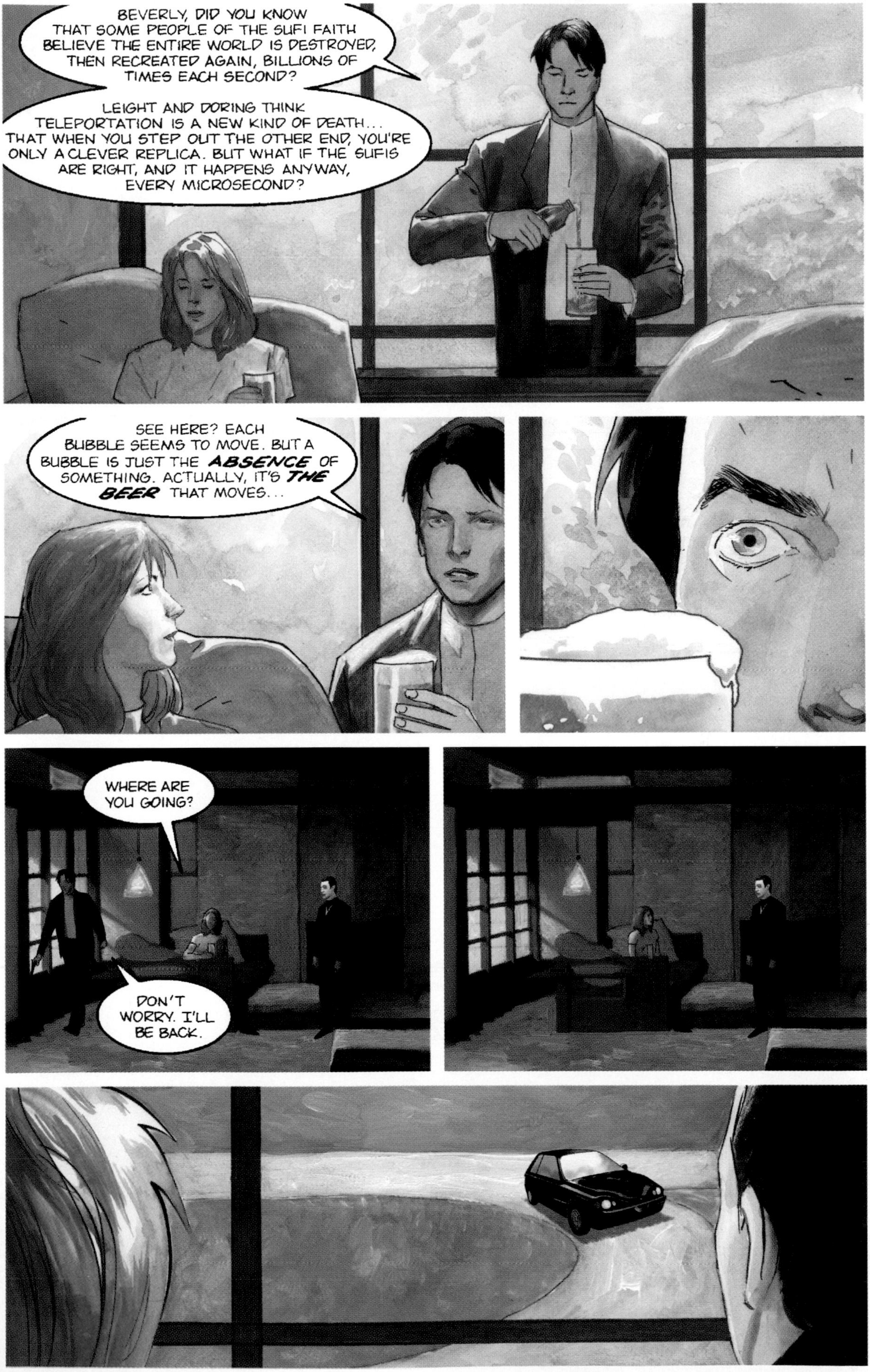
BEVERLY, DID YOU KNOW THAT SOME PEOPLE OF THE SUFI FAITH BELIEVE THE ENTIRE WORLD IS DESTROYED, THEN RECREATED AGAIN, BILLIONS OF TIMES EACH SECOND?
LEIGHT AND DORING THINK TELEPORTATION IS A NEW KIND OF DEATH... THAT WHEN YOU STEP OUT THE OTHER END, YOU'RE ONLY A CLEVER REPLICA. BUT WHAT IF THE SUFIS ARE RIGHT, AND IT HAPPENS ANYWAY, EVERY MICROSECOND?
SEE HERE? EACH BUBBLE SEEMS TO MOVE. BUT A BUBBLE IS JUST THE ***ABSENCE*** OF SOMETHING. ACTUALLY, IT'S ***THE BEER*** THAT MOVES...
WHERE ARE YOU GOING?
DON'T WORRY. I'LL BE BACK.

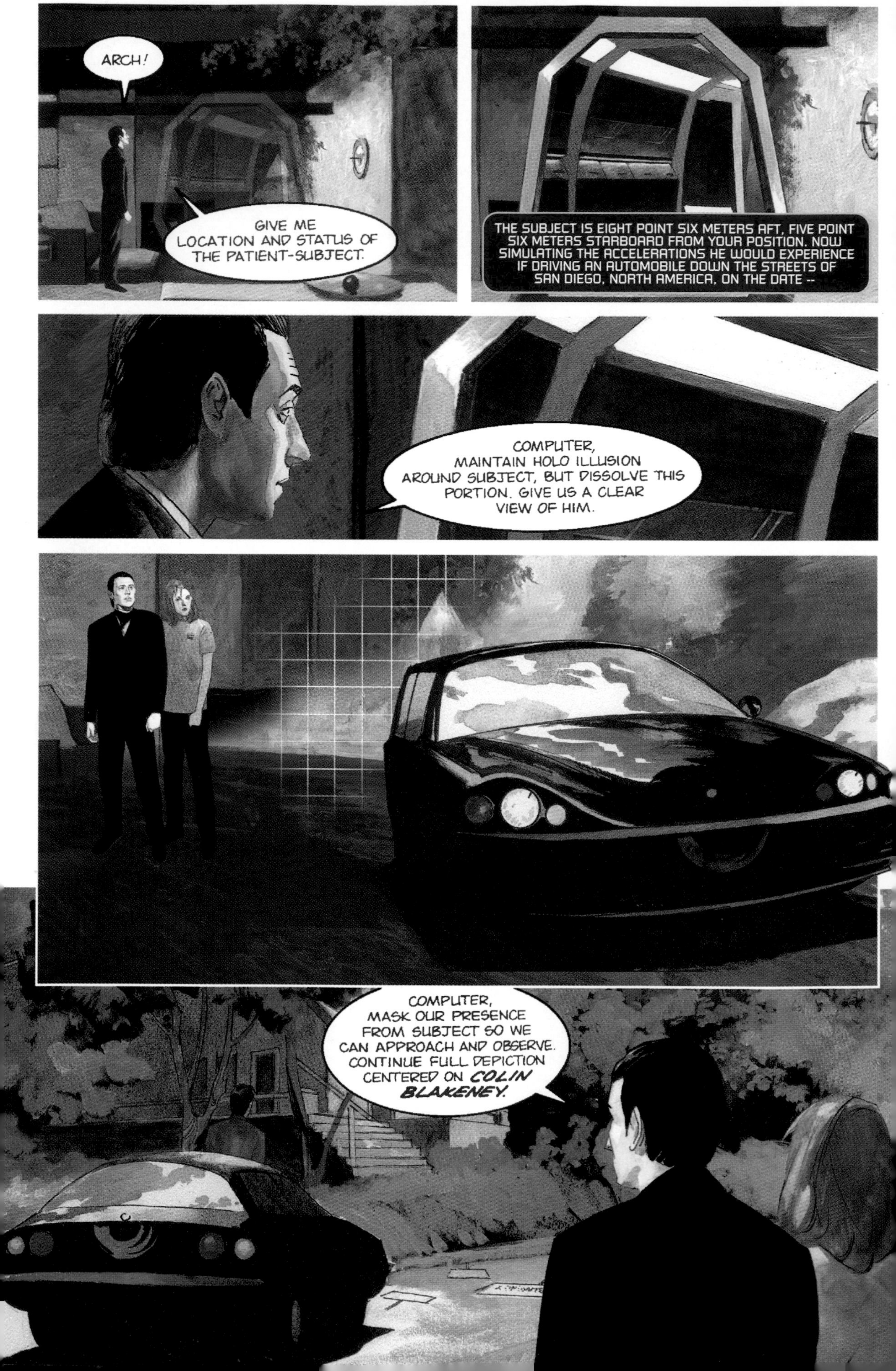
ARCH!
GIVE ME LOCATION AND STATUS OF THE PATIENT-SUBJECT.
THE SUBJECT IS EIGHT POINT SIX METERS AFT, FIVE POINT SIX METERS STARBOARD FROM YOUR POSITION. NOW SIMULATING THE ACCELERATIONS HE WOULD EXPERIENCE IF DRIVING AN AUTOMOBILE DOWN THE STREETS OF SAN DIEGO, NORTH AMERICA, ON THE DATE --
COMPUTER, MAINTAIN HOLO ILLUSION AROUND SUBJECT, BUT DISSOLVE THIS PORTION. GIVE US A CLEAR VIEW OF HIM.
COMPUTER, MASK OUR PRESENCE FROM SUBJECT SO WE CAN APPROACH AND OBSERVE. CONTINUE FULL DEPICTION CENTERED ON *COLIN BLAKENEY.*

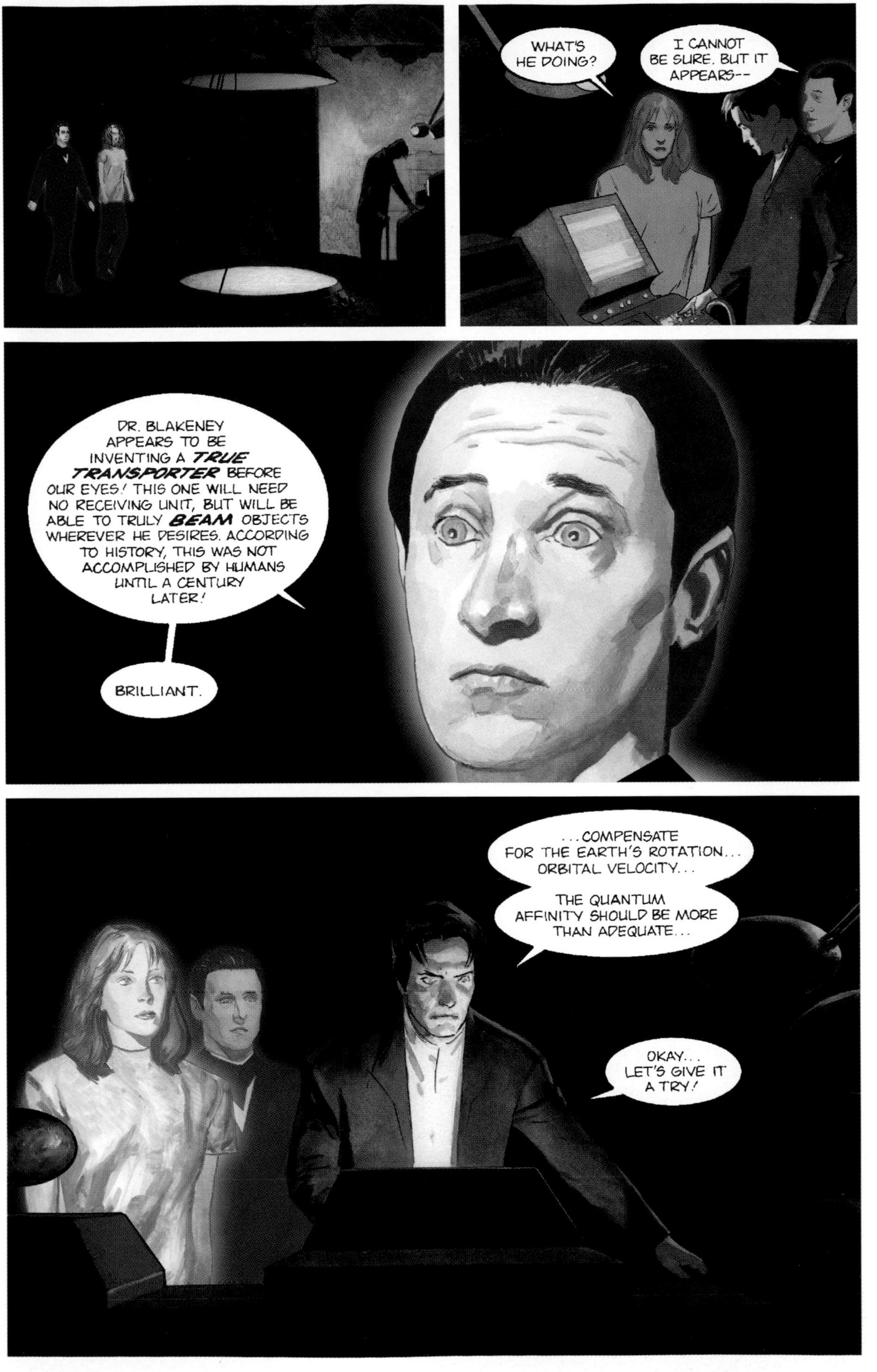
WHAT'S HE DOING?
I CANNOT BE SURE. BUT IT APPEARS--
DR. BLAKENEY APPEARS TO BE INVENTING A TRUE TRANSPORTER BEFORE OUR EYES! THIS ONE WILL NEED NO RECEIVING UNIT, BUT WILL BE ABLE TO TRULY BEAM OBJECTS WHEREVER HE DESIRES. ACCORDING TO HISTORY, THIS WAS NOT ACCOMPLISHED BY HUMANS UNTIL A CENTURY LATER!
BRILLIANT.
...COMPENSATE FOR THE EARTH'S ROTATION... ORBITAL VELOCITY...
THE QUANTUM AFFINITY SHOULD BE MORE THAN ADEQUATE...
OKAY... LET'S GIVE IT A TRY!

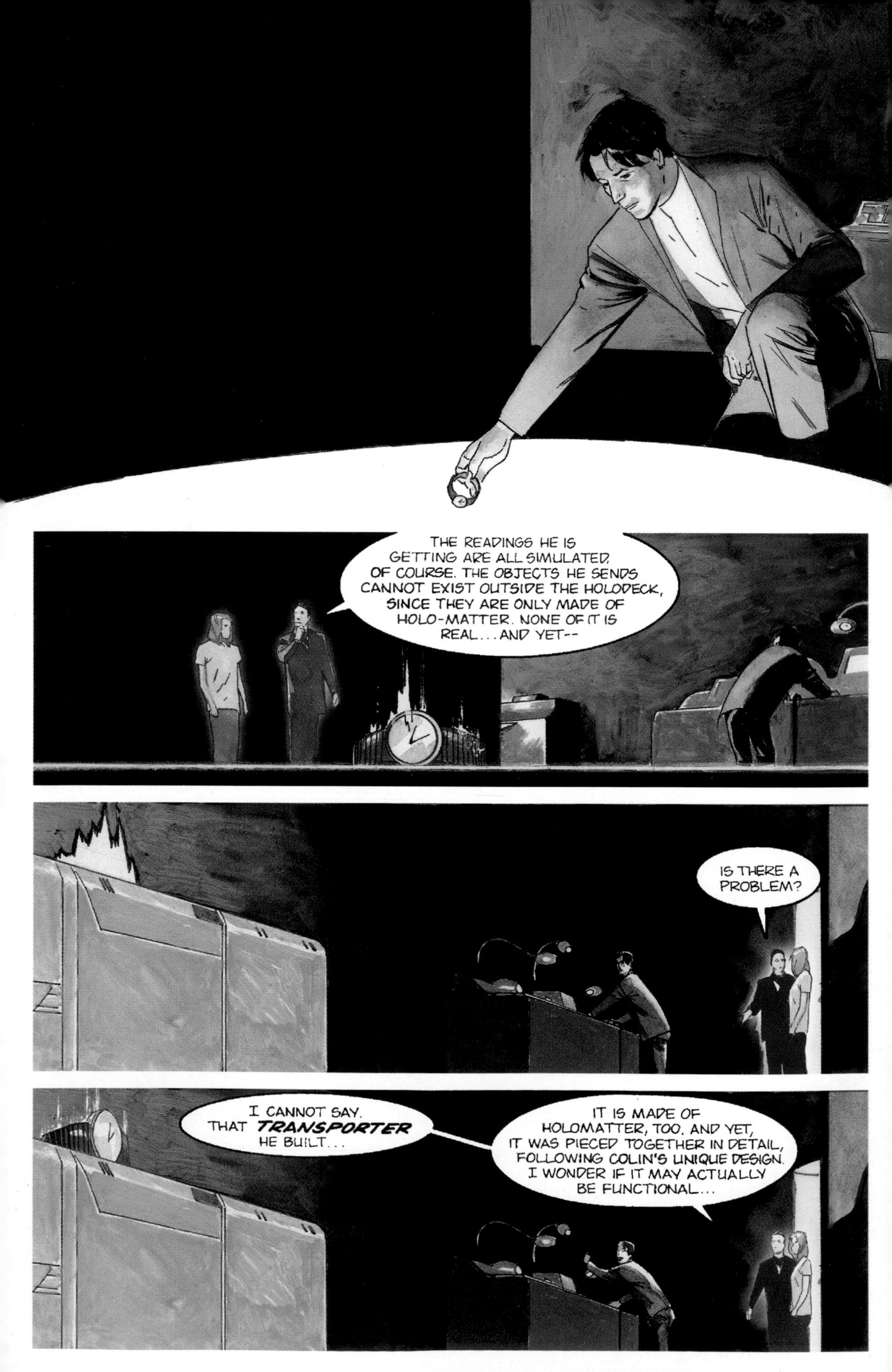
THE READINGS HE IS GETTING ARE ALL SIMULATED, OF COURSE. THE OBJECTS HE SENDS CANNOT EXIST OUTSIDE THE HOLODECK, SINCE THEY ARE ONLY MADE OF HOLO-MATTER. NONE OF IT IS REAL... AND YET--
IS THERE A PROBLEM?
I CANNOT SAY. THAT TRANSPORTER HE BUILT...
IT IS MADE OF HOLOMATTER, TOO. AND YET, IT WAS PIECED TOGETHER IN DETAIL, FOLLOWING COLIN'S UNIQUE DESIGN. I WONDER IF IT MAY ACTUALLY BE FUNCTIONAL...

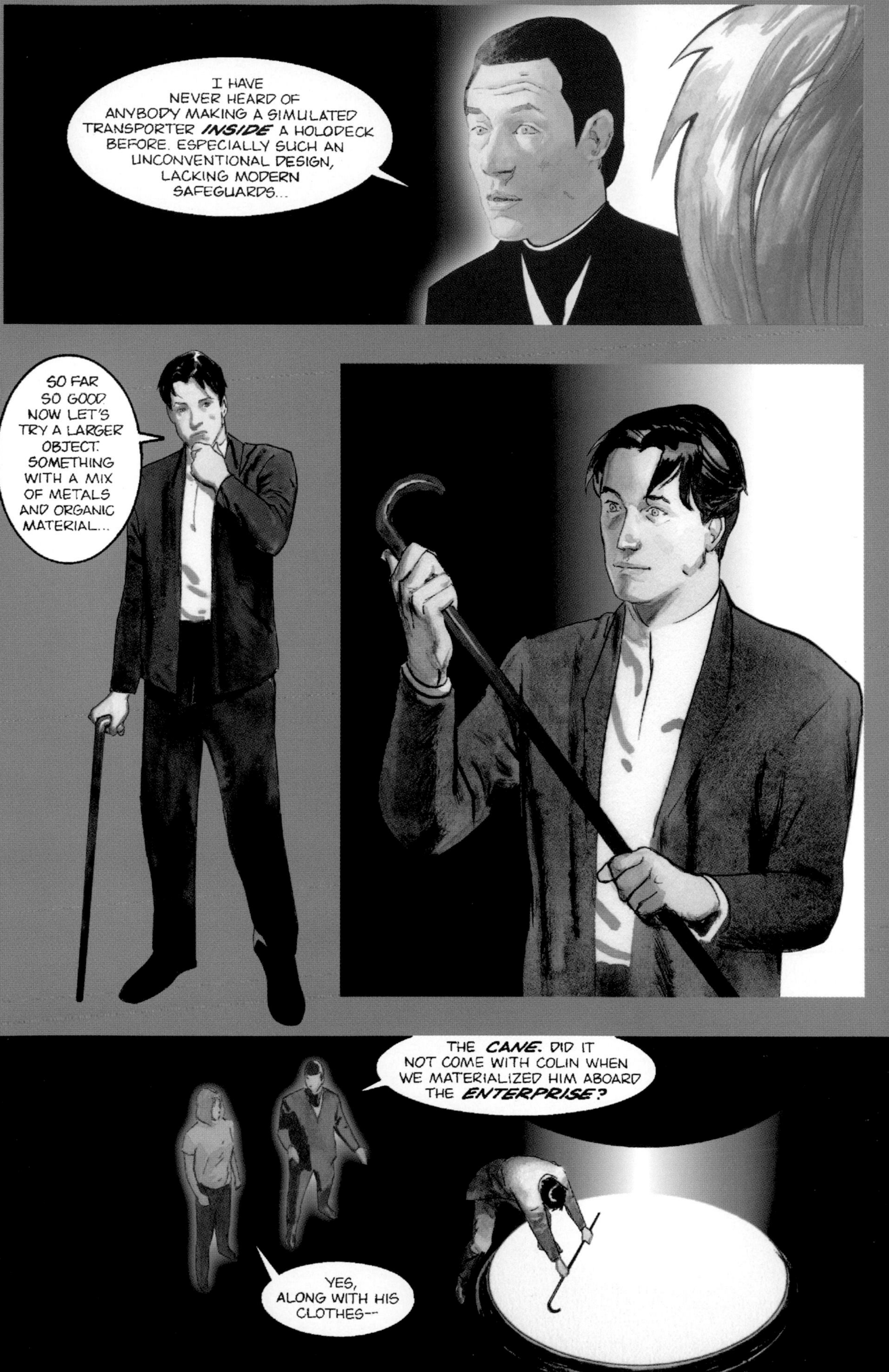
I HAVE NEVER HEARD OF ANYBODY MAKING A SIMULATED TRANSPORTER *INSIDE* A HOLODECK BEFORE. ESPECIALLY SUCH AN UNCONVENTIONAL DESIGN, LACKING MODERN SAFEGUARDS...
SO FAR SO GOOD. NOW LET'S TRY A LARGER OBJECT. SOMETHING WITH A MIX OF METALS AND ORGANIC MATERIAL...
THE *CANE*. DID IT NOT COME WITH COLIN WHEN WE MATERIALIZED HIM ABOARD THE *ENTERPRISE*?
YES, ALONG WITH HIS CLOTHES--

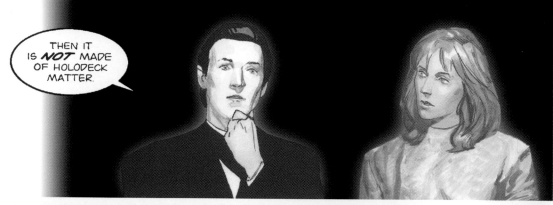

THEN IT IS *NOT* MADE OF HOLODECK MATTER.

DOES THAT MEAN HE WON'T BE ABLE TO SEND IT?

I AM NOT SURE. THE READINGS HE IS GETTING ARE FICTITIOUS. IN REALITY, HE IS NOT IN SAN DIEGO, BUT ABOARD THE *ENTERPRISE*. SO IF HIS CANE *DOES* TRANSPORT--

IT COULD MATERIALIZE IN THE MIDDLE OF SOLID--

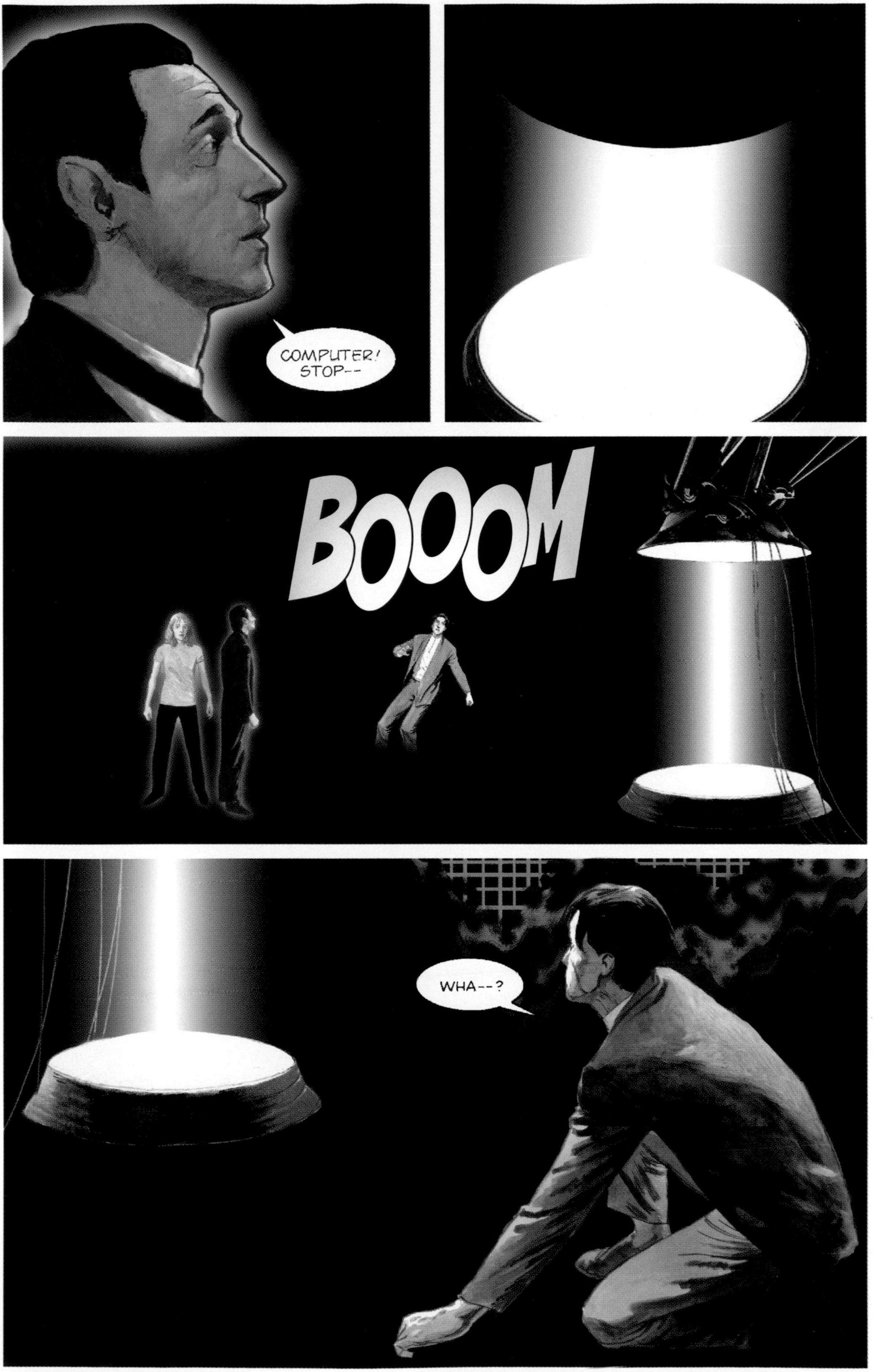

COMPUTER! STOP--
BOOOM
WHA--?

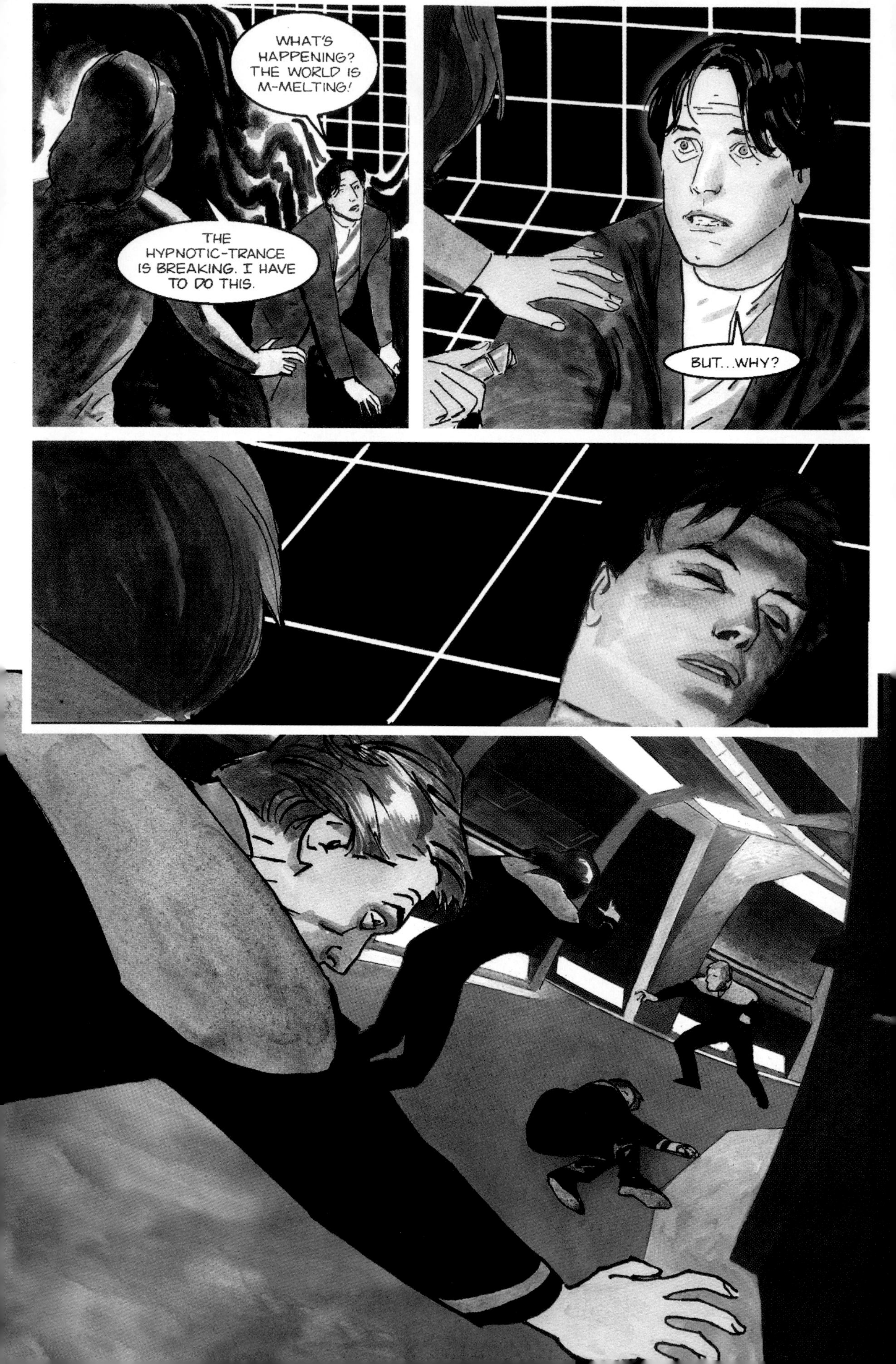
WHAT'S HAPPENING? THE WORLD IS M-MELTING!
THE HYPNOTIC-TRANCE IS BREAKING. I HAVE TO DO THIS.
BUT...WHY?

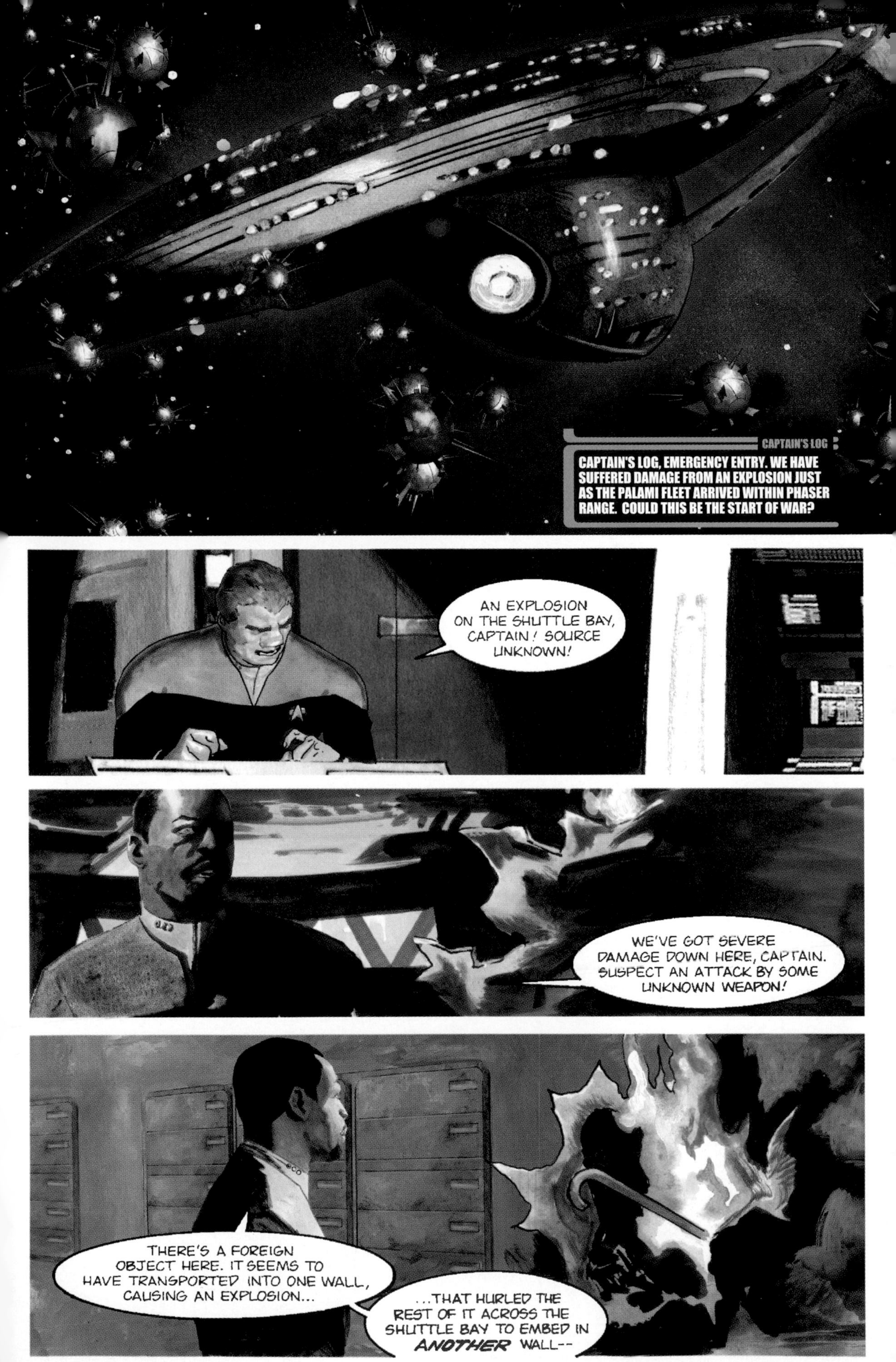
CAPTAIN'S LOG
CAPTAIN'S LOG, EMERGENCY ENTRY. WE HAVE SUFFERED DAMAGE FROM AN EXPLOSION JUST AS THE PALAMI FLEET ARRIVED WITHIN PHASER RANGE. COULD THIS BE THE START OF WAR?
AN EXPLOSION ON THE SHUTTLE BAY, CAPTAIN! SOURCE UNKNOWN!
WE'VE GOT SEVERE DAMAGE DOWN HERE, CAPTAIN. SUSPECT AN ATTACK BY SOME UNKNOWN WEAPON!
THERE'S A FOREIGN OBJECT HERE. IT SEEMS TO HAVE TRANSPORTED INTO ONE WALL, CAUSING AN EXPLOSION...
...THAT HURLED THE REST OF IT ACROSS THE SHUTTLE BAY TO EMBED IN *ANOTHER* WALL--

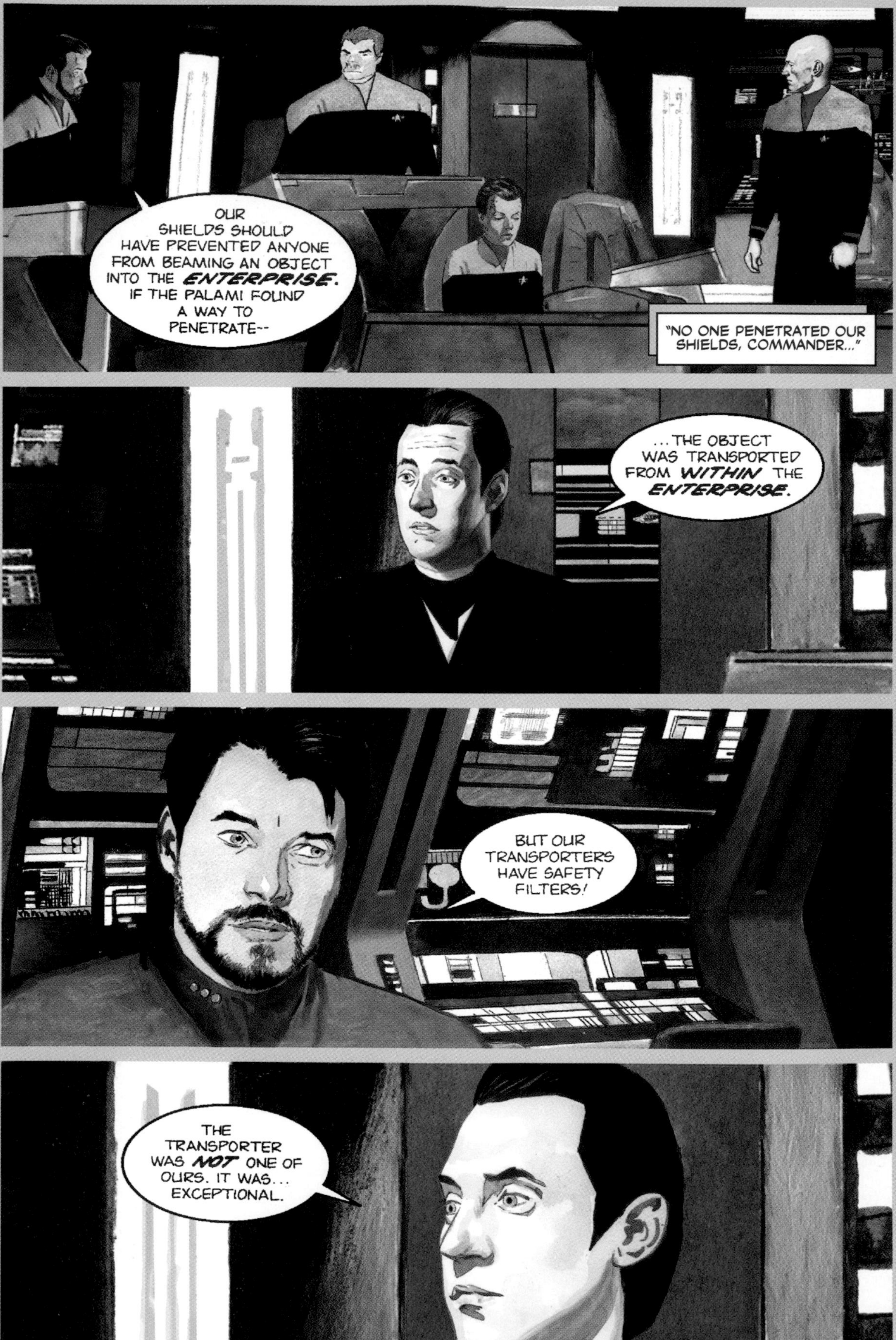
OUR SHIELDS SHOULD HAVE PREVENTED ANYONE FROM BEAMING AN OBJECT INTO THE *ENTERPRISE*. IF THE PALAMI FOUND A WAY TO PENETRATE--
"NO ONE PENETRATED OUR SHIELDS, COMMANDER..."
...THE OBJECT WAS TRANSPORTED FROM *WITHIN* THE *ENTERPRISE*.
BUT OUR TRANSPORTERS HAVE SAFETY FILTERS!
THE TRANSPORTER WAS *NOT* ONE OF OURS. IT WAS... EXCEPTIONAL.

DATA'S EXPLANATION TAKES A LITTLE TIME. MEANWHILE, THE PALAMI SHIPS DRAW NEAR. HUGE, OMINOUS AND ALMOST TOO NUMEROUS TO COUNT...

ENOUGH! WE FACE A CRISIS WITH THE PALAMI. I CANNOT AFFORD ANY MORE DISTRACTIONS.

DOES DR. CRUSHER STILL FEEL THIS PROCEDURE IN THE HOLODECK IS URGENT?

SHE DOES, CAPTAIN, AND I CAN PROMISE THE ACCIDENT WILL NOT BE REPEATED. WE HAVE REPLACED ALL OF THE PATIENT'S MATERIAL POSSESSIONS-- HIS CANE AND CLOTHING-- WITH SUBSTITUTES MADE OF HOLOMATTER.

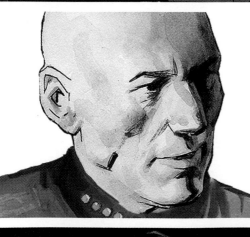

THEN MAKE IT SO, DATA. AND RETURN TO THE BRIDGE AS SOON AS YOU CAN. I WANT YOU HERE.

REPORT! TELL ME ABOUT THE PALAMI. WHAT ARE THEY DOING?

THE ARMADA HAS CHANGED CONFIGURATION SINCE WE SHIFTED TO COMBAT ALERT.

I DETECT SIGNS THAT THEY ARE TAKING UP A WARLIKE POSTURE THEMSELVES, JUST BEYOND THE BARRIER OF QUARANTINE MINES.

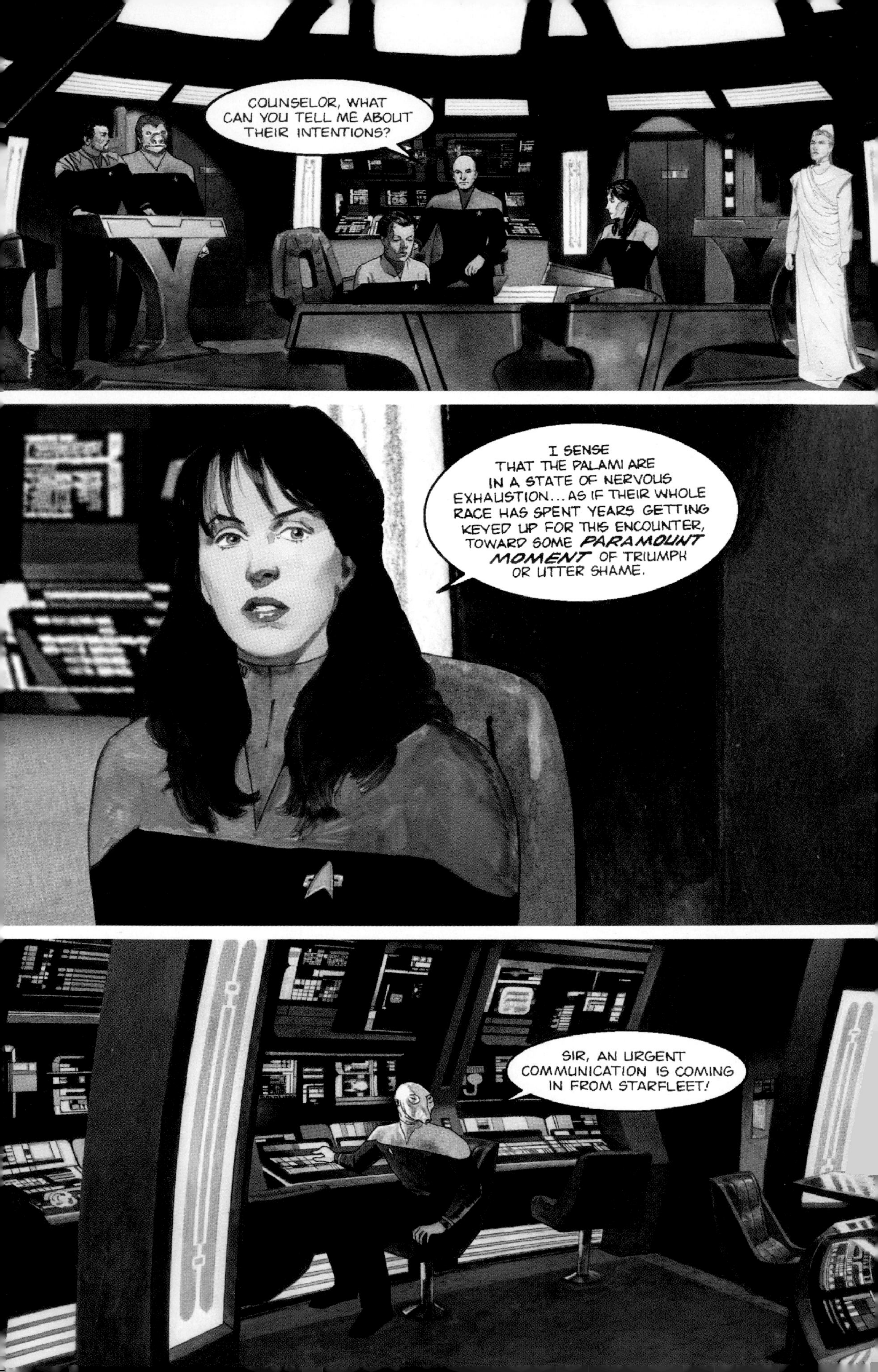
COUNSELOR, WHAT CAN YOU TELL ME ABOUT THEIR INTENTIONS?
I SENSE THAT THE PALAMI ARE IN A STATE OF NERVOUS EXHAUSTION... AS IF THEIR WHOLE RACE HAS SPENT YEARS GETTING KEYED UP FOR THIS ENCOUNTER, TOWARD SOME PARAMOUNT MOMENT OF TRIUMPH OR UTTER SHAME.
SIR, AN URGENT COMMUNICATION IS COMING IN FROM STARFLEET!

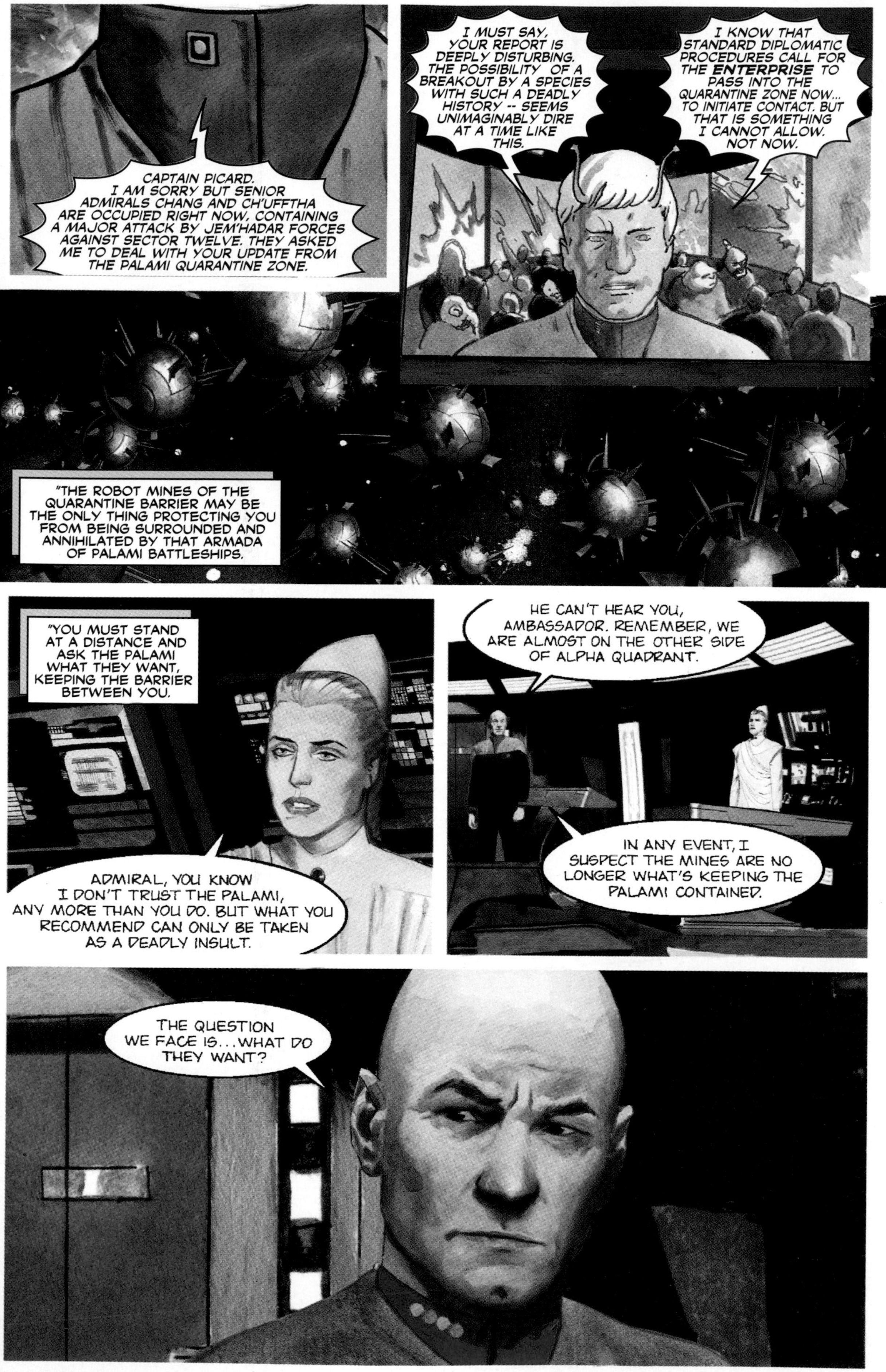
CAPTAIN PICARD. I AM SORRY BUT SENIOR ADMIRALS CHANG AND CH'UFFTHA ARE OCCUPIED RIGHT NOW, CONTAINING A MAJOR ATTACK BY JEM'HADAR FORCES AGAINST SECTOR TWELVE. THEY ASKED ME TO DEAL WITH YOUR UPDATE FROM THE PALAMI QUARANTINE ZONE.
I MUST SAY, YOUR REPORT IS DEEPLY DISTURBING. THE POSSIBILITY OF A BREAKOUT BY A SPECIES WITH SUCH A DEADLY HISTORY -- SEEMS UNIMAGINABLY DIRE AT A TIME LIKE THIS.
I KNOW THAT STANDARD DIPLOMATIC PROCEDURES CALL FOR THE ENTERPRISE TO PASS INTO THE QUARANTINE ZONE NOW... TO INITIATE CONTACT. BUT THAT IS SOMETHING I CANNOT ALLOW. NOT NOW.
"THE ROBOT MINES OF THE QUARANTINE BARRIER MAY BE THE ONLY THING PROTECTING YOU FROM BEING SURROUNDED AND ANNIHILATED BY THAT ARMADA OF PALAMI BATTLESHIPS.
"YOU MUST STAND AT A DISTANCE AND ASK THE PALAMI WHAT THEY WANT, KEEPING THE BARRIER BETWEEN YOU.
ADMIRAL, YOU KNOW I DON'T TRUST THE PALAMI, ANY MORE THAN YOU DO. BUT WHAT YOU RECOMMEND CAN ONLY BE TAKEN AS A DEADLY INSULT.
HE CAN'T HEAR YOU, AMBASSADOR. REMEMBER, WE ARE ALMOST ON THE OTHER SIDE OF ALPHA QUADRANT.
IN ANY EVENT, I SUSPECT THE MINES ARE NO LONGER WHAT'S KEEPING THE PALAMI CONTAINED.
THE QUESTION WE FACE IS... WHAT DO THEY WANT?

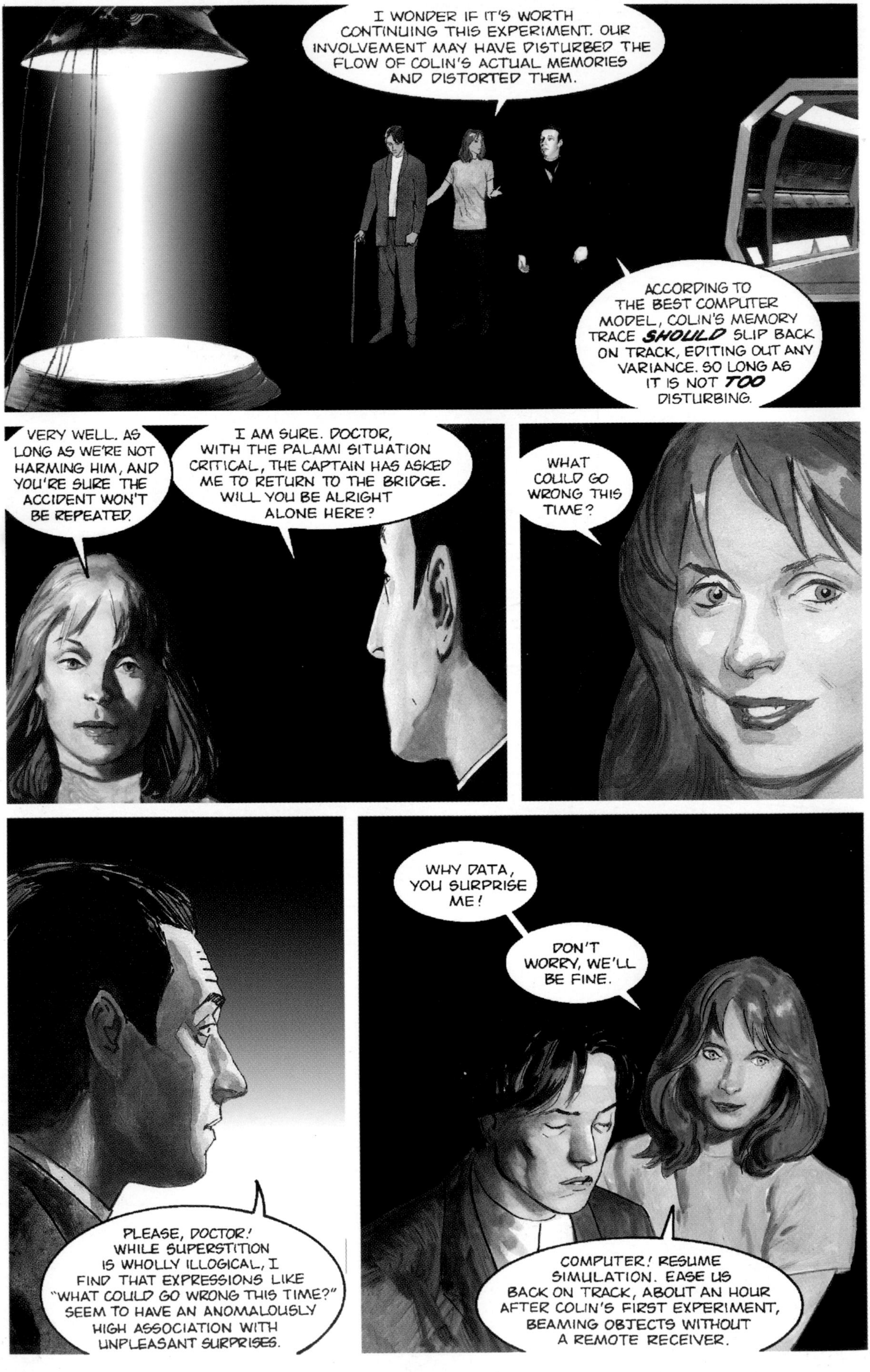
I WONDER IF IT'S WORTH CONTINUING THIS EXPERIMENT. OUR INVOLVEMENT MAY HAVE DISTURBED THE FLOW OF COLIN'S ACTUAL MEMORIES AND DISTORTED THEM.
ACCORDING TO THE BEST COMPUTER MODEL, COLIN'S MEMORY TRACE SHOULD SLIP BACK ON TRACK, EDITING OUT ANY VARIANCE. SO LONG AS IT IS NOT TOO DISTURBING.
VERY WELL. AS LONG AS WE'RE NOT HARMING HIM, AND YOU'RE SURE THE ACCIDENT WON'T BE REPEATED.
I AM SURE. DOCTOR, WITH THE PALAMI SITUATION CRITICAL, THE CAPTAIN HAS ASKED ME TO RETURN TO THE BRIDGE. WILL YOU BE ALRIGHT ALONE HERE?
WHAT COULD GO WRONG THIS TIME?
PLEASE, DOCTOR! WHILE SUPERSTITION IS WHOLLY ILLOGICAL, I FIND THAT EXPRESSIONS LIKE "WHAT COULD GO WRONG THIS TIME?" SEEM TO HAVE AN ANOMALOUSLY HIGH ASSOCIATION WITH UNPLEASANT SURPRISES.
WHY DATA, YOU SURPRISE ME!
DON'T WORRY, WE'LL BE FINE.
COMPUTER! RESUME SIMULATION. EASE US BACK ON TRACK, ABOUT AN HOUR AFTER COLIN'S FIRST EXPERIMENT, BEAMING OBJECTS WITHOUT A REMOTE RECEIVER.

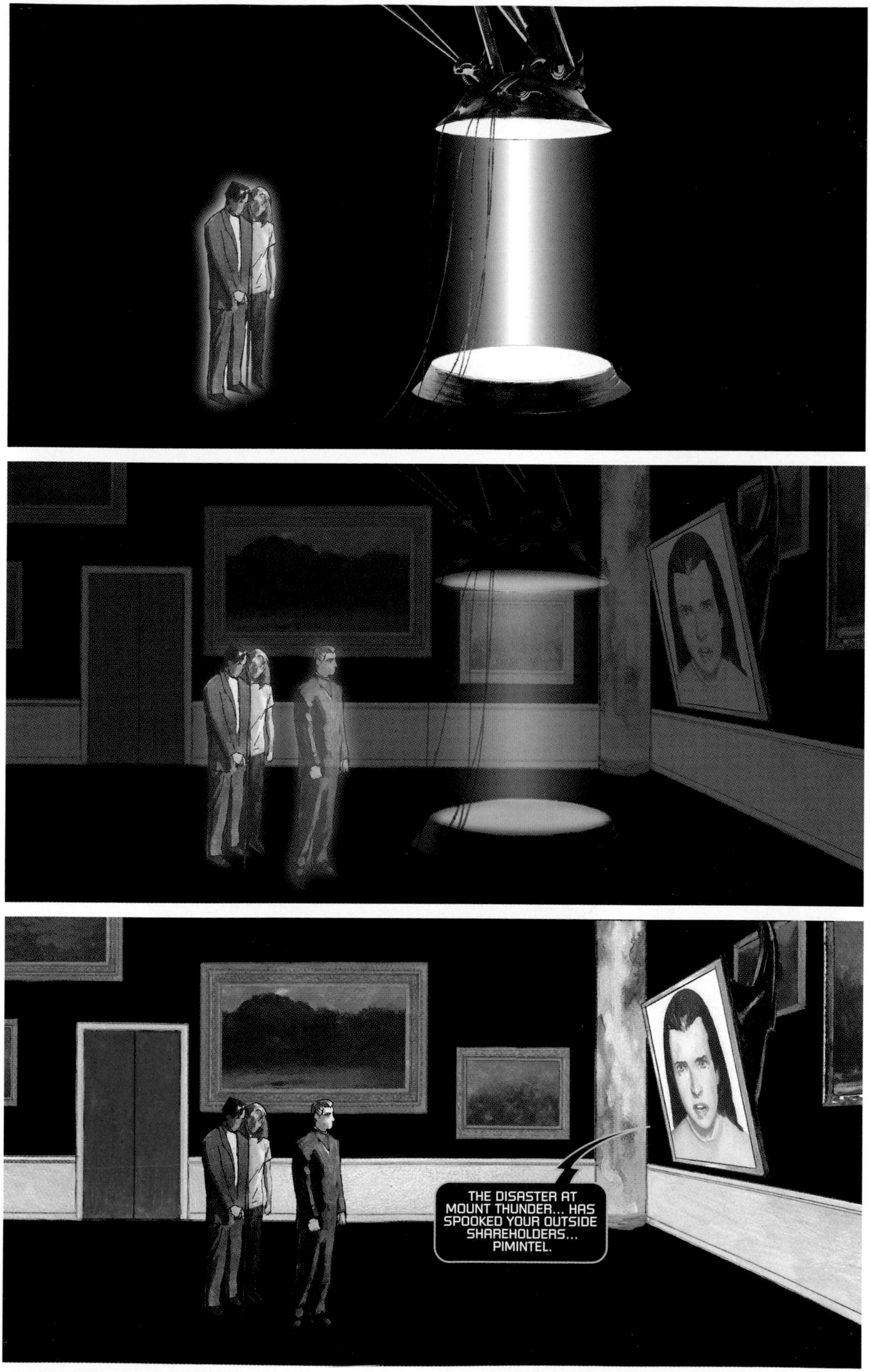
THE DISASTER AT MOUNT THUNDER... HAS SPOOKED YOUR OUTSIDE SHAREHOLDERS... PIMINTEL.

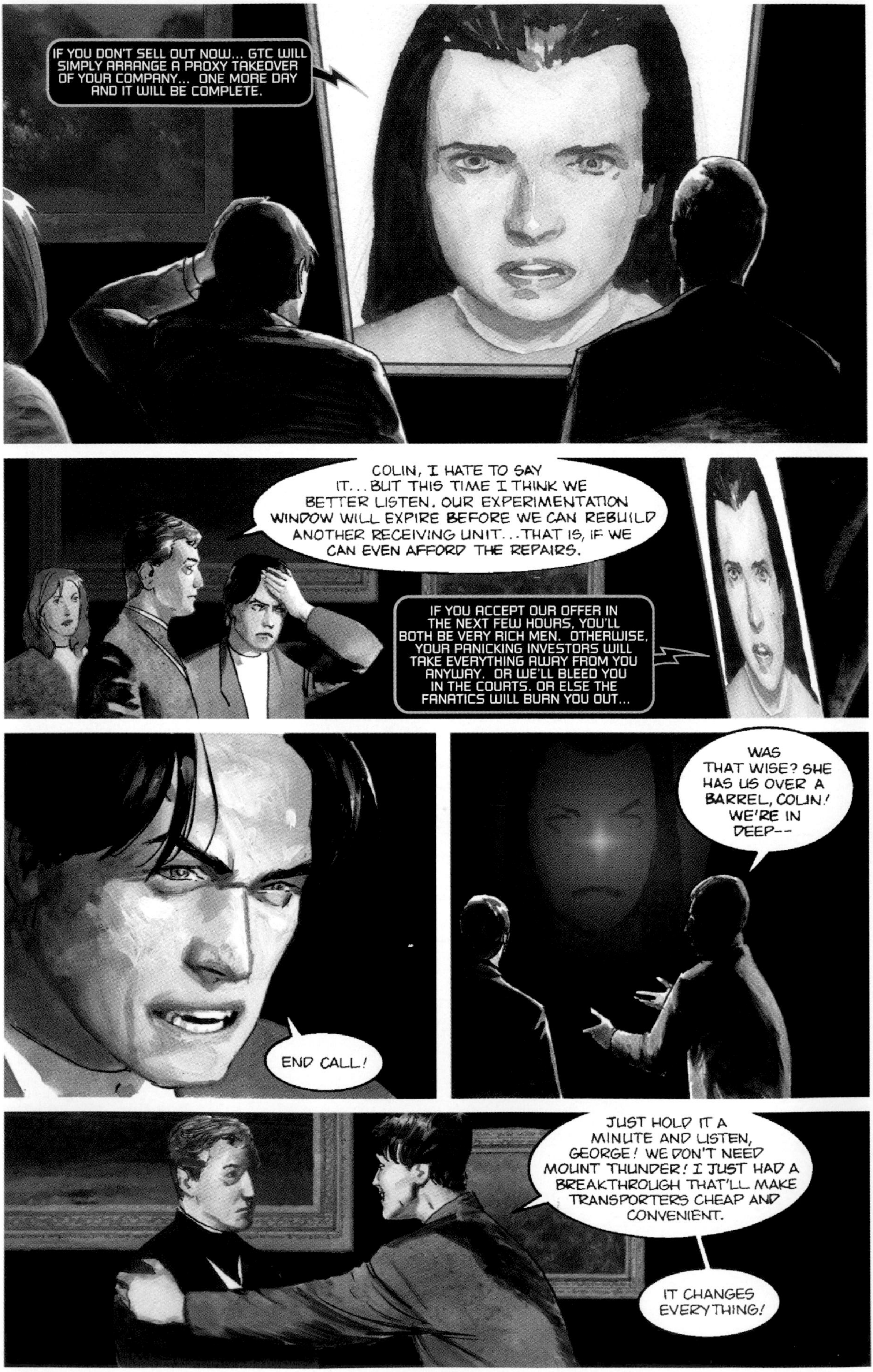
IF YOU DON'T SELL OUT NOW... GTC WILL SIMPLY ARRANGE A PROXY TAKEOVER OF YOUR COMPANY... ONE MORE DAY AND IT WILL BE COMPLETE.
COLIN, I HATE TO SAY IT... BUT THIS TIME I THINK WE BETTER LISTEN. OUR EXPERIMENTATION WINDOW WILL EXPIRE BEFORE WE CAN REBUILD ANOTHER RECEIVING UNIT...THAT IS, IF WE CAN EVEN AFFORD THE REPAIRS.
IF YOU ACCEPT OUR OFFER IN THE NEXT FEW HOURS, YOU'LL BOTH BE VERY RICH MEN. OTHERWISE, YOUR PANICKING INVESTORS WILL TAKE EVERYTHING AWAY FROM YOU ANYWAY. OR WE'LL BLEED YOU IN THE COURTS. OR ELSE THE FANATICS WILL BURN YOU OUT...
END CALL!
WAS THAT WISE? SHE HAS US OVER A BARREL, COLIN! WE'RE IN DEEP--
JUST HOLD IT A MINUTE AND LISTEN, GEORGE! WE DON'T NEED MOUNT THUNDER! I JUST HAD A BREAKTHROUGH THAT'LL MAKE TRANSPORTERS CHEAP AND CONVENIENT.
IT CHANGES EVERYTHING!

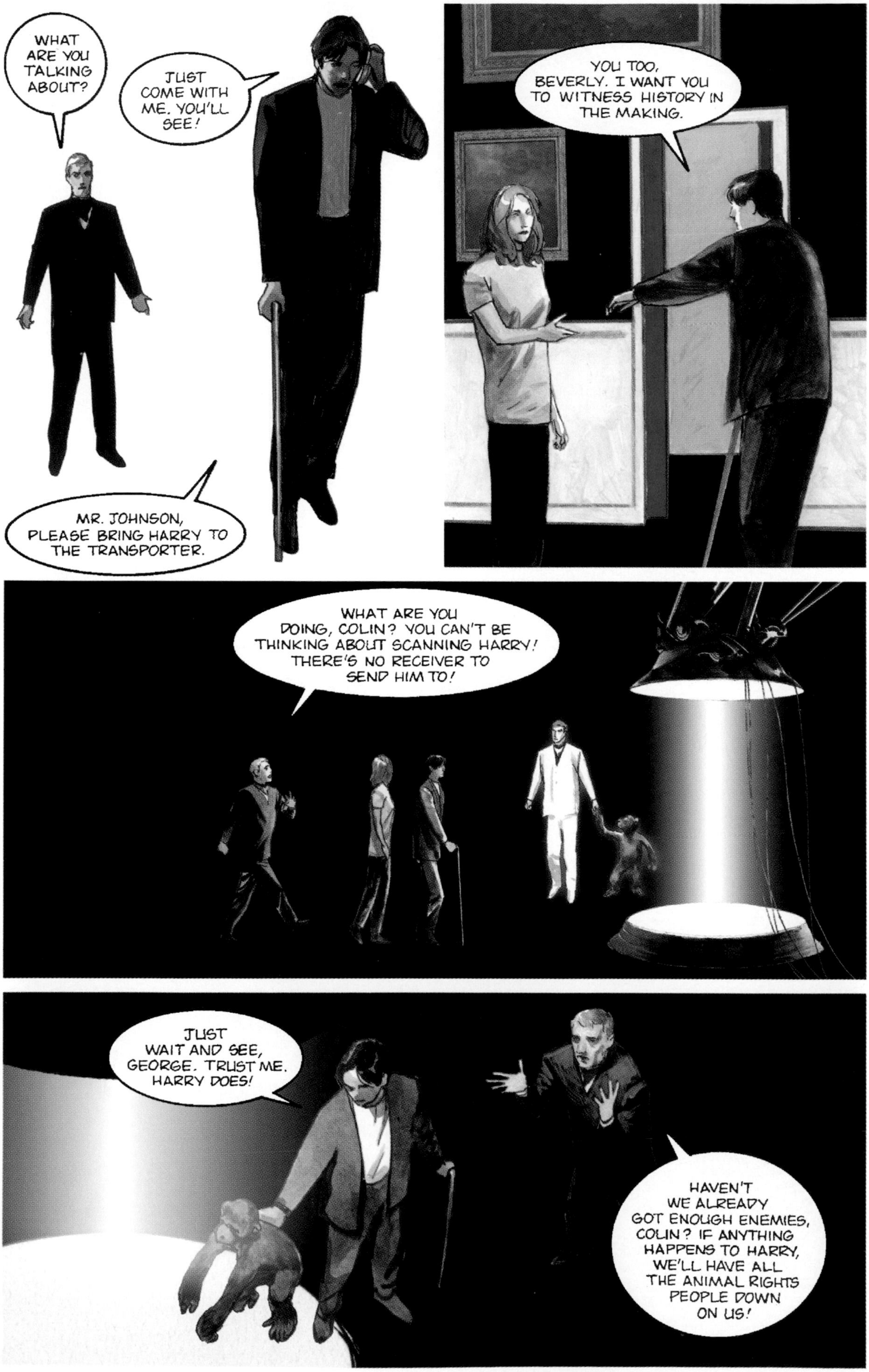
WHAT ARE YOU TALKING ABOUT?
JUST COME WITH ME. YOU'LL SEE!
MR. JOHNSON, PLEASE BRING HARRY TO THE TRANSPORTER.
YOU TOO, BEVERLY. I WANT YOU TO WITNESS HISTORY IN THE MAKING.
WHAT ARE YOU DOING, COLIN? YOU CAN'T BE THINKING ABOUT SCANNING HARRY! THERE'S NO RECEIVER TO SEND HIM TO!
JUST WAIT AND SEE, GEORGE. TRUST ME. HARRY DOES!
HAVEN'T WE ALREADY GOT ENOUGH ENEMIES, COLIN? IF ANYTHING HAPPENS TO HARRY, WE'LL HAVE ALL THE ANIMAL RIGHTS PEOPLE DOWN ON US!

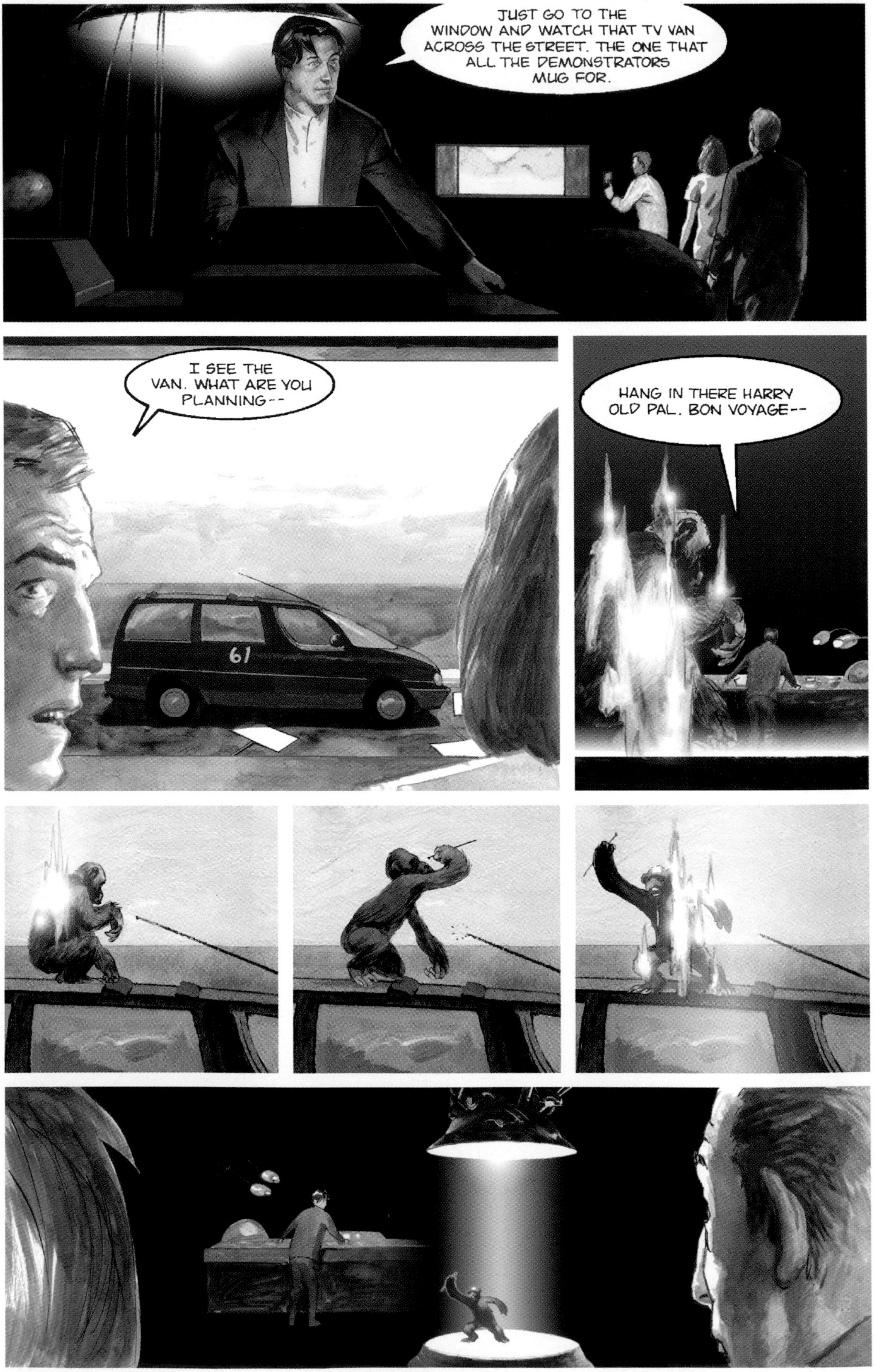
JUST GO TO THE WINDOW AND WATCH THAT TV VAN ACROSS THE STREET. THE ONE THAT ALL THE DEMONSTRATORS MUG FOR.
I SEE THE VAN. WHAT ARE YOU PLANNING--
61
HANG IN THERE HARRY OLD PAL. BON VOYAGE--

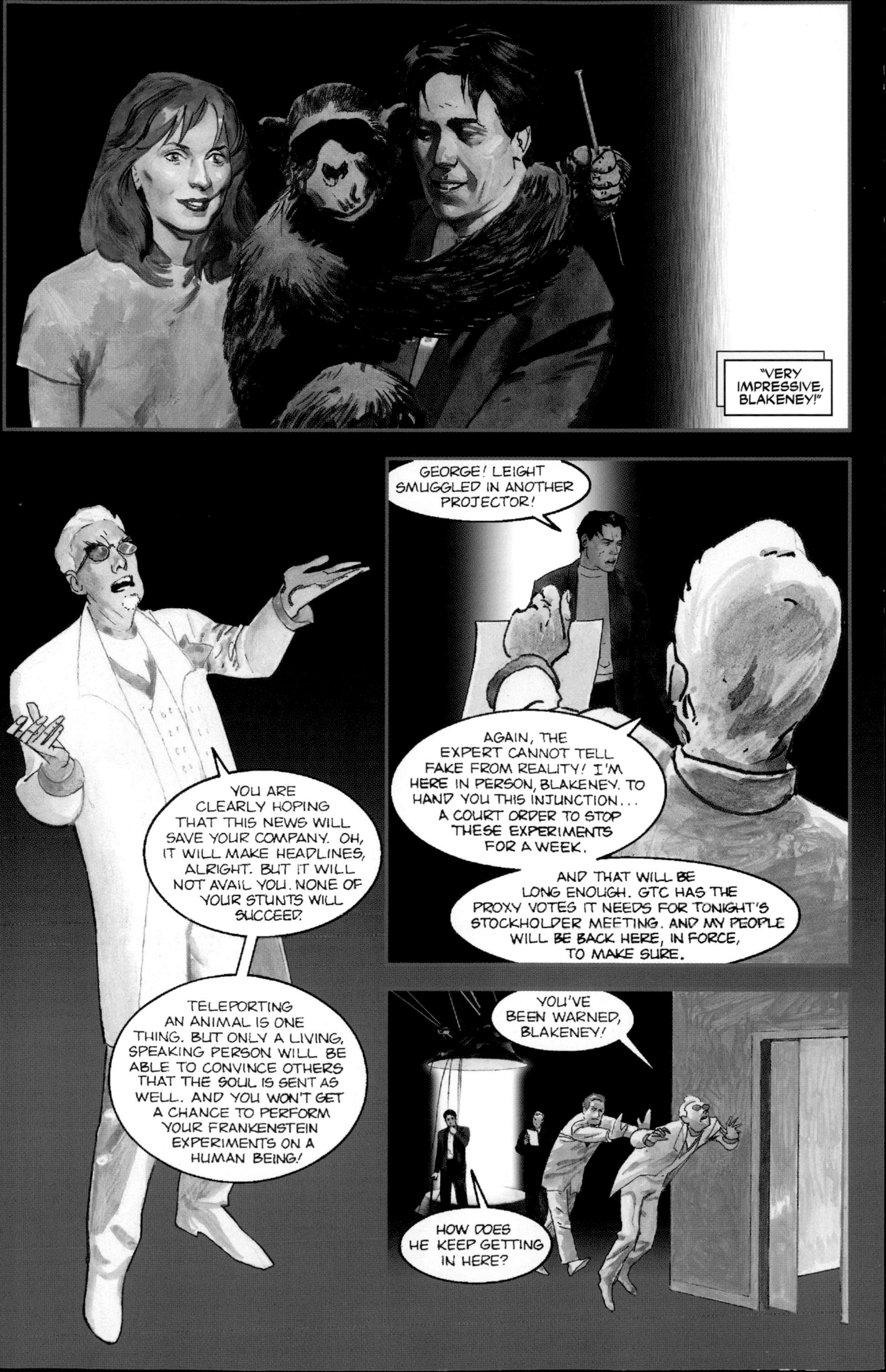
"VERY IMPRESSIVE, BLAKENEY!"
GEORGE! LEIGHT SMUGGLED IN ANOTHER PROJECTOR!
YOU ARE CLEARLY HOPING THAT THIS NEWS WILL SAVE YOUR COMPANY. OH, IT WILL MAKE HEADLINES, ALRIGHT. BUT IT WILL NOT AVAIL YOU. NONE OF YOUR STUNTS WILL SUCCEED.
AGAIN, THE EXPERT CANNOT TELL FAKE FROM REALITY! I'M HERE IN PERSON, BLAKENEY. TO HAND YOU THIS INJUNCTION... A COURT ORDER TO STOP THESE EXPERIMENTS FOR A WEEK.
AND THAT WILL BE LONG ENOUGH. GTC HAS THE PROXY VOTES IT NEEDS FOR TONIGHT'S STOCKHOLDER MEETING. AND MY PEOPLE WILL BE BACK HERE, IN FORCE, TO MAKE SURE.
TELEPORTING AN ANIMAL IS ONE THING. BUT ONLY A LIVING, SPEAKING PERSON WILL BE ABLE TO CONVINCE OTHERS THAT THE SOUL IS SENT AS WELL. AND YOU WON'T GET A CHANCE TO PERFORM YOUR FRANKENSTEIN EXPERIMENTS ON A HUMAN BEING!
YOU'VE BEEN WARNED, BLAKENEY!
HOW DOES HE KEEP GETTING IN HERE?

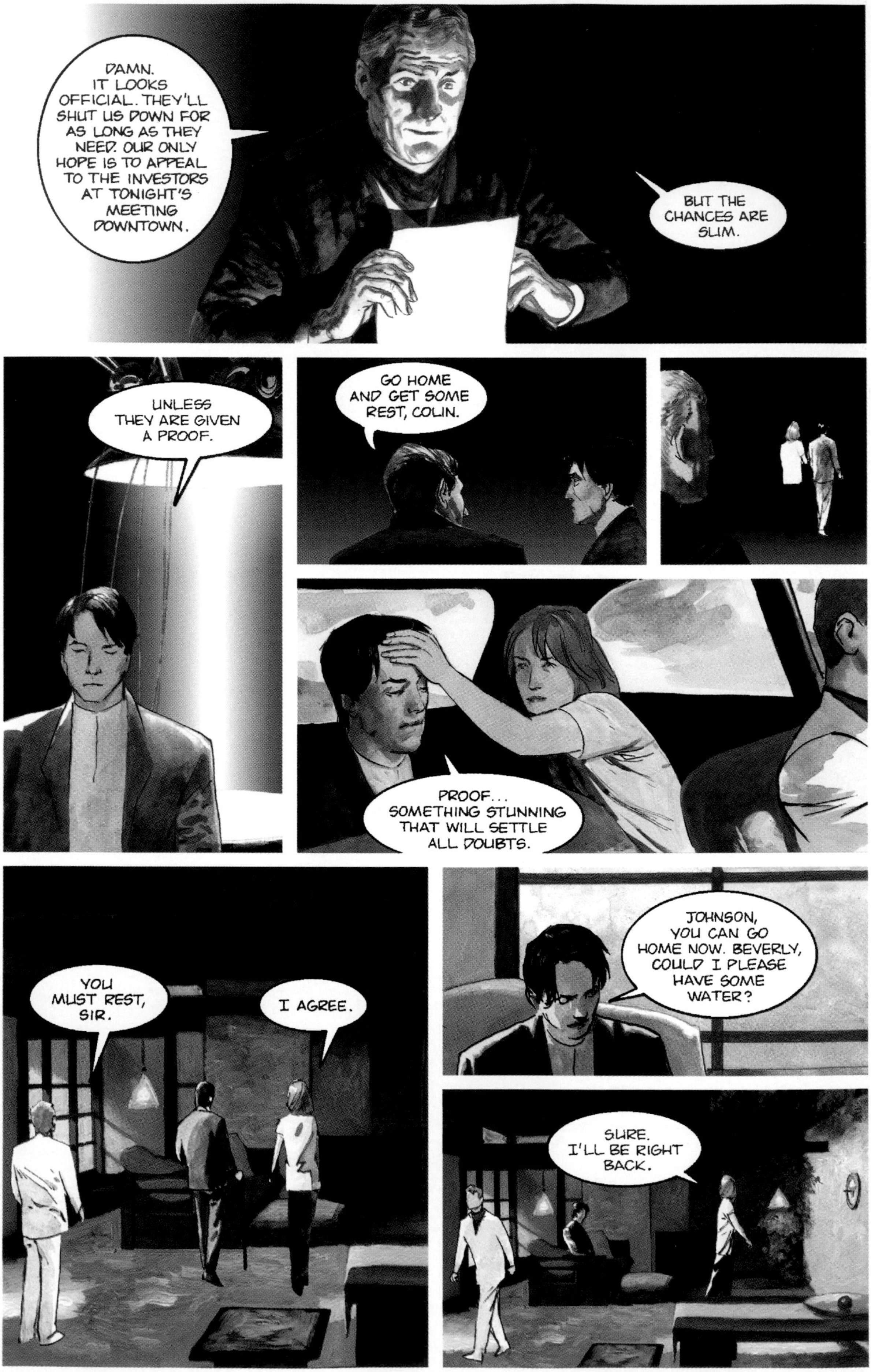
DAMN. IT LOOKS OFFICIAL. THEY'LL SHUT US DOWN FOR AS LONG AS THEY NEED. OUR ONLY HOPE IS TO APPEAL TO THE INVESTORS AT TONIGHT'S MEETING DOWNTOWN.
BUT THE CHANCES ARE SLIM.
UNLESS THEY ARE GIVEN A PROOF.
GO HOME AND GET SOME REST, COLIN.
PROOF... SOMETHING STUNNING THAT WILL SETTLE ALL DOUBTS.
YOU MUST REST, SIR.
I AGREE.
JOHNSON, YOU CAN GO HOME NOW. BEVERLY, COULD I PLEASE HAVE SOME WATER?
SURE. I'LL BE RIGHT BACK.

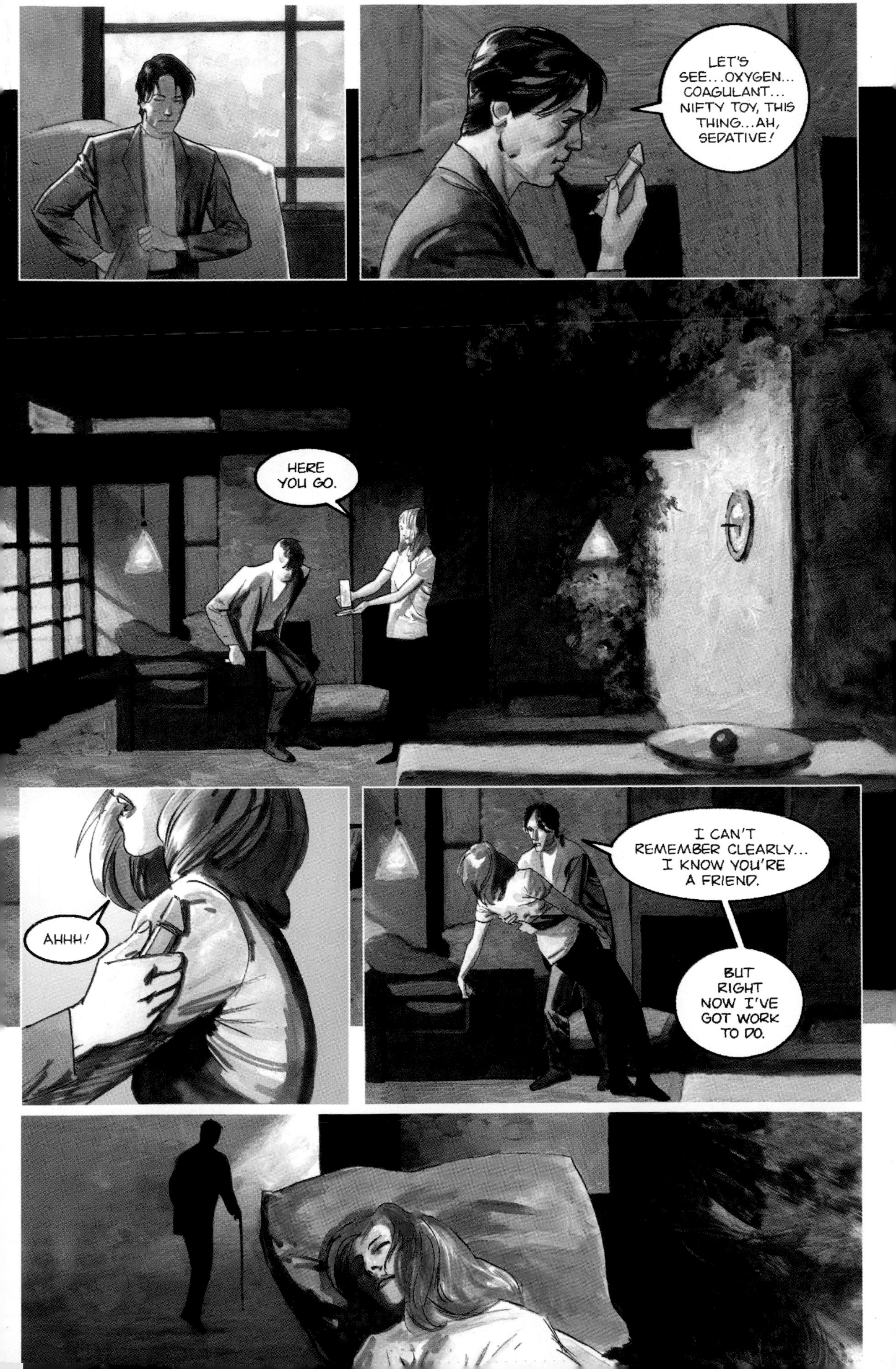
LET'S SEE...OXYGEN... COAGULANT... NIFTY TOY, THIS THING...AH, SEDATIVE!
HERE YOU GO.
AHHH!
I CAN'T REMEMBER CLEARLY... I KNOW YOU'RE A FRIEND.
BUT RIGHT NOW I'VE GOT WORK TO DO.

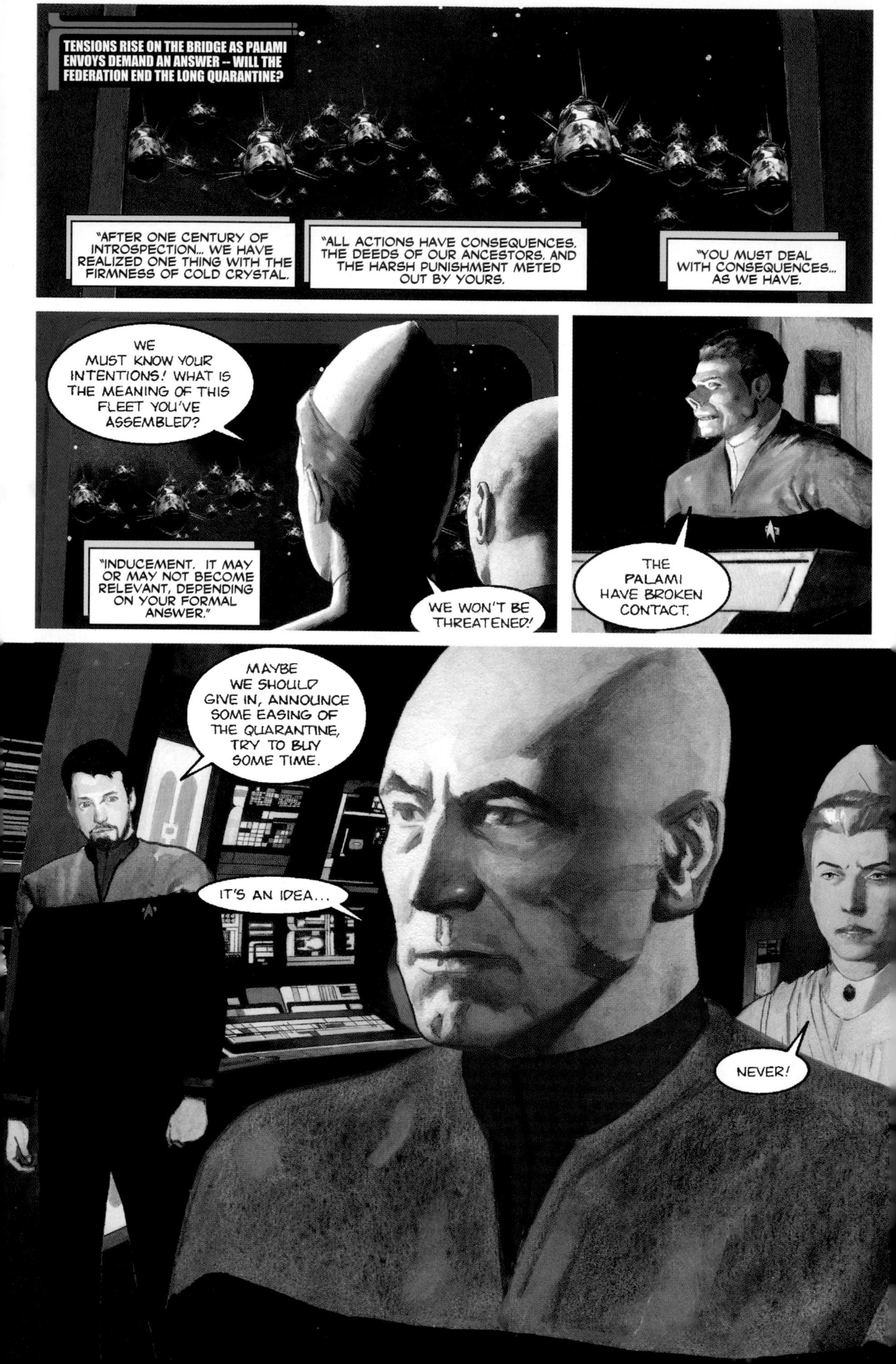
TENSIONS RISE ON THE BRIDGE AS PALAMI ENVOYS DEMAND AN ANSWER -- WILL THE FEDERATION END THE LONG QUARANTINE?
"AFTER ONE CENTURY OF INTROSPECTION... WE HAVE REALIZED ONE THING WITH THE FIRMNESS OF COLD CRYSTAL.
"ALL ACTIONS HAVE CONSEQUENCES. THE DEEDS OF OUR ANCESTORS, AND THE HARSH PUNISHMENT METED OUT BY YOURS.
"YOU MUST DEAL WITH CONSEQUENCES... AS WE HAVE.
WE MUST KNOW YOUR INTENTIONS! WHAT IS THE MEANING OF THIS FLEET YOU'VE ASSEMBLED?
"INDUCEMENT. IT MAY OR MAY NOT BECOME RELEVANT, DEPENDING ON YOUR FORMAL ANSWER."
WE WON'T BE THREATENED!
THE PALAMI HAVE BROKEN CONTACT.
MAYBE WE SHOULD GIVE IN, ANNOUNCE SOME EASING OF THE QUARANTINE, TRY TO BUY SOME TIME.
IT'S AN IDEA...
NEVER!

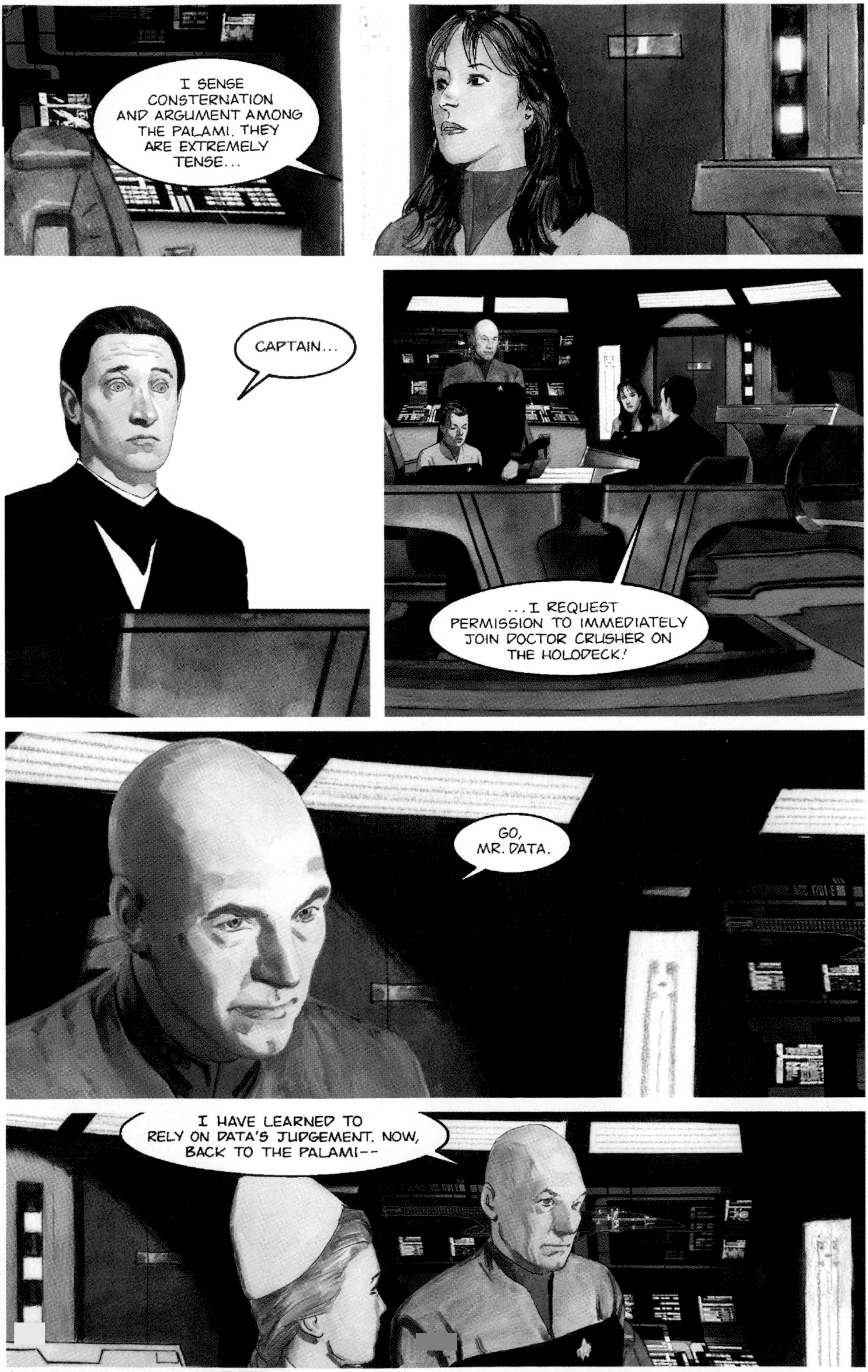
I SENSE CONSTERNATION AND ARGUMENT AMONG THE PALAMI. THEY ARE EXTREMELY TENSE...
CAPTAIN...
...I REQUEST PERMISSION TO IMMEDIATELY JOIN DOCTOR CRUSHER ON THE HOLODECK!
GO, MR. DATA.
I HAVE LEARNED TO RELY ON DATA'S JUDGEMENT. NOW, BACK TO THE PALAMI--

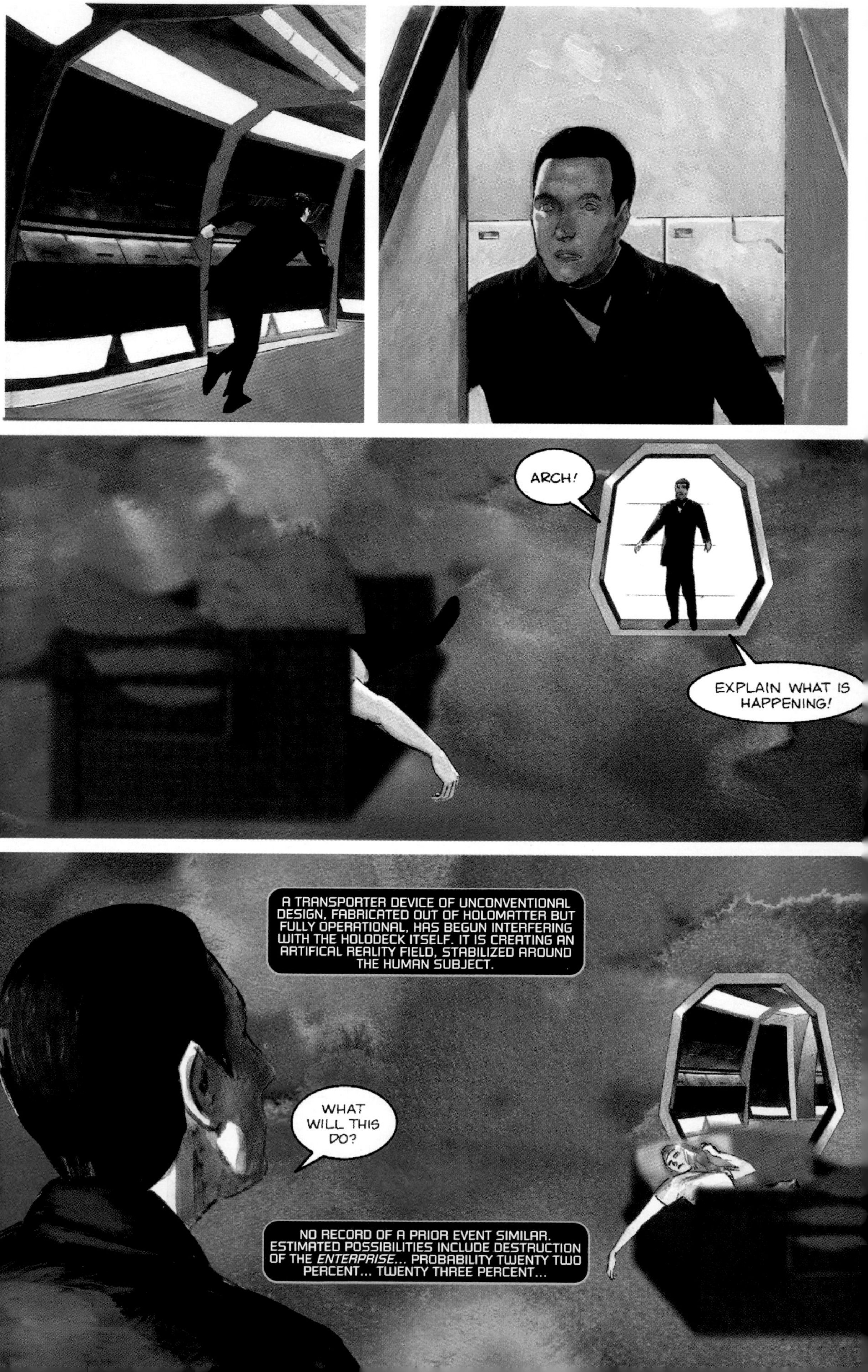
ARCH!
EXPLAIN WHAT IS HAPPENING!
A TRANSPORTER DEVICE OF UNCONVENTIONAL DESIGN, FABRICATED OUT OF HOLOMATTER BUT FULLY OPERATIONAL, HAS BEGUN INTERFERING WITH THE HOLODECK ITSELF. IT IS CREATING AN ARTIFICAL REALITY FIELD, STABILIZED AROUND THE HUMAN SUBJECT.
WHAT WILL THIS DO?
NO RECORD OF A PRIOR EVENT SIMILAR. ESTIMATED POSSIBILITIES INCLUDE DESTRUCTION OF THE *ENTERPRISE*... PROBABILITY TWENTY TWO PERCENT... TWENTY THREE PERCENT...

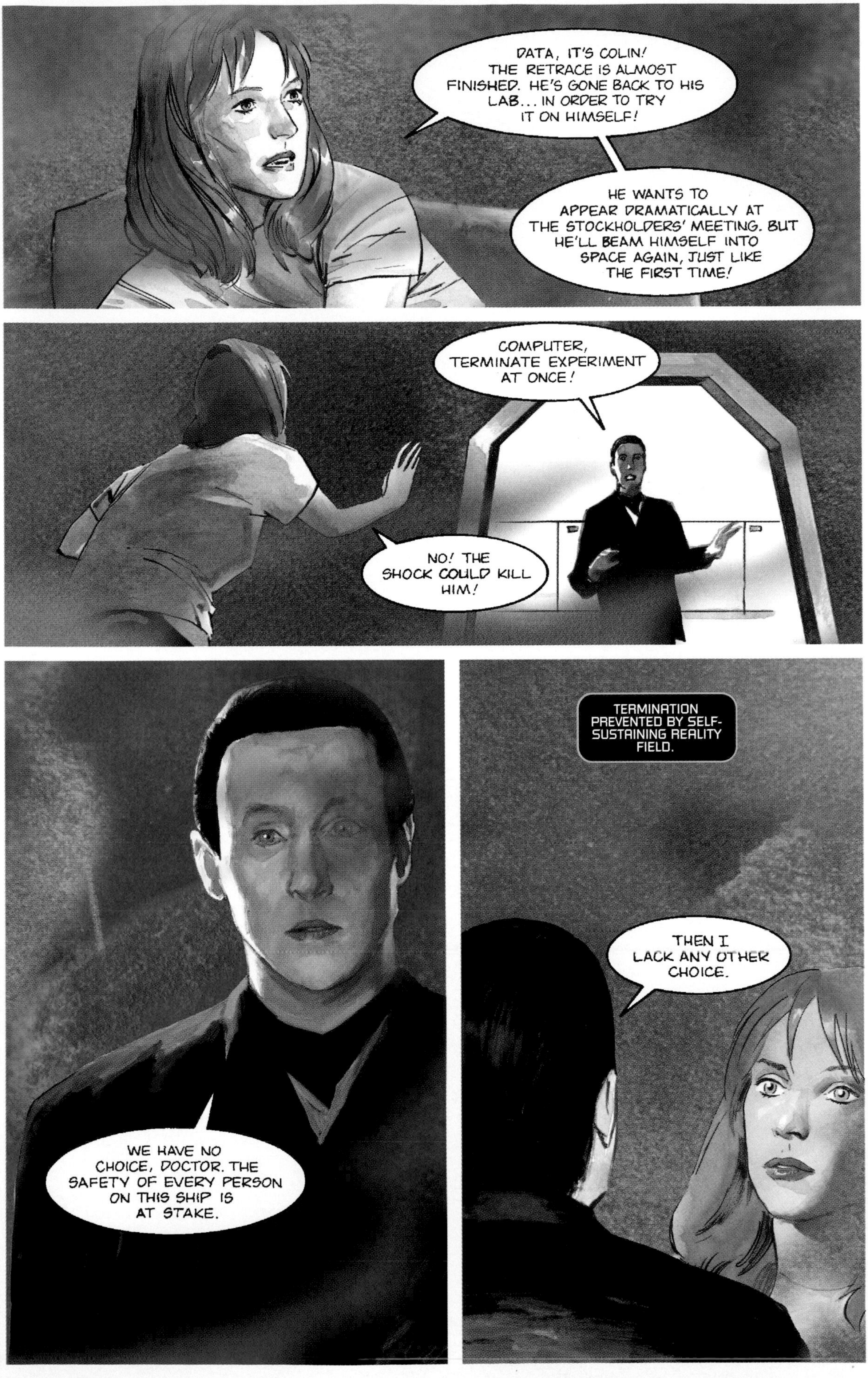
DATA, IT'S COLIN! THE RETRACE IS ALMOST FINISHED. HE'S GONE BACK TO HIS LAB... IN ORDER TO TRY IT ON HIMSELF!
HE WANTS TO APPEAR DRAMATICALLY AT THE STOCKHOLDERS' MEETING. BUT HE'LL BEAM HIMSELF INTO SPACE AGAIN, JUST LIKE THE FIRST TIME!
COMPUTER, TERMINATE EXPERIMENT AT ONCE!
NO! THE SHOCK COULD KILL HIM!
WE HAVE NO CHOICE, DOCTOR. THE SAFETY OF EVERY PERSON ON THIS SHIP IS AT STAKE.
TERMINATION PREVENTED BY SELF-SUSTAINING REALITY FIELD.
THEN I LACK ANY OTHER CHOICE.

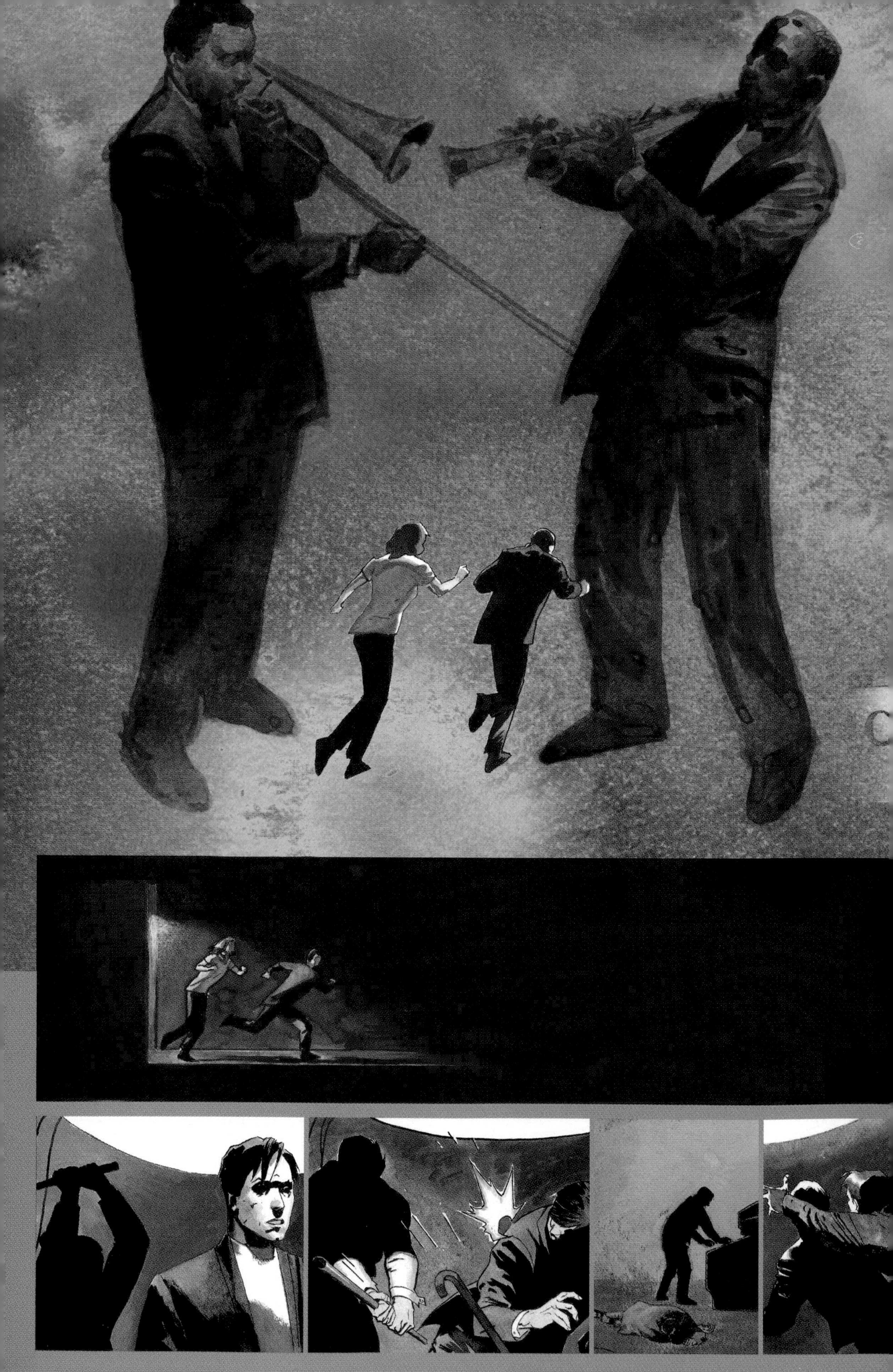

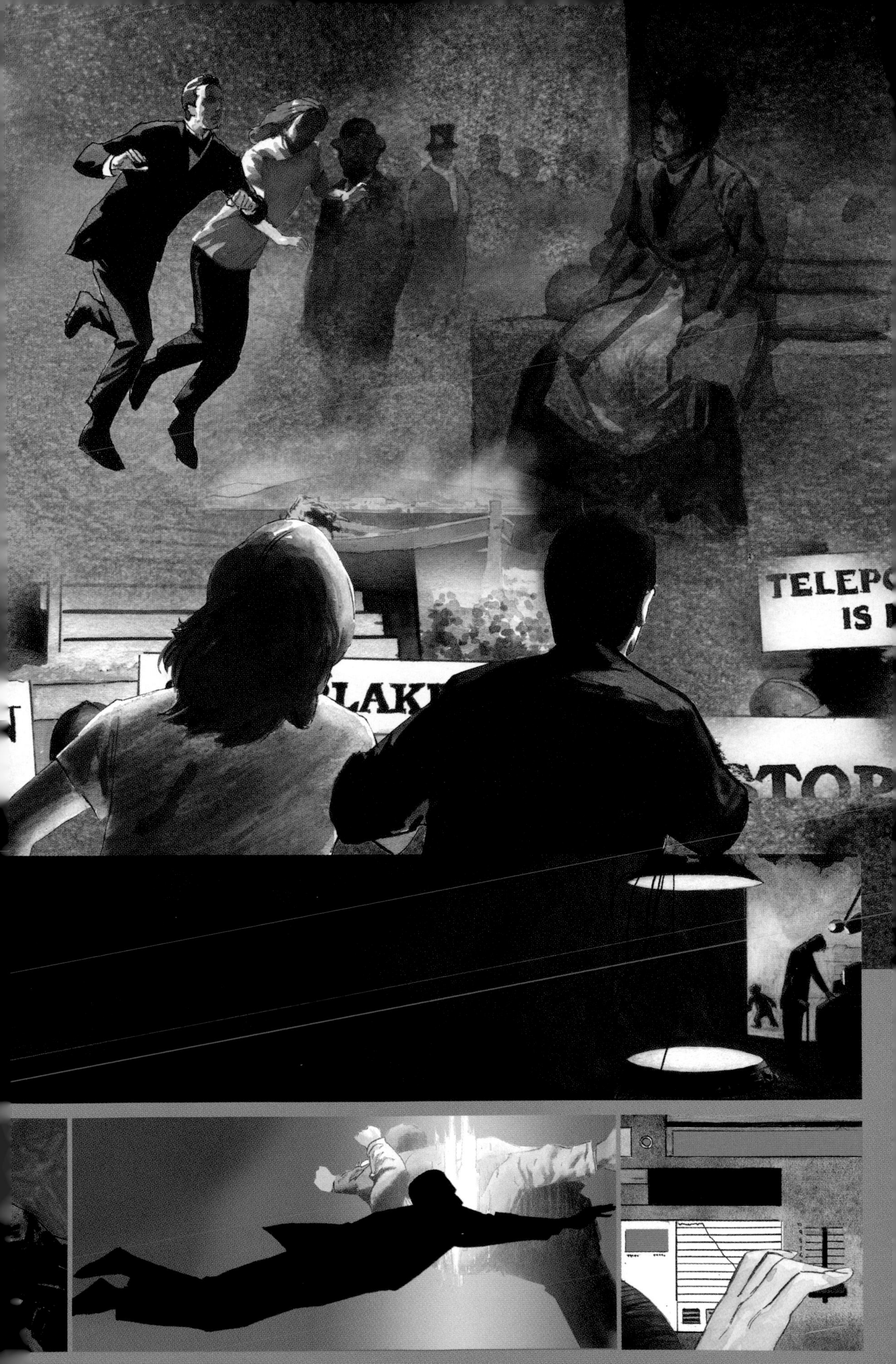

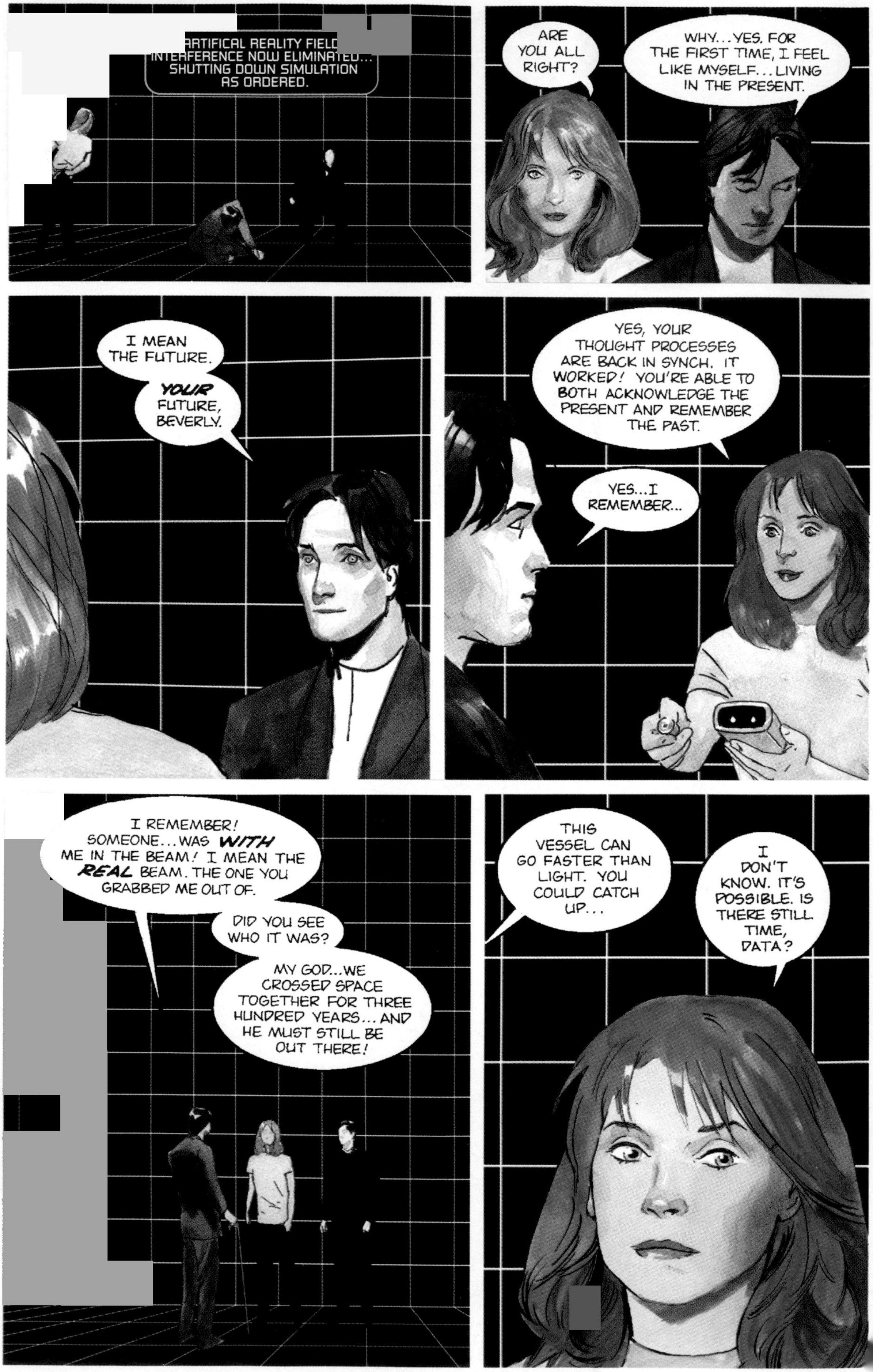
ARTIFICAL REALITY FIELD INTERFERENCE NOW ELIMINATED... SHUTTING DOWN SIMULATION AS ORDERED.
ARE YOU ALL RIGHT?
WHY... YES. FOR THE FIRST TIME, I FEEL LIKE MYSELF... LIVING IN THE PRESENT.
I MEAN THE FUTURE.
YOUR FUTURE, BEVERLY.
YES, YOUR THOUGHT PROCESSES ARE BACK IN SYNCH. IT WORKED! YOU'RE ABLE TO BOTH ACKNOWLEDGE THE PRESENT AND REMEMBER THE PAST.
YES... I REMEMBER...
I REMEMBER! SOMEONE... WAS WITH ME IN THE BEAM! I MEAN THE REAL BEAM. THE ONE YOU GRABBED ME OUT OF.
DID YOU SEE WHO IT WAS?
MY GOD... WE CROSSED SPACE TOGETHER FOR THREE HUNDRED YEARS... AND HE MUST STILL BE OUT THERE!
THIS VESSEL CAN GO FASTER THAN LIGHT. YOU COULD CATCH UP...
I DON'T KNOW. IT'S POSSIBLE. IS THERE STILL TIME, DATA?

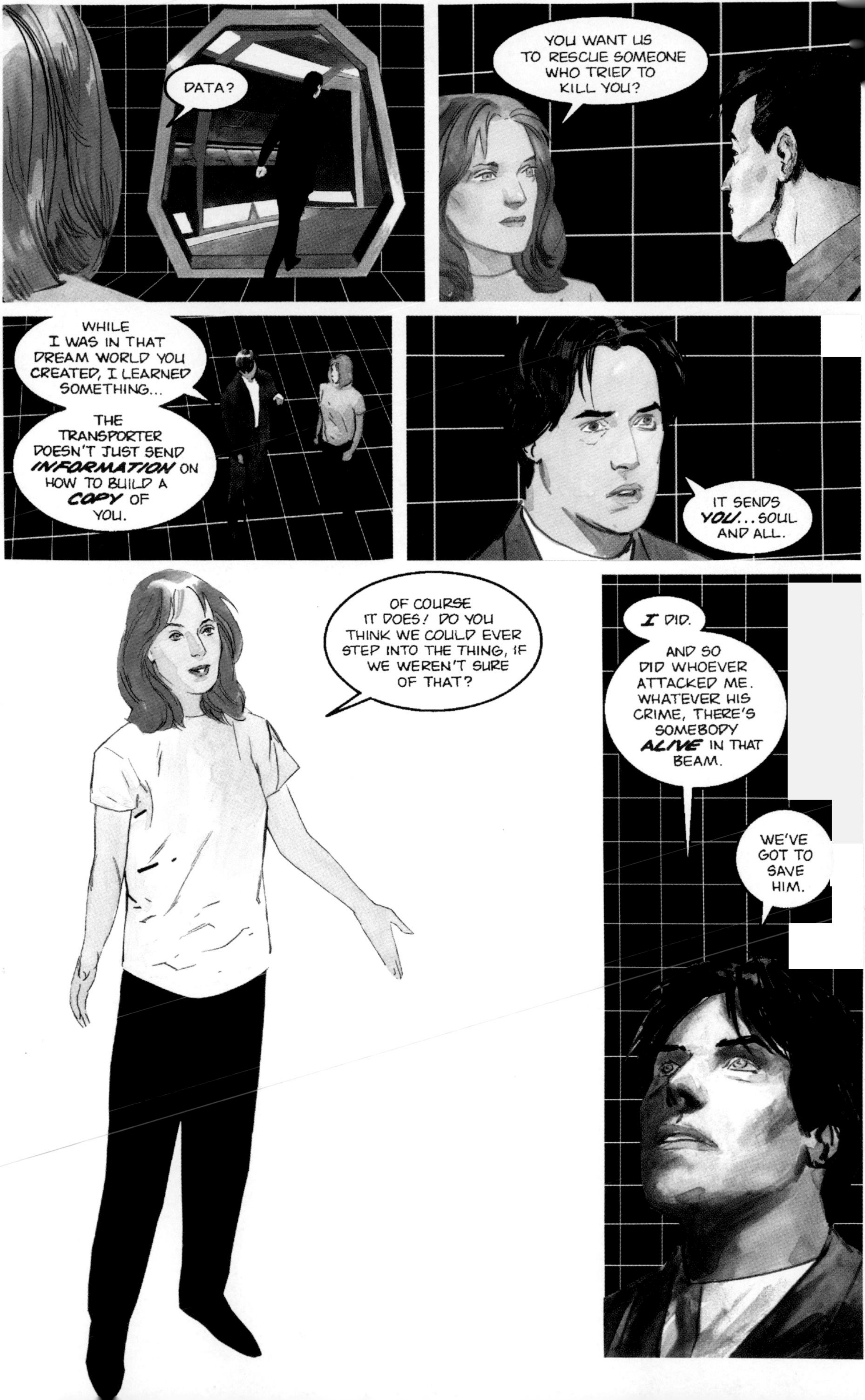

DATA?
YOU WANT US TO RESCUE SOMEONE WHO TRIED TO KILL YOU?
WHILE I WAS IN THAT DREAM WORLD YOU CREATED, I LEARNED SOMETHING...
THE TRANSPORTER DOESN'T JUST SEND INFORMATION ON HOW TO BUILD A COPY OF YOU.
IT SENDS YOU... SOUL AND ALL.
OF COURSE IT DOES! DO YOU THINK WE COULD EVER STEP INTO THE THING, IF WE WEREN'T SURE OF THAT?
I DID.
AND SO DID WHOEVER ATTACKED ME. WHATEVER HIS CRIME, THERE'S SOMEBODY ALIVE IN THAT BEAM.
WE'VE GOT TO SAVE HIM.

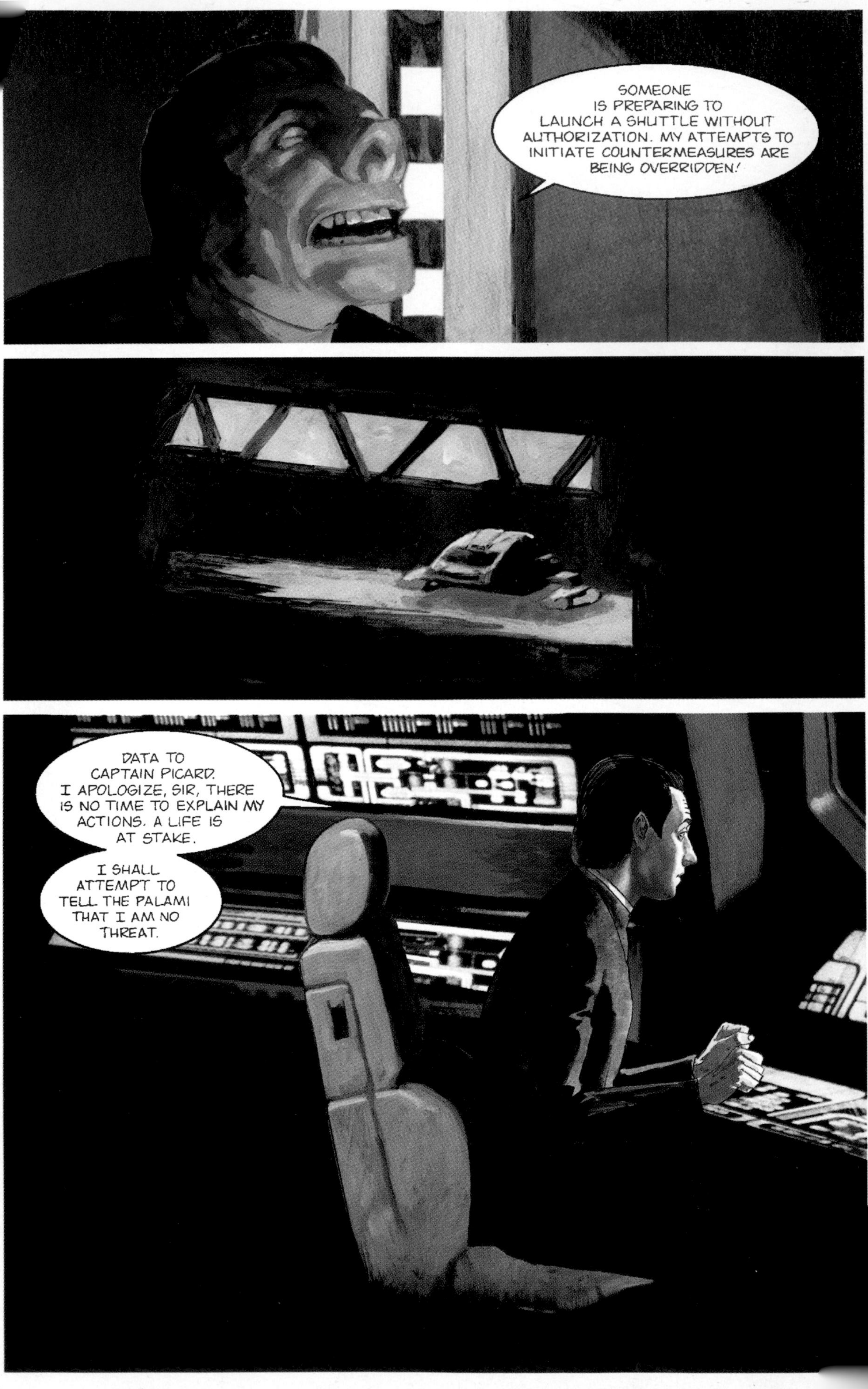
SOMEONE IS PREPARING TO LAUNCH A SHUTTLE WITHOUT AUTHORIZATION. MY ATTEMPTS TO INITIATE COUNTERMEASURES ARE BEING OVERRIDDEN!
DATA TO CAPTAIN PICARD. I APOLOGIZE, SIR, THERE IS NO TIME TO EXPLAIN MY ACTIONS. A LIFE IS AT STAKE.
I SHALL ATTEMPT TO TELL THE PALAMI THAT I AM NO THREAT.

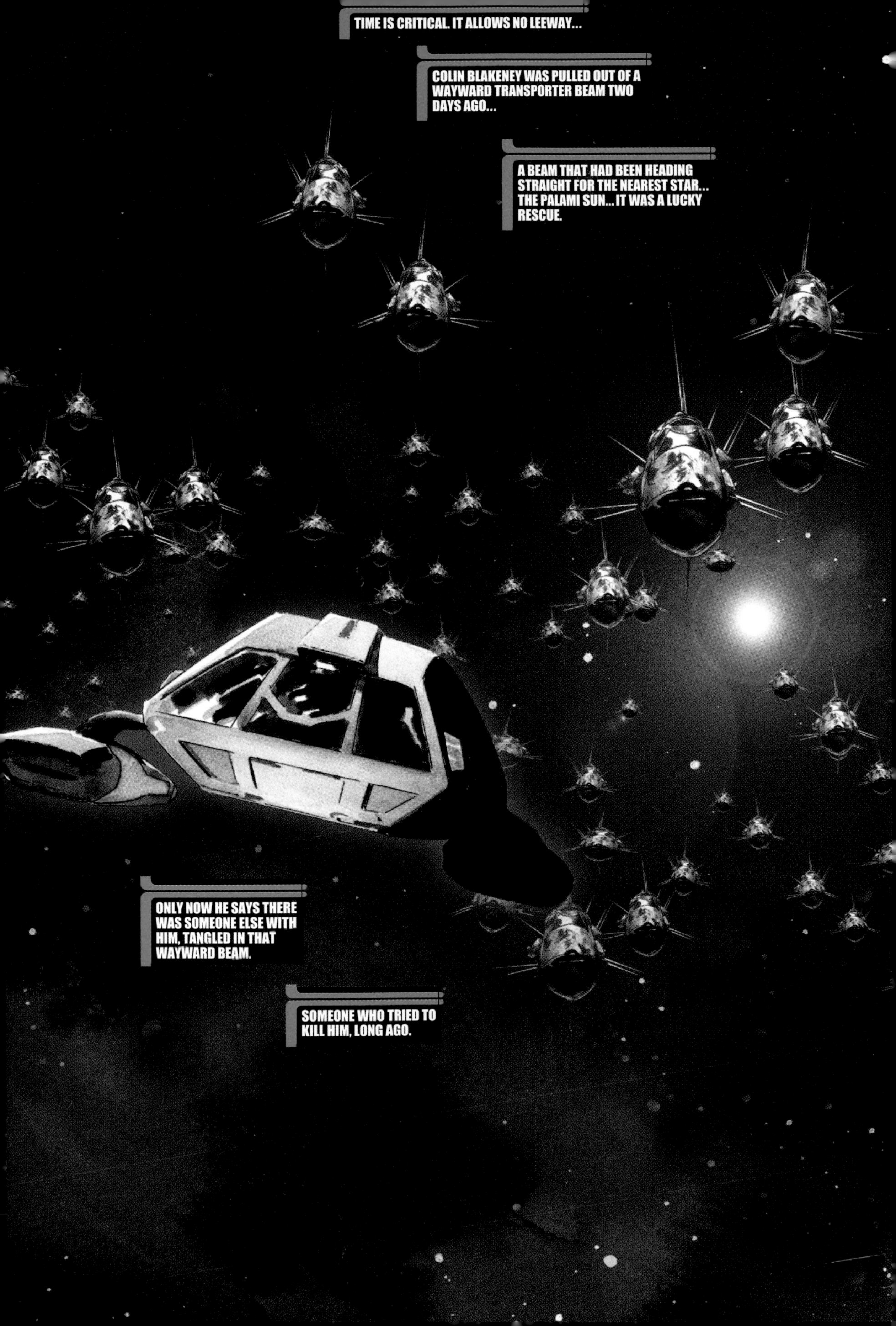
TIME IS CRITICAL. IT ALLOWS NO LEEWAY...
COLIN BLAKENEY WAS PULLED OUT OF A WAYWARD TRANSPORTER BEAM TWO DAYS AGO...
A BEAM THAT HAD BEEN HEADING STRAIGHT FOR THE NEAREST STAR... THE PALAMI SUN... IT WAS A LUCKY RESCUE.
ONLY NOW HE SAYS THERE WAS SOMEONE ELSE WITH HIM, TANGLED IN THAT WAYWARD BEAM.
SOMEONE WHO TRIED TO KILL HIM, LONG AGO.

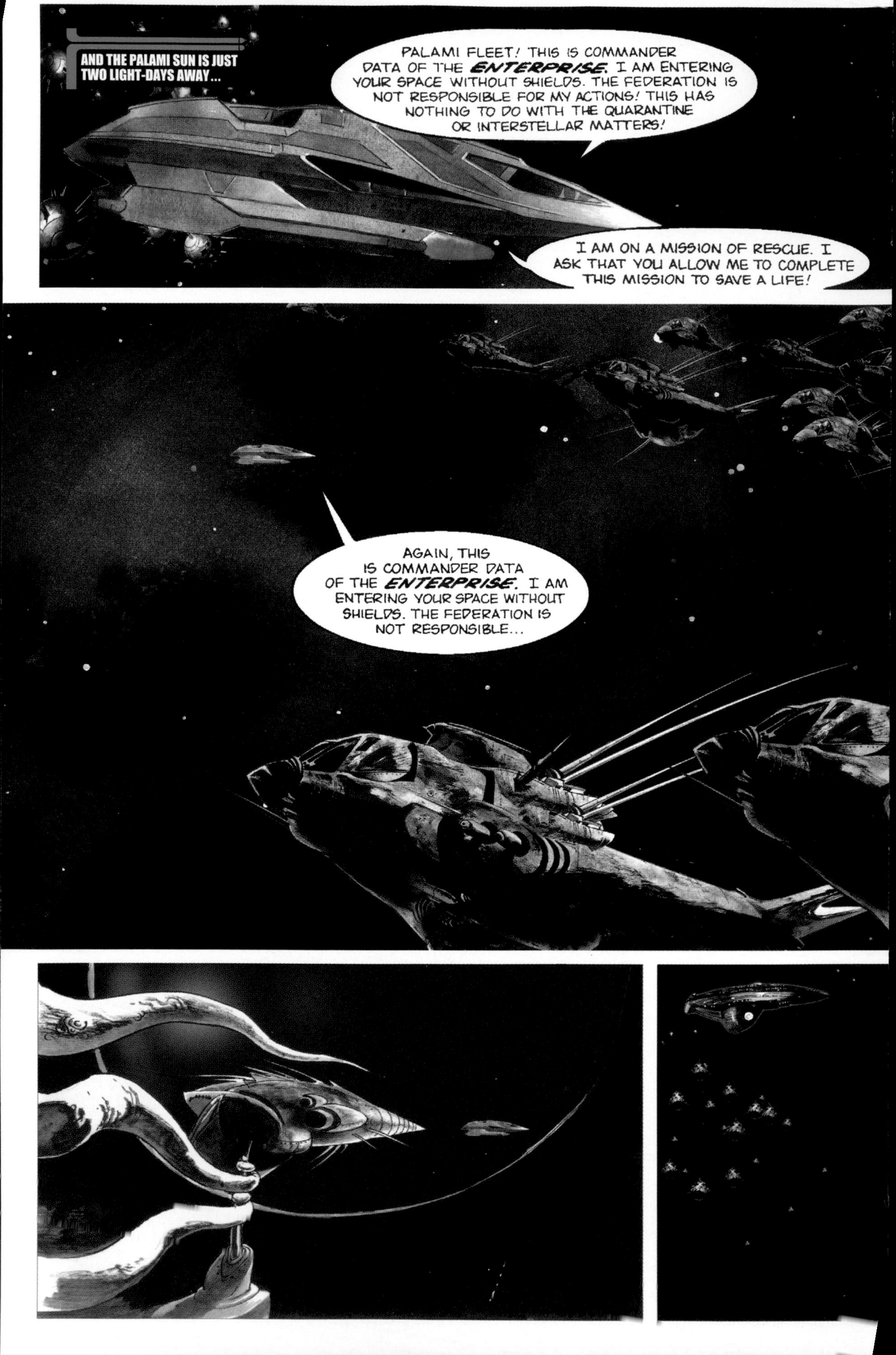
AND THE PALAMI SUN IS JUST TWO LIGHT-DAYS AWAY...
PALAMI FLEET! THIS IS COMMANDER DATA OF THE ENTERPRISE. I AM ENTERING YOUR SPACE WITHOUT SHIELDS. THE FEDERATION IS NOT RESPONSIBLE FOR MY ACTIONS! THIS HAS NOTHING TO DO WITH THE QUARANTINE OR INTERSTELLAR MATTERS!
I AM ON A MISSION OF RESCUE. I ASK THAT YOU ALLOW ME TO COMPLETE THIS MISSION TO SAVE A LIFE!
AGAIN, THIS IS COMMANDER DATA OF THE ENTERPRISE. I AM ENTERING YOUR SPACE WITHOUT SHIELDS. THE FEDERATION IS NOT RESPONSIBLE...

I SENSE RISING TENSION... SOMETHING LIKE PANIC AMONG THE PALAMI!

THEY DON'T LIKE SURPRISES.

SENSORS SHOW SOME OF THEIR SHIPS PUTTING WEAPONS ONLINE! PREPARING TO FIRE!

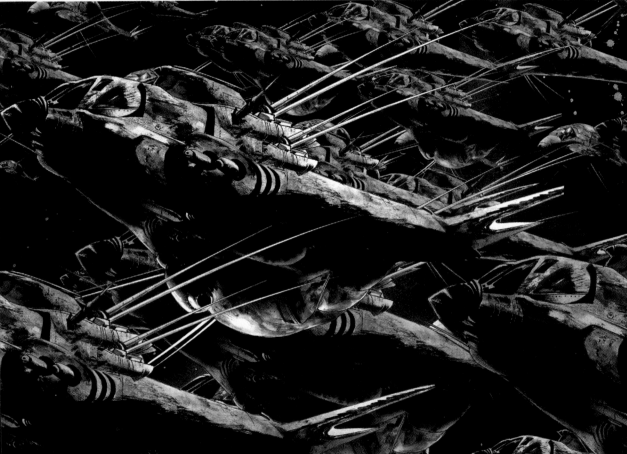

THANK YOU.

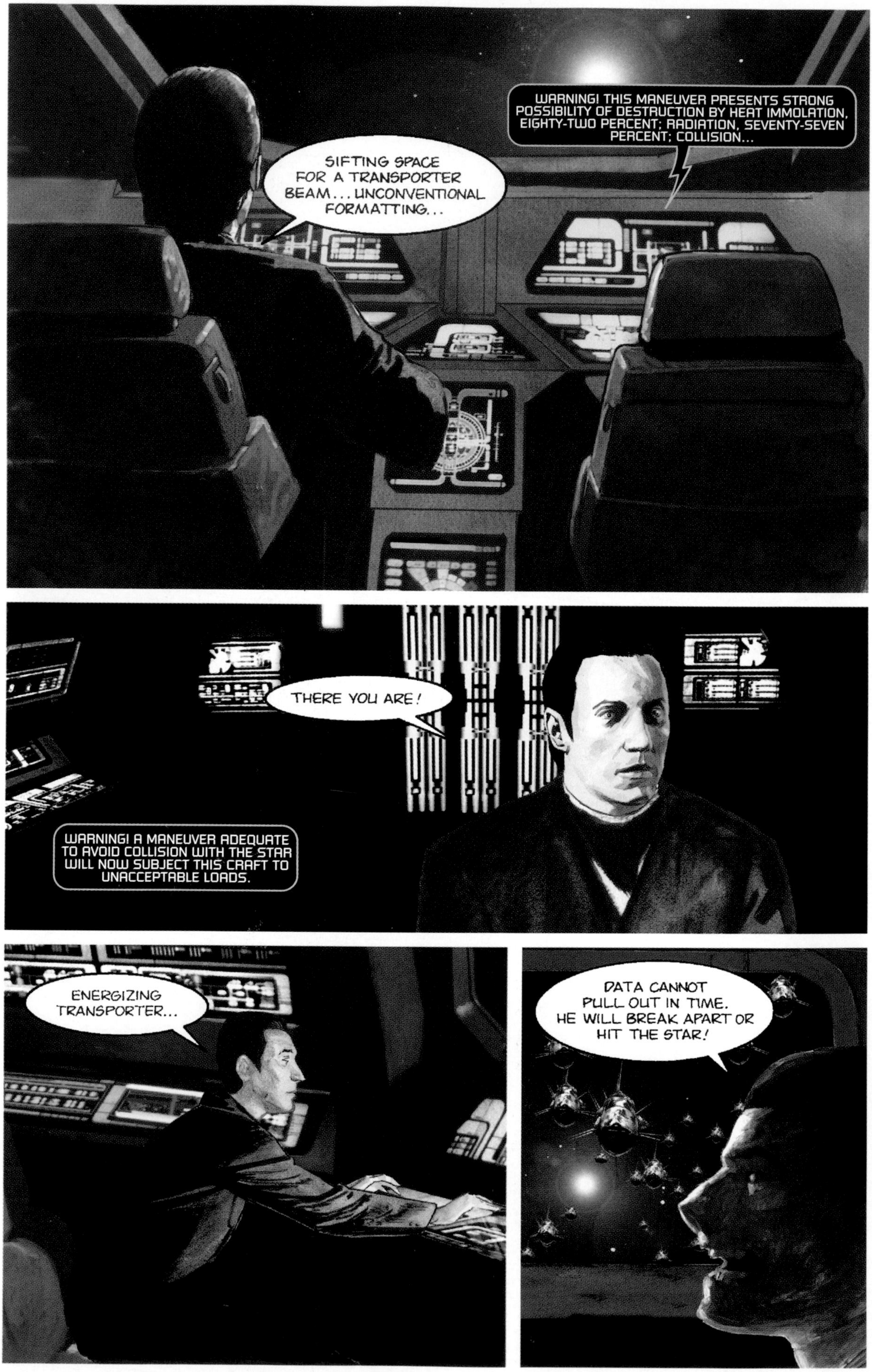

SIFTING SPACE FOR A TRANSPORTER BEAM... UNCONVENTIONAL FORMATTING...
WARNING! THIS MANEUVER PRESENTS STRONG POSSIBILITY OF DESTRUCTION BY HEAT IMMOLATION, EIGHTY-TWO PERCENT; RADIATION, SEVENTY-SEVEN PERCENT; COLLISION...
THERE YOU ARE!
WARNING! A MANEUVER ADEQUATE TO AVOID COLLISION WITH THE STAR WILL NOW SUBJECT THIS CRAFT TO UNACCEPTABLE LOADS.
ENERGIZING TRANSPORTER...
DATA CANNOT PULL OUT IN TIME. HE WILL BREAK APART OR HIT THE STAR!

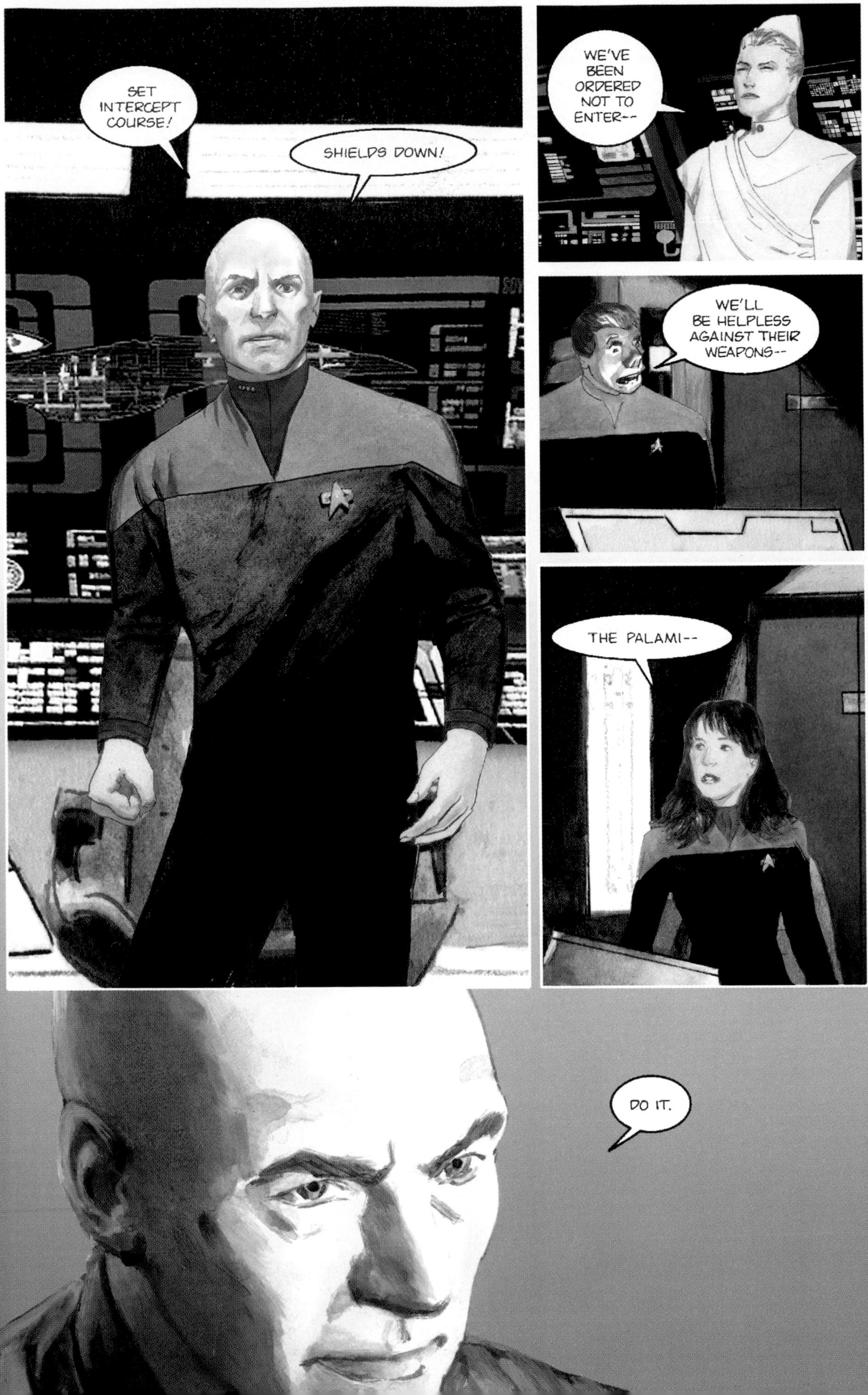
SET INTERCEPT COURSE!
SHIELDS DOWN!
WE'VE BEEN ORDERED NOT TO ENTER--
WE'LL BE HELPLESS AGAINST THEIR WEAPONS--
THE PALAMI--
DO IT.

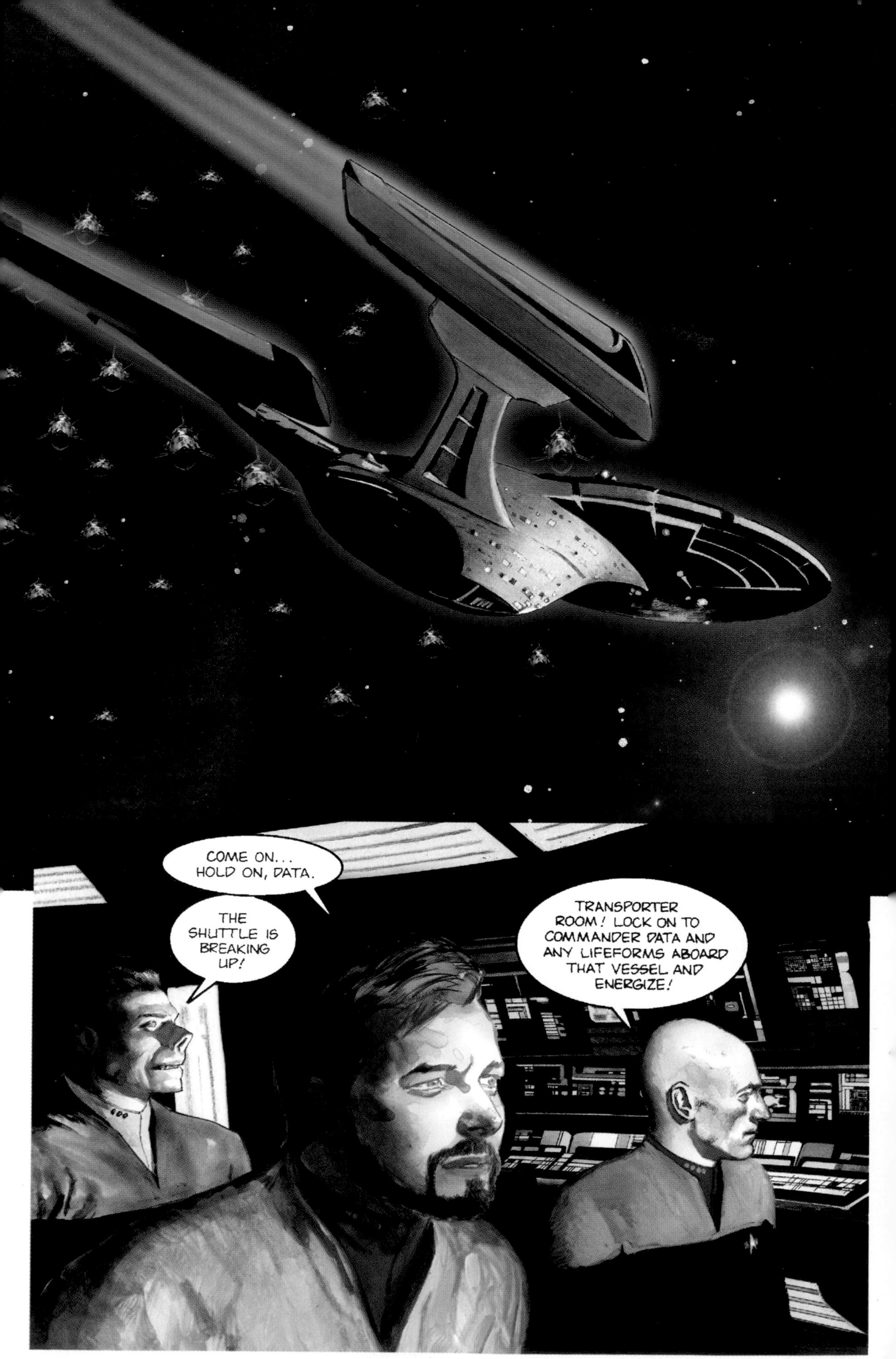
COME ON... HOLD ON, DATA.
THE SHUTTLE IS BREAKING UP!
TRANSPORTER ROOM! LOCK ON TO COMMANDER DATA AND ANY LIFEFORMS ABOARD THAT VESSEL AND ENERGIZE!

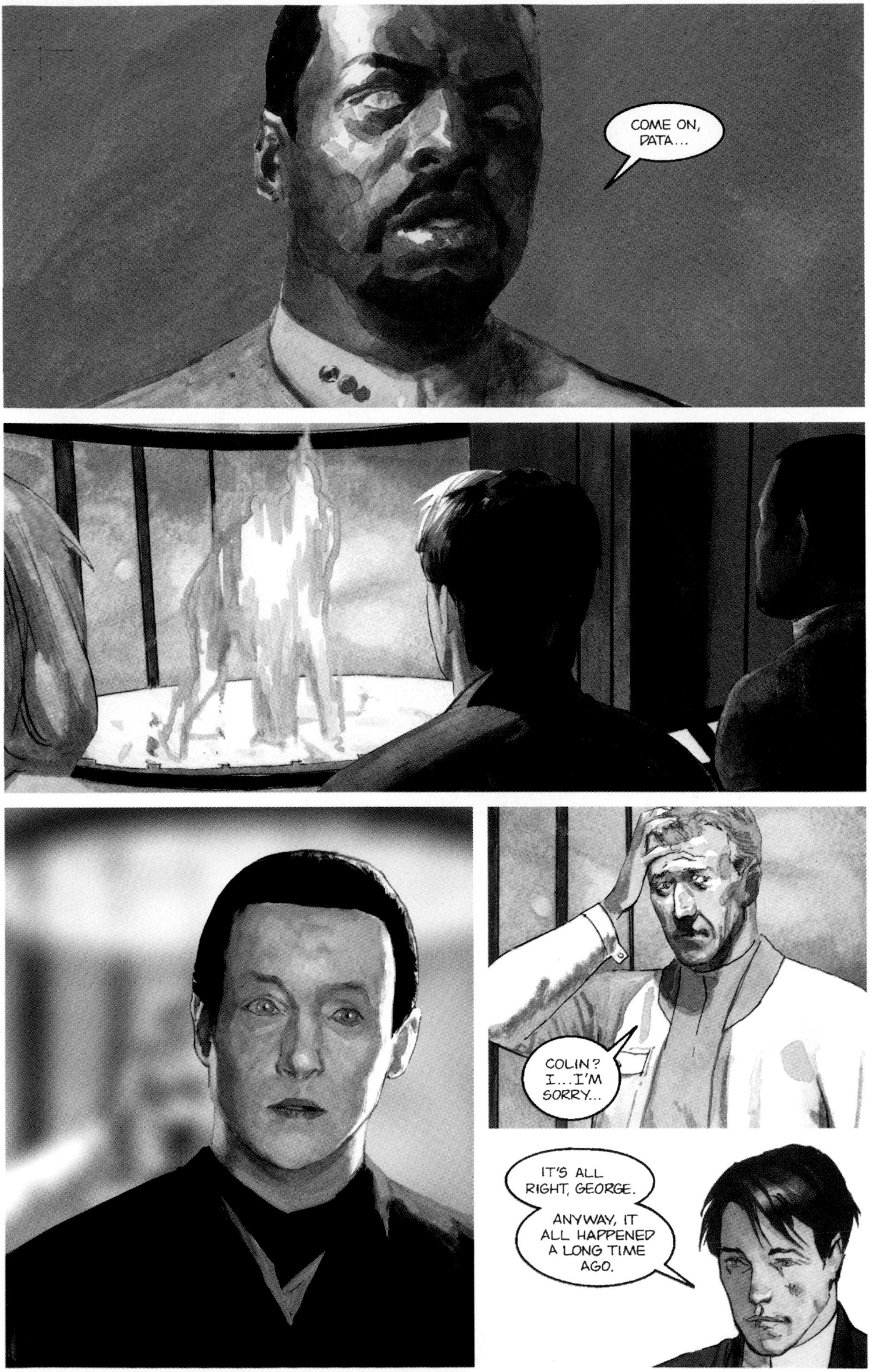
COME ON, DATA...
COLIN? I...I'M SORRY...
IT'S ALL RIGHT, GEORGE.
ANYWAY, IT ALL HAPPENED A LONG TIME AGO.

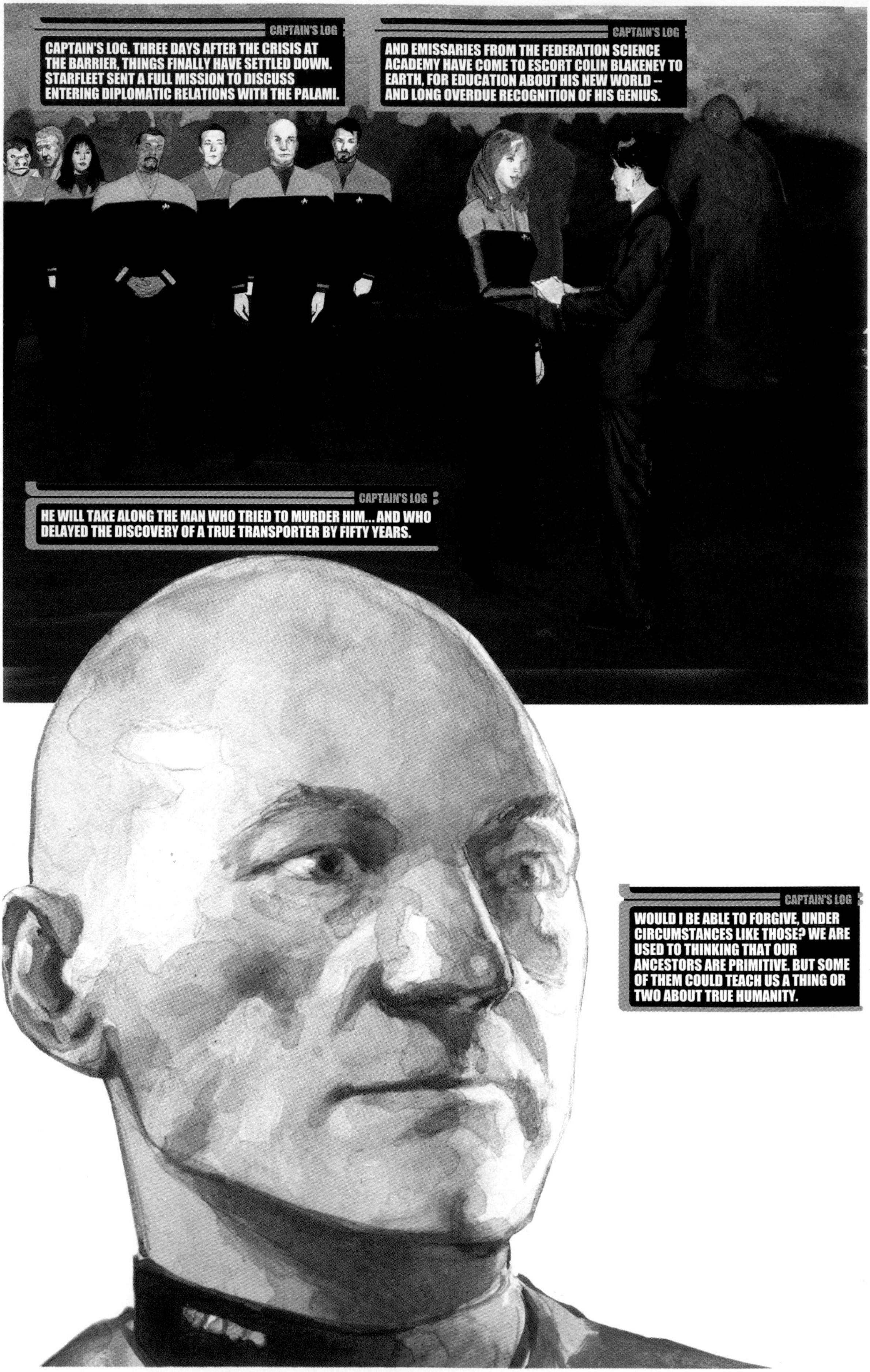
CAPTAIN'S LOG
CAPTAIN'S LOG. THREE DAYS AFTER THE CRISIS AT THE BARRIER, THINGS FINALLY HAVE SETTLED DOWN. STARFLEET SENT A FULL MISSION TO DISCUSS ENTERING DIPLOMATIC RELATIONS WITH THE PALAMI.
CAPTAIN'S LOG
AND EMISSARIES FROM THE FEDERATION SCIENCE ACADEMY HAVE COME TO ESCORT COLIN BLAKENEY TO EARTH, FOR EDUCATION ABOUT HIS NEW WORLD -- AND LONG OVERDUE RECOGNITION OF HIS GENIUS.
CAPTAIN'S LOG
HE WILL TAKE ALONG THE MAN WHO TRIED TO MURDER HIM... AND WHO DELAYED THE DISCOVERY OF A TRUE TRANSPORTER BY FIFTY YEARS.
CAPTAIN'S LOG
WOULD I BE ABLE TO FORGIVE, UNDER CIRCUMSTANCES LIKE THOSE? WE ARE USED TO THINKING THAT OUR ANCESTORS ARE PRIMITIVE. BUT SOME OF THEM COULD TEACH US A THING OR TWO ABOUT TRUE HUMANITY.

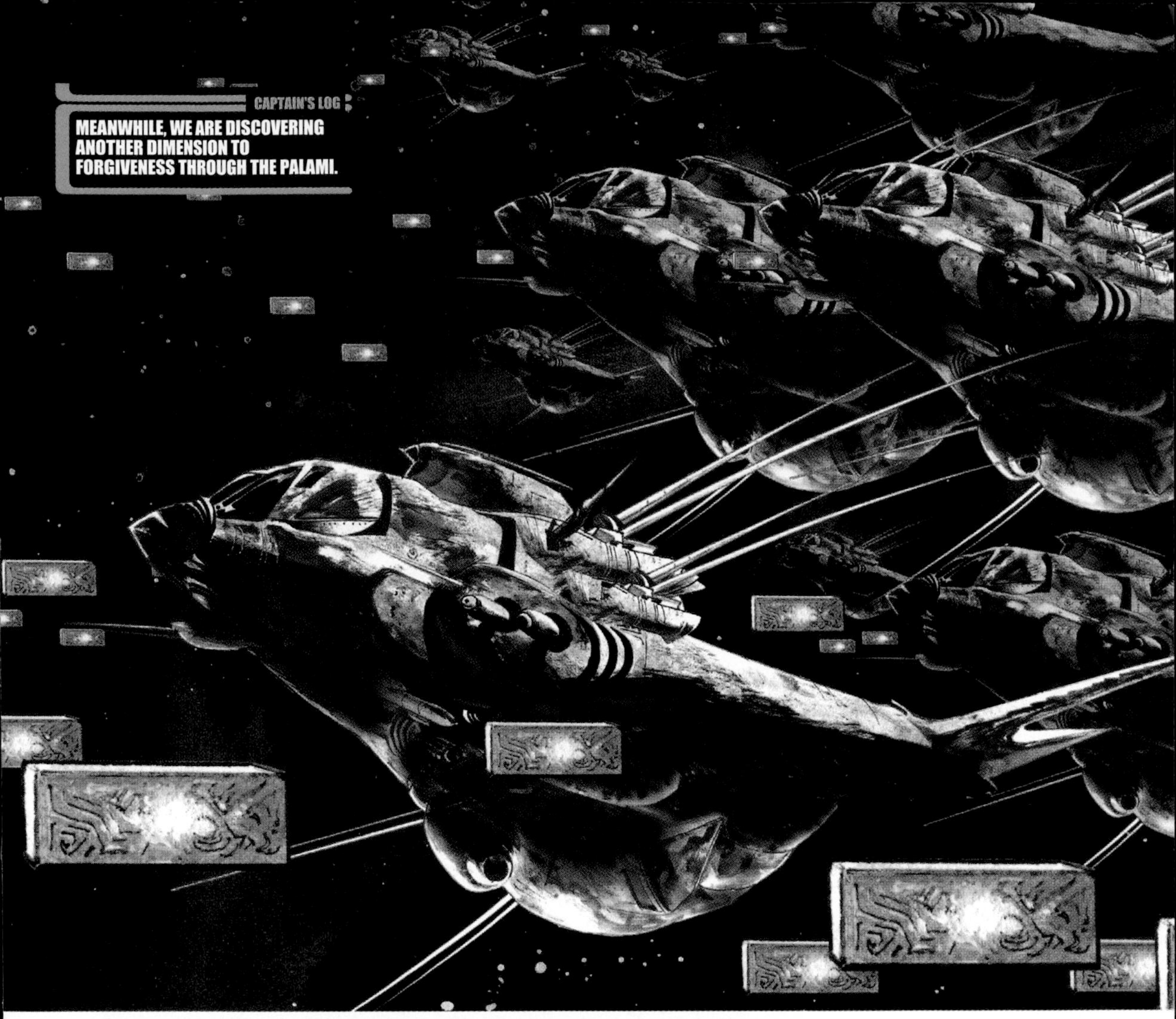
CAPTAIN'S LOG
MEANWHILE, WE ARE DISCOVERING ANOTHER DIMENSION TO FORGIVENESS THROUGH THE PALAMI.

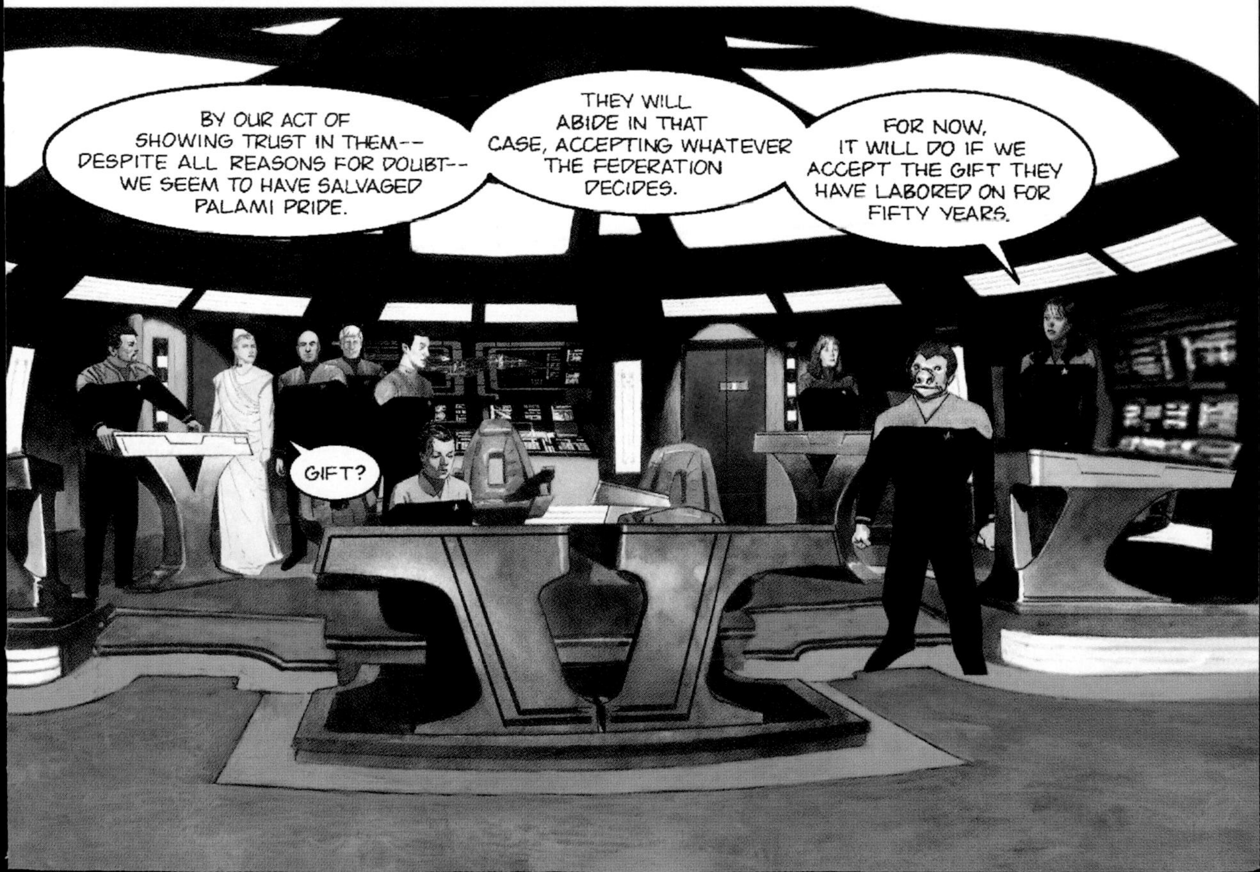
BY OUR ACT OF SHOWING TRUST IN THEM-- DESPITE ALL REASONS FOR DOUBT-- WE SEEM TO HAVE SALVAGED PALAMI PRIDE.
THEY WILL ABIDE IN THAT CASE, ACCEPTING WHATEVER THE FEDERATION DECIDES.
FOR NOW, IT WILL DO IF WE ACCEPT THE GIFT THEY HAVE LABORED ON FOR FIFTY YEARS.
GIFT?

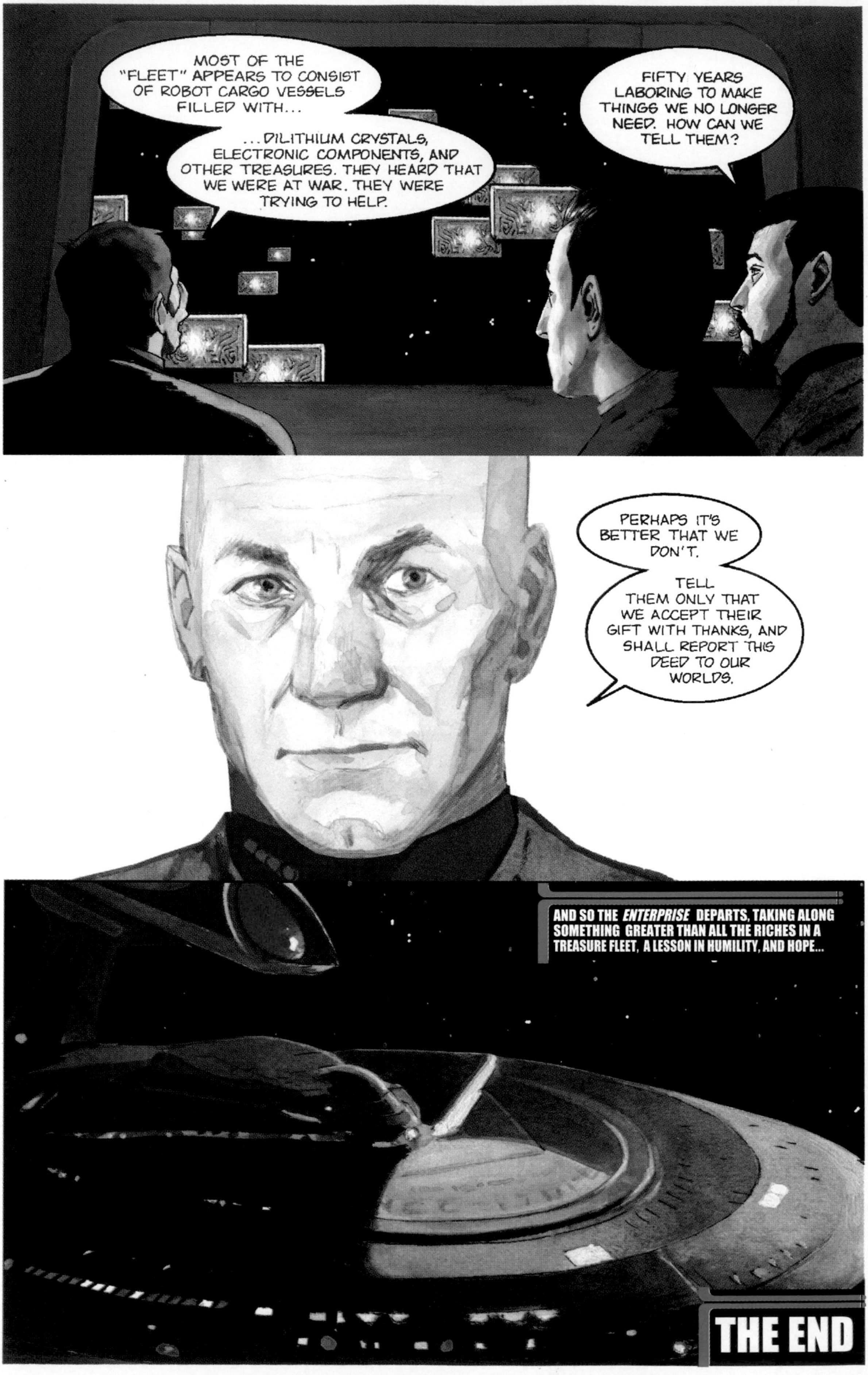
MOST OF THE "FLEET" APPEARS TO CONSIST OF ROBOT CARGO VESSELS FILLED WITH...
...DILITHIUM CRYSTALS, ELECTRONIC COMPONENTS, AND OTHER TREASURES. THEY HEARD THAT WE WERE AT WAR. THEY WERE TRYING TO HELP.
FIFTY YEARS LABORING TO MAKE THINGS WE NO LONGER NEED. HOW CAN WE TELL THEM?
PERHAPS IT'S BETTER THAT WE DON'T.
TELL THEM ONLY THAT WE ACCEPT THEIR GIFT WITH THANKS, AND SHALL REPORT THIS DEED TO OUR WORLDS.
AND SO THE *ENTERPRISE* DEPARTS, TAKING ALONG SOMETHING GREATER THAN ALL THE RICHES IN A TREASURE FLEET, A LESSON IN HUMILITY, AND HOPE...
THE END

# USS ENTERPRISE NCC-1701-E

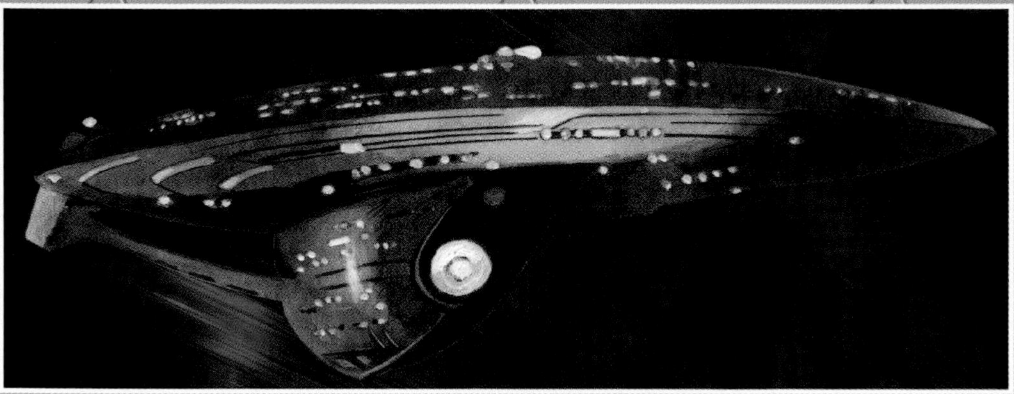

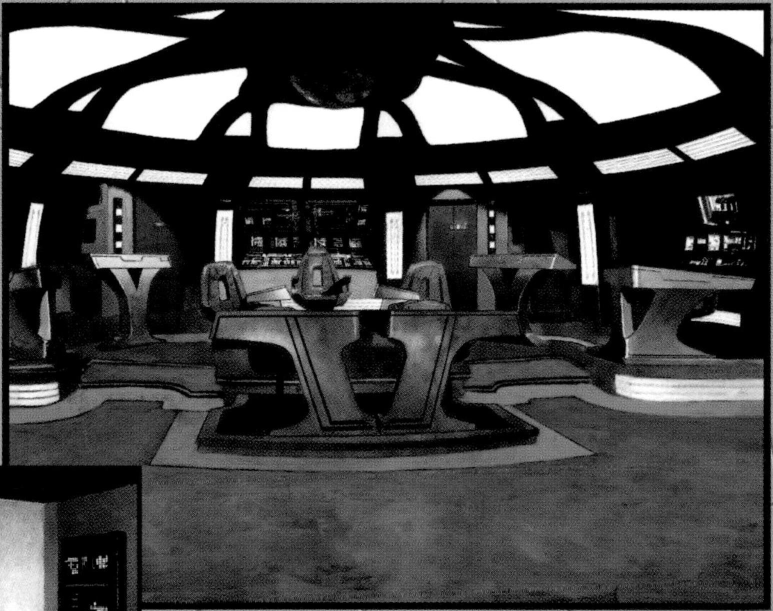

The Bridge

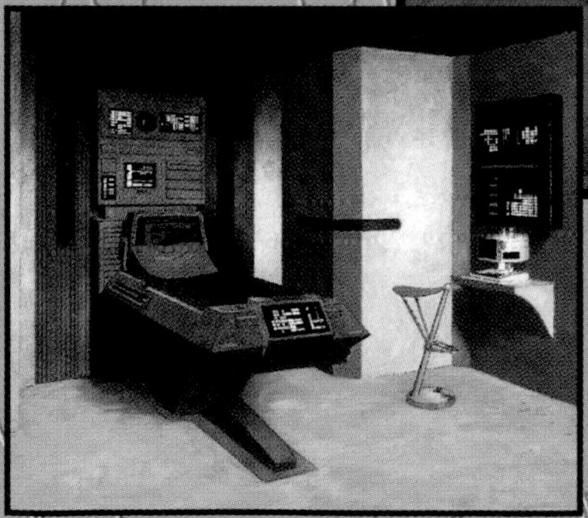

Sickbay

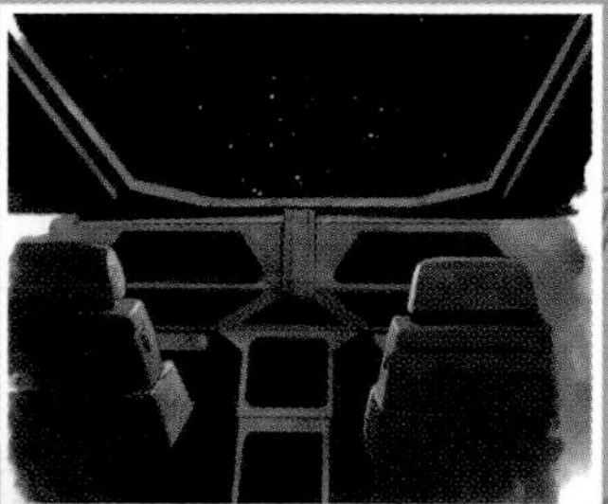

Enterprise Shuttlecraft

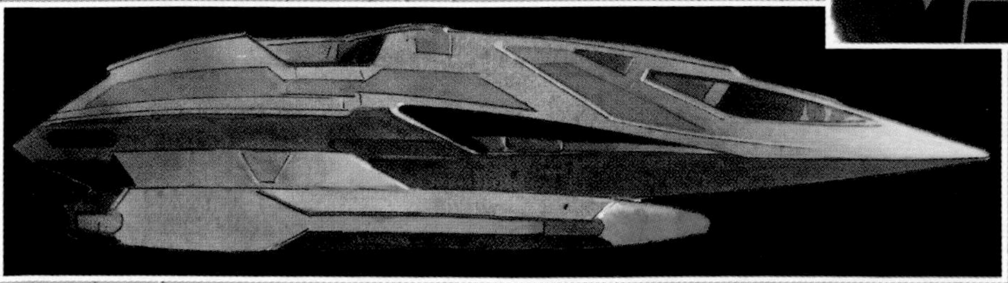

Captain
Jean-Luc
Picard

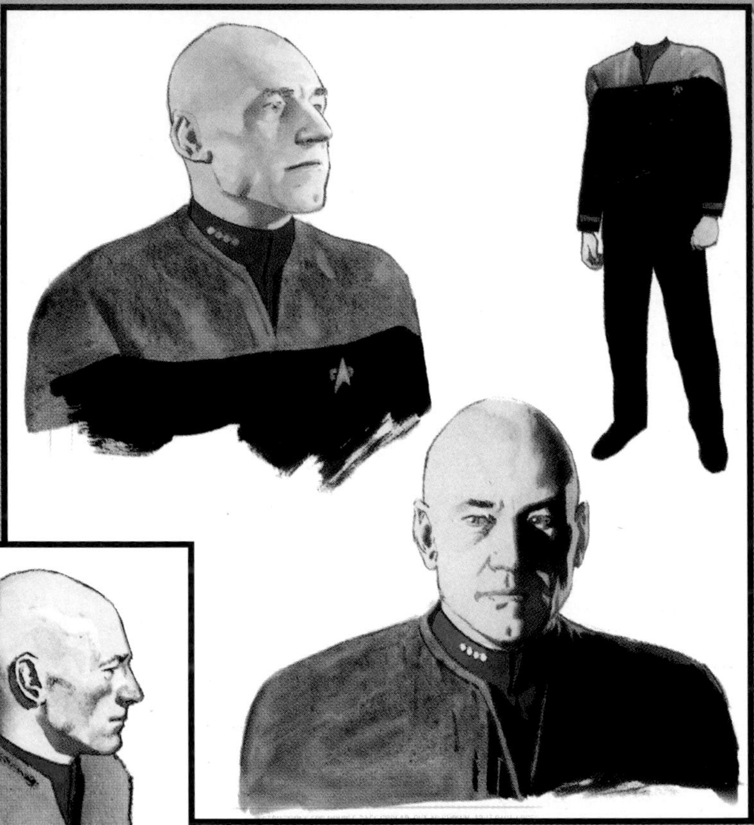

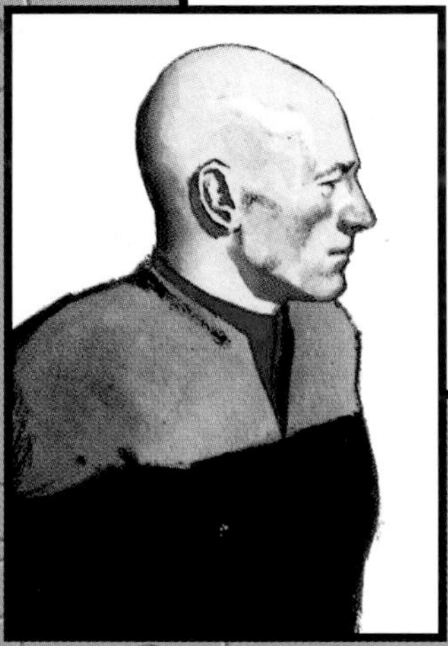

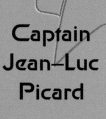

Lieutenant
Commander
Data

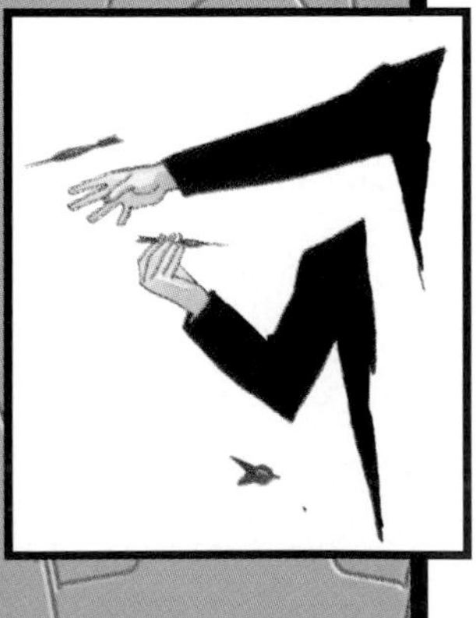

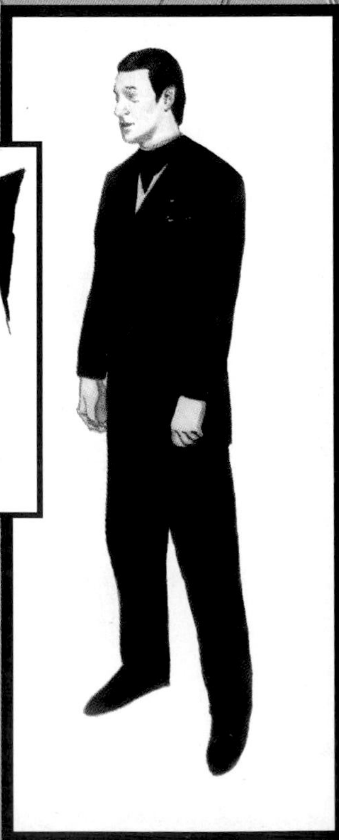

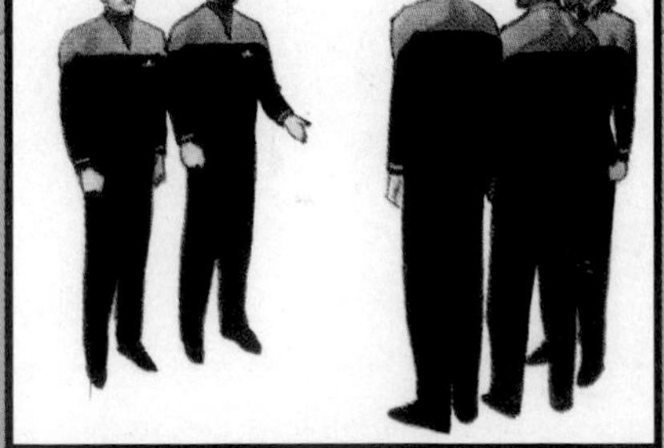

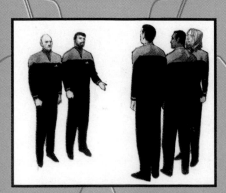

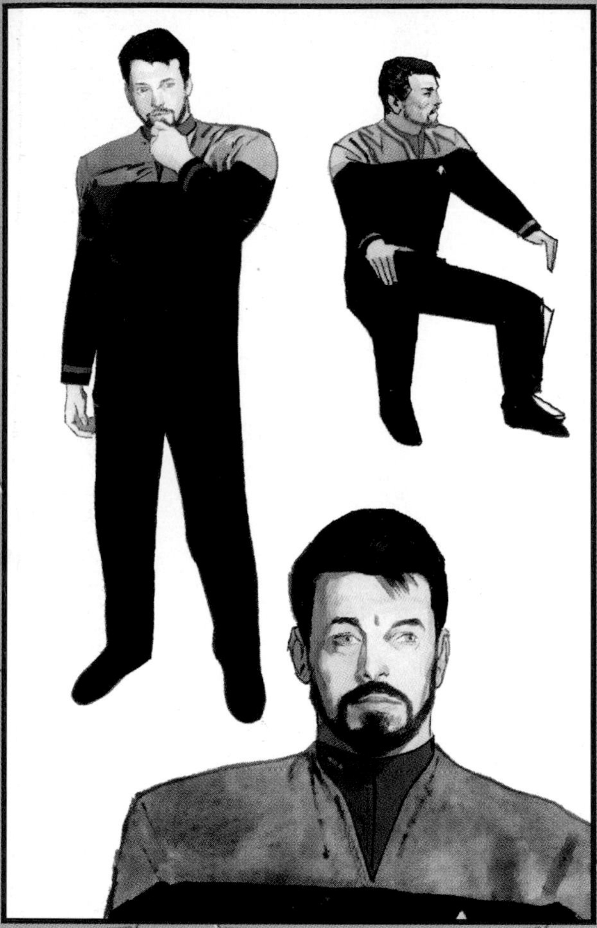

Commander William T. Riker

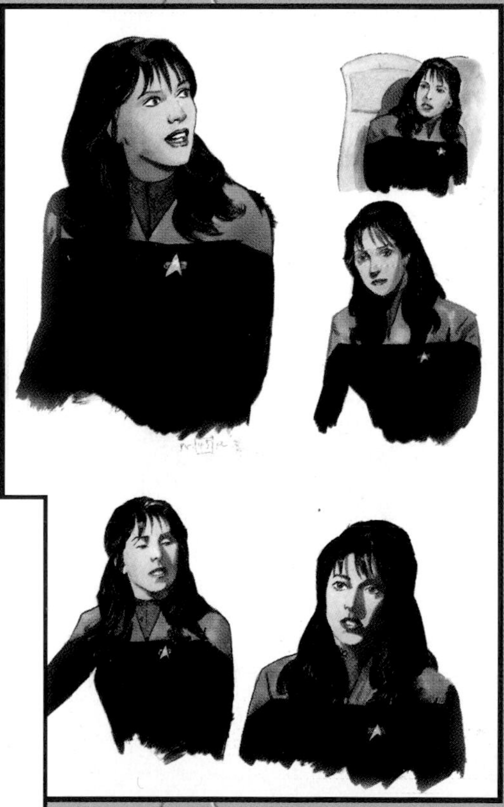

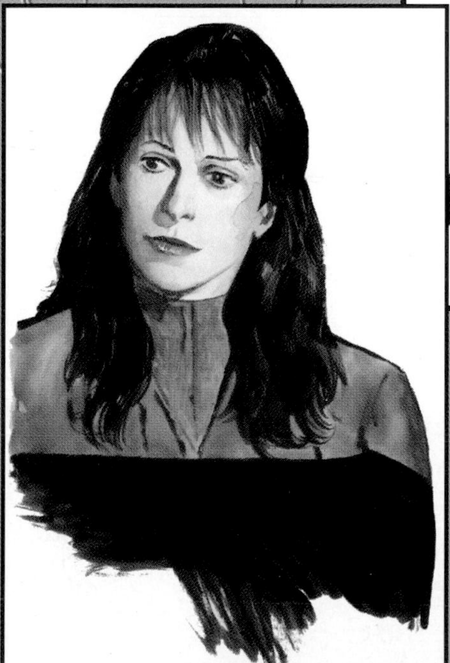

Ship's Counselor Deanna Troi

## CONTINUE THE ADVENTURE WITH THESE OTHER BOOKS FROM WILDSTORM AND DC:

### STAR TREK COLLECTIONS

**Star Trek: All of Me**
Isabella & Ingersoll/
Lopresti/Emberlin

**Star Trek:**
**Other Realities**
Various

**Star Trek:**
**The Next Generation**
**Embrace the Wolf**
Golden & Sniegoski/
Hoover/Hubbs

**Star Trek:**
**The Next Generation**
**Enemy Unseen**
Various

**Star Trek:**
**The Next Generation**
**Gorn Crisis**
Anderson & Moesta/Kordey

**Star Trek: Voyager**
**Avalon Rising**
Young & Young/Roach

**Star Trek: Voyager**
**Elite Force**
Abnett & Lanning/
Moy/Carani

**Star Trek: Voyager**
**False Colors**
Archer/Moy/Carani

**Star Trek: New Frontier**
**Double Time**
David/Collins/Roach

### WILDSTORM COLLECTIONS

**The Authority:**
**Relentless**
Ellis/Hitch/Neary

**The Authority:**
**Under New Management**
Ellis/Millar/Hitch/Quitely

**Crimson: Loyalty & Loss**
Augustyn/Ramos/Hope

**Crimson: Heaven & Earth**
Augustyn/Ramos/Hope

**Crimson: Earth Angel**
Augustyn/Ramos/Hope

**Crimson: Redemption**
Augustyn/Ramos/Hope

**Deathblow:**
**Sinners and Saints**
Choi/Lee/Sale/Scott

**Danger Girl:**
**The Dangerous Collection #1-3**
Campbell/Hartnell/Garner

**Divine Right:**
**Collected Edition #1-3**
Lee/Williams

**Gen13**
Choi/Lee/Campbell/Garner

**Gen13: #13 ABC**
Choi/Lee/Campbell/Garner

**Gen13: Bootleg Vol. 1**
Various writers and artists

**Gen13:**
**Grunge the Movie**
Warren

**Gen13:**
**I Love New York**
Arcudi/Frank/Smith

**Gen13:**
**Interactive Plus**
Various writers and artists

**Gen13: Starting Over**
Choi/Lee/Campbell/Garner

**Gen13:**
**We'll Take Manhattan**
Lobdell/Benes/Sibal

**Gen13/ Superman**
Hughes/Bermejo

**Kurt Busiek's Astro City:**
**Life in the Big City**
Busiek/Anderson

**Kurt Busiek's Astro City:**
**Confession**
Busiek/Anderson/Blyberg

**Kurt Busiek's Astro City:**
**Family Album**
Busiek/Anderson/Blyberg

**Kurt Busiek's Astro City:**
**Tarnished Angel**
Busiek/Anderson/Blyberg

**Leave It to Chance:**
**Shaman's Rain**
Robinson/Smith

**Leave It to Chance:**
**Trick or Threat**
Robinson/Smith/Freeman

**Wetworks: Rebirth**
Portacio/Choi/Williams

**Planetary/Authority:**
**Ruling the World**
Ellis/Jimenez/Lanning

**Planetary:**
**All Over the World and Other Stories**
Ellis/Cassaday

**Planetary:**
**The Fourth Man**
Ellis/Cassaday

**StormWatch:**
**Force of Nature**
Ellis/Raney/Elliott

**StormWatch:**
**Lightning Strikes**
Ellis/Raney/Lee/
Elliott/Williams

**StormWatch:**
**Change or Die**
Ellis/Raney/Jimenez

**StormWatch:**
**A Finer World**
Ellis/Hitch/Neary

**StormWatch:**
**Final Orbit**
Ellis/Various

**WildC.A.T.s: Gang War**
Moore/Various

**WildC.A.T.s:**
**Gathering of Eagles**
Claremont/Lee/Williams

**WildC.A.T.s: Homecoming**
Moore/Various

**WildC.A.T.s/X-Men**
Various writers and artis

**Wildcats: Street Smart**
Lobdell/Charest/Friend

**Wildcats:**
**Vicious Circles**
Casey/Phillips

**Wildcats:**
**Serial Boxes**
Casey/Phillips

### AMERICA'S BEST COMICS

**ABC Special**
Moore/ Various

**League of Extraordinary Gentlemen**
Moore/O'Neill

**Promethea Book One**
Moore/Williams/Gray

**Promethea Book Two**
Moore/Williams/Gray

**Tom Strong Book One**
Moore/Sprouse

**Top 10**
Moore/Ha/Cannon

For the nearest comics shop carrying collected editions and monthly titles from WildStorm, call 1-888-COMIC BOOK.